FRENCH FANCY

Putting on her most formal manner, Celeste addressed him coldly. "If you are come to see M. le Vicar, you cannot. He takes the nap."

Still bemused, Geoff continued to stare. "Then he errs. He is missing a beautiful sight."

She drew herself up. "Sir, you shall not kiss me," she said.

Geoff had, by now, regained his senses. "Why would I do that? On second thought, since the coast is clear, why should I not?"

"Because I am the housekeeper here as you can see, and not a maid. You are therefore not to kiss me." She moved back a step at the expression on his face.

Was she being coy? This was a new and intriguing approach, tantamount to an invitation. In the lexicon of Rake Cole, maids and Frenchwomen were fair game, and here were both in one enchanting package. It had been some time since he had kissed a housemaid so lovely. And never, could he recall, had he kissed a housekeeper. The novel idea appealed to Rake Cole. He wasted no more time. Stepping into the room, he swept the housekeeper-maid into his arms and kissed her soundly.

ZEBRA REGENCIES
ARE
THE TALK OF THE TON!

A REFORMED RAKE (4499, $3.99)
by Jeanne Savery

After governess Harriet Cole helped her young charge flee to France—and the designs of a despicable suitor, more trouble soon arrived in the person of a London rake. Sir Frederick Carrington insisted on providing safe escort back to England. Harriet deemed Carrington more dangerous than any band of brigands, but secretly relished matching wits with him. But after being taken in his arms for a tender kiss, she found herself wondering—*could* a lady find love with an irresistible rogue?

A SCANDALOUS PROPOSAL (4504, $4.99)
by Teresa DesJardien

After only two weeks into the London season, Lady Pamela Premington has already received her first offer of marriage. If only it hadn't come from the *ton's* most notorious rake, Lord Marchmont. Pamela had already set her sights on the distinguished Lieutenant Penford, who had the heroism and honor that made him the ideal match. Now she had to keep from falling under the spell of the seductive Lord so she could pursue the man more worthy of her love. Or was he?

A LADY'S CHAMPION (4535, $3.99)
by Janice Bennett

Miss Daphne, art mistress of the Selwood Academy for Young Ladies, greeted the notion of ghosts haunting the academy with skepticism. However, to avoid rumors frightening off students, she found herself turning to Mr. Adrian Carstairs, sent by her uncle to be her "protector" against the "ghosts." Although, Daphne would accept no interference in her life, she *would* accept aid in exposing any spectral spirits. What she never expected was for Adrian to expose the secret wishes of her hidden heart . . .

CHARITY'S GAMBIT (4537, $3.99)
by Marcy Stewart

Charity Abercrombie reluctantly embarks on a London season in hopes of making a suitable match. However she cannot forget the mysterious Dominic Castille—and the kiss they shared—when he fell from a tree as she strolled through the woods. Charity does not know that the dark and dashing captain harbors a dangerous secret that will ensnare them both in its web—leaving Charity to risk certain ruin and losing the man she so passionately loves . . .

The Duke's Double

Winifred Witton

ZEBRA BOOKS
KENSINGTON PUBLISHING CORP.

For Russell, always.

ZEBRA BOOKS are published by

Kensington Publishing Corp.
850 Third Avenue
New York, NY 10022

First Printing: February, 1995

Printed in the United States of America

One

Mlle. Celeste Moreau sat in the window of her tiny parlor in the cottage next door to the *boulangerie,* and ruthlessly trimmed two inches from the décolletage of her best lavender *peau de soie* mourning gown.

She held up the dress, and a satisfied dimple deepened in her peach-bloom cheek as she considered her handiwork.

"Ah. *C'est beaucoup mieux.* Much better." It was all very well to be demure and of the most respectable, but it was *de rigueur* to have at least one *formidable toilette,* if one meant to travel to London and capture the heart of an English *milor'.*

She drew a deep breath as the delicious odor of fresh baked bread drifted in through the lace curtains at her open window. The loaves were out. She'd best send Madeleine—no, the enticing aroma must already have reached her plump, sweet-faced cousin. Led by her nose—and her *tendre* for M. Guillaume Gagny, the *boulanger*—Madeleine would be waiting in his shop for the first of the hot, crusty *miches de pain.*

Celeste went back to work. The tip of her pink tongue protruded between her even, white teeth, as she concentrated on the delicate task of cutting without destroying the pattern of the lace covering the short bodice.

During the past year of her mourning for poor Papa, Celeste had spent much time reading English novels to improve her command of the language. From the writings of Fanny Burney, Mrs. Ann Radcliffe, and particularly Maria Edgeworth—whose *Castle Rackrent* was nearly worn to flinders—she had made a careful study of the English aristocracy and felt herself an authority.

Counts were to be shunned, she had learned, at least those of Italy, though she had met several French *comtes* and they seemed quite gentlemanly. There were no counts in England, all were foreign to that country in books she read, probably for the reason of their dastardly reputations. There were countesses, but their husbands were known as earls, who were invariably respected and worthy gentlemen. Thus the clever English averted danger.

An earl would suit her purpose admirably, except those she encountered in the novels were elderly and possessed only of daughters. She would not bank on an earl.

Barons also appeared to be wicked, and one must avoid at all costs the English baronet, the one whose title was "Sir." All baronets were evil, and it was a title impossible for a French tongue to pronounce properly anyway.

That left dukes; and the son of the Duchess of Ault, her uncle's employer in England, was a duke, and at last knowledge, unwed.

She heard the creak of her front gate and glanced out the window. Madeleine was latching it again with difficulty, a basket of early fruit hampering one arm, and a long, golden brown loaf tucked under the other. Though only a few years older, Madeleine had served as her companion and chaperone since the death of Celeste's father. Unfortunately, besides being both short and plump, dear Madeleine was without beauty, quite the opposite of her tall, elegant cousin, who had dark chestnut curls and deceptively limpid brown eyes in a lovely heart-shaped face.

Celeste rose and opened the door for her, relieving her of the basket. "Madeleine, this is not all fruit! Why have you bought pastries? I will become as round as you!"

Madeleine blushed, tucking back the wisps of soft brown hair that had escaped from her ruffled mobcap. "M. Gagny is to blame, not I. He insisted on giving me the cakes."

Celeste saw that there were three on top of the fruit in the basket as she set it down.

She knew what that meant. Now that the bread was out of his ovens, the *boulanger* could leave the shop in the hands of his assistant and make a morning call.

M. Gagny was the most eligible bachelor in the village, and Celeste knew Madeleine to be the ideal wife for him. Unhappily, she also knew that he waited only for the end of the official year of her mourning before offering for herself, not Madeleine. M. Gagny lived in two cramped rooms above the bakery, and he desired not her—well, perhaps a little—but her small house, adjoining his shop as it did.

Madeleine had by now taken in the condition of the usually tidy parlor, and she dropped the loaf. Celeste's mourning attire lay draped over every chair and table, all her black, dove gray, and lavender gowns. Two bonnets, one black, the other a charming chip straw trimmed with lavender ruching, lay on the floor beside her, both shorn of their black veils. A series of fashion plates, fresh from Paris, were scattered about the room.

"*Chérie,* what are you doing?" Madeleine exclaimed. "You cannot mean to remake these so dismal garments! I thought you would now be preparing to burn them."

Celeste rescued the chip straw bonnet from beneath the bread and looked about for a place to put them both. "I shall need them, every one," she explained, sweeping a gown from a table, "for I intend to become a most respectable governess."

Her cousin gasped. "But why? Your papa has not left you destitute."

"Very nearly." She caught up the lavender *peau de soie* and pirouetted with it. "I intend to change all that. I have decided to leave France and marry an English duke possessed of great wealth."

Madeleine sank into a chair, sadly crushing a black bombazine carriage dress before Celeste could rescue it. "What are you saying?" she wailed. "What duke?"

"How can I know until I meet him? This is not a new thought, my love. I have had it in mind for many months. Do you remember the billet from Henriette, who went to the island of England last year? She wrote that since M. Bonaparte is no longer a threat to that country, the French *emigrée* is now all the vogue. The taste is for the brunette, the preference for pale-golden hair a thing of the past. I shall be all the most in style!"

"But—but to be a governess!" Madeleine shook her head, her mobcap slipping askew. "I do not understand."

"Why, I have read that in England, the eldest son of the lord of the castle always marries the governess. The only other solution is for the heroine to wed her guardian, but, for one more year, I am the ward of our uncle, and he, after all, is a priest."

Madeleine nodded dumbly, and Celeste pulled the black bombazine from beneath her and tried to plump out the creased skirt. Truly, it was difficult at times to explain the simplest of schemes to Madeleine. She tried another tack.

"It is not only Henriette who brings this about." She swept a dove gray walking gown from the desk and ruffled through an untidy pile of papers, until she located a folded sheet. "Madeleine, I have been going through Papa's correspondence, and I have found a letter from our uncle who, you must know, is the priest of the Duchess of Ault in England. A duchess will know many rich dukes."

She returned with the letter to her seat by the window, the only empty chair. "Listen to his words: 'I have dispatched the key to the solution to the one to whom it matters most—' no, not there. 'I pray, dearest brother, that he will solve the riddle I am bound by the laws of the confessional never to reveal—' that is of no importance to us." She turned the page. "Ah, here. 'I am so alone in my travail. I would that I had my family about me in this strange, unfriendly land.' You see?" Celeste waved the letter triumphantly. "I am almost the only one left of his family. He wants me. So I go to him at the castle of Ault, and I meet this duchess."

Madeleine moaned softly. Celeste paid no heed. "No children are mentioned, but the duchess is, of course, Catholic. There may be many in need of a governess. I believe her son, *M. le Duc,* is already of age."

She did not say aloud that the Duke of Ault was the *parti* she had in mind. Celeste was not overly superstitious, but it never hurt to be careful. Voicing one's plans could only tempt capricious Fate to throw a spoke in one's wheel.

"If there are no small children at the castle," she went on briskly, "I am sure our uncle will know of some other delightful English family in need of one who can teach the French language, the pianoforte, and the proper use of water colors."

"But you cannot play or make sketches," Madeleine complained faintly.

"And who is to know until I have tried?"

"But a governess! Celeste, you would not like it at all."

"I have thought it all out, and I have no other choice." She bent to pick up the letter which had dropped from her lap. "I do not wish to become an actress in the Covent Garden, for I suspect that road does not lead to marriage. It is quite the thing to wed one's guardian, but that I cannot do. The lord of the manor may trifle with a maidservant, but he will not wed her, either. No, a governess I must be."

Madeleine gazed at her in wonder. "Where have you acquired this great knowledge?"

From the table beside her, Celeste picked up a novel covered in marbled paper. "I have here a book to guide me. I shall take it with me, so that I will know just how to go on. It is called *Glenarvon*, and it is written by a lady of the English aristocracy, and therefore all within it must be true."

She gathered up the gown on which she had been

working, following the details of one of the Parisian fashion plates, and held it up for Madeleine's admiration. "Is it not now beautiful? It is in the latest stare, as they say in my books of the English. The garments of my mourning with but a bit of refurbishing will be perfect for a governess. The lavender and dove gray, most demure, most suitable and, I have found, most becoming, if I but rouge a trifle the cheeks and the lips."

"You will not paint your face!" Madeleine squeaked, shocked.

"No, no, not so it will be noticed, for I plan to become a Lady of Quality."

Letting the gown fall, she rose and caught her cousin's hands, pulling her to her feet and whirling her about. "Should I fail to catch a duke, my Madeleine, I can always become a modiste. One way or another, as soon as I am settled, I shall send for you. Perhaps we shall be modistes together."

But Celeste had no intention of failing. She was going to become the Duchess of Ault.

The front gate creaked, and she released her breathless cousin and ran to the window. As she had feared, M. Guillaume Gagny proceeded in his stately manner up the garden path, his tubby figure garbed in his Sunday best, and a tight nosegay of spring flowers in his pudgy hand. Madeleine, her round cheeks pink-flushed, hurried to open the door.

Celeste smoothed her somber skirts and prepared to receive her difficult visitor. At least he would not propose to her as yet. She had two weeks respite before the end of her mourning, and M. Gagny was anything if not punctilious on every point of convention. But on the day that year ended . . . on that day, she would be on her way to England.

Madeleine vanished into the kitchen, and M. Gagny came toward Celeste, wafting the delectable aroma of fresh baked bread in his wake. He bent over the hand she extended and planted a moist kiss on her fingertips.

"Not long now, eh, *ma petite?*" he reminded her with a coy glance better suited to one ten years his junior. She wiped the fingers surreptitiously in a fold of her gown, as she seated herself and motioned him to the chair vacated by Madeleine and the black bombazine. Politely, he ignored the disorder of the parlor.

While they made desultory conversation about the clement weather, his eyes, gleaming with anticipation, roamed about the comfortable room. Celeste watched as those acquisitive eyes came to rest on Madeleine, who entered carrying a tray, and she saw the anticipation fade to regret. She noted the wistful glint, but as she well knew, French businessmen were a practical race when it came to romance. Poor Madeleine . . .

Her cousin brushed the fashion plates from a table and set down the tray. She cleared another chair of gowns and began quietly pouring hot chocolate into the delicate fluted cups that had belonged to their grandmother.

M. Gagny, a smile once more on his chubby face, began to prattle of village gossip. Celeste settled her features in an expression of vivid interest, and let her mind return to the far more important task of remodeling her wardrobe. The grays and lavenders would do very well much as they were, even the good, black bombazine . . . but surely, one more, perhaps her rose lustring from last year with new lace puffed sleeves . . . just in case. . . .

Her late father once visited his brother in England, and she had heard much from him of the cold, unemotional nature of the gentlemen of quality. She would need to warm one up.

She let Madeleine carry the conversation, and M. Gagny did not seem to notice her preoccupation. After half an hour, replete with pastry and hot chocolate, he correctly took his leave of the ladies.

Madeleine walked slowly back from seeing him to the door. "Celeste, are you sure you would not rather remain here and marry M. Gagny? He is so very nice."

"He is fat!"

"So am I, and you do not hold me in disgust . . . do you?"

Celeste bounced from her chair and swooped on her, kissing both her cheeks. *"Ma dodu poupée!* Silly little doll! I adore you! You are a wooly lamb. But he does not love me, or I him."

"Love will come after marriage. How could it help but do so?"

"It is this cottage he wants, so close to his shop."

"Oh, no!" Madeleine was genuinely distressed. "That cannot be true. He is all that is amiable and kind, and will make an ideal husband."

Celeste smiled and patted her shoulder. "And you have a *tendre* for him, have you not? If it were you who owns this house, I know the one he would be courting." She waggled a teasing finger. "It is you he prefers. I have too much volatility for the so sedate *M. le Boulanger.*"

"But you are so beautiful!"

"Beautiful! He would marry me if I were—" Her gaze centered on her cousin's plain features. "Madeleine, I have it! I shall not send for you after all." She laughed at Madeleine's suddenly crestfallen face. "No, no. This is so much better. M. Gagny wants this house. I shall have no use for it when I marry my wealthy Englishman, and it should not go out of the family. Madeleine, I give it to you. It is yours. Now you shall become madame, the wife of the baker, and both become as round as two balls together!"

Madeleine collapsed onto the heap of gowns that had been swept from the chairs and stared at her, her mouth agape.

"But yes, Madeleine! It is the solution. I go in the morning to the house of *M. l'Avocat* and sign over a deed to you! Come now, get up off my wardrobe and help me ready all for my journey."

Thus having decided to burn her last bridge, Celeste threw herself into her preparations to capture the heart of the Duke of Ault.

Two

Rake Cole slipped back into the hall by a side door from the terrace. There was a mirror there, and he needed to straighten his neckcloth and rearrange his carefully tousled curls before returning to the ballroom. Confound it, why couldn't Francoise Gaudet kiss a man without rumpling his hair?

He should never have yielded to her coy invitation, but the devil was in it, she was damned attractive. He poked at the creases in his Oriental and fiddled with his short, dark curls. Neither would look quite the same, but he persevered until instead of Rake Cole, Sir Geoffrey Cole, Bart., looked back at him.

Since unexpectedly succeeding two years before to the baronetcy of his elder brother—and the guardianship of that brother's young daughter—Geoff was seriously attempting to be more circumspect in his actions. As head of his family, he felt it behooved him to become a pattern card of respectability, but women like Francoise made it difficult. Frenchwomen, those of her cut at any rate, were vastly more demonstrative than their English sisters. And far freer with their favors.

His appearance reasonably repaired, he waited by the door to the ball, watching the dancing, until he was sure

Francoise was safely inside. She might not be a lady, but he strove to be a gentleman.

He had been gone longer than he intended. It was high time he checked on his ward before Miss Marianna Cole committed some ghastly social *faux pas.* He looked about the room, growing uneasy. With her volatile spirits combined with his shady reputation, he eyed the future with foreboding. Already she had proved to be a handful, awake on every suit and ripe for any lark. He had dreaded turning her loose on the *ton,* for she had blossomed almost overnight into a confoundedly pretty girl.

Already she had captured the eye of the young Duke of Ault, who only that morning had begged permission to pay his addresses to her in form. Marianna, however, was far too young to marry, only weeks from the schoolroom. Next season, perhaps, he'd reconsider Ault's offer. If only the man were not so frippery a rattle . . . and if only Marianna could be kept from crossing the line. His sister Augusta was not worth tuppence as a chaperone.

He never should have let Marianna come out this Season. Only with that engaging little chit, he had soon learned it was easier to submit to her demands than to put up with her wan face and silent suffering. And where was the blasted girl now?

"Oh, the devil," he muttered as he searched in vain for his ward among the dancers. Irritably flicking up the lid of a dainty, enameled snuffbox, he took a pinch of his special sort between thumb and forefinger—and paused, his hand only partway to his aristocratic nose.

His scowl became more pronounced as he completed the act. A movement of the quadrille in progress afforded him an excellent view of his young niece slipping, in a manner that could only be construed as surreptitious, from behind a long, brocaded curtain that enclosed the embrasure of one of the twelve French windows opening onto the garden. Rake Cole knew only too well what went on within the draped alcoves of a ballroom.

In her open robe of celestial blue sarcenet embroidered with rosebuds and knots of silver twist, worn over an undergown of misty ivory satin, Marianna presented an enchanting picture. There was no admiration, however, in her uncle's expression as he snapped the tiny box shut. Damn it all, he shouldn't have stayed out so long. And where was Augusta? She was supposed to be chaperoning Marianna, not cavorting with one of her cicisbeos.

He gritted his teeth. Ever since their nursery days, his sister had been frivolous. Why couldn't Augusta hold the line? Chaperones did not dance, they kept an eye on their charges.

As he glowered, Marianna patted her dusky curls into place and moved quickly to join an animated group of young people, her laughing face becomingly flushed. The lights blazing from nearly a thousand candles in the glittering chandeliers picked up sparkles from her dress as she ran.

Their hostess, Lady Bentley, stopped before Geoff, nodding her silver head and setting the ostrich plumes in her lilac turban to swaying.

"You must allow me to congratulate you on your charming ward, Sir Geoffrey." Her smile was rather thin. "She is quite the belle of my ball."

He thanked her, and the ostrich plumes waved at him as she passed on to greet a late-coming guest.

Still frowning, Sir Geoffrey remained where he was,

his eyes on the curtained embrasure. Within a few minutes, his patience was rewarded. The draperies stirred again, then were brushed aside to reveal a young gentleman in full, scarlet regimentals stepping in through the open French window. He paused to glance around, and then walked off in the opposite direction from Marianna.

Every inch Sir Geoffrey, Rake clenched his fists at his sides, his blood pressure shot up, and he muttered words he had not used since his days as London's reigning care-for-nobody. If she received the reputation of being fast—as she surely would if she continued behaving in this reprehensible manner—no gentleman of rank would consider her an eligible wife, let alone his Grace, the Duke of Ault.

His fulminating eyes returned to his niece, who was now flirting outrageously with another rather dashing officer. Out for barely three weeks, she already seemed to have the entire regiment at her feet, and that sort of connection would never do. Her social success had obviously gone to her head. If he didn't step in, the silly child was bound to entangle herself with some handsome half-pay officer.

She didn't need to make a wealthy match, not with her fortune, but he was determined to see that she married someone worthy of his late elder brother's only daughter. Although Geoff had merely inherited a baronetcy on the death of old Charles, the girl stood a good chance of becoming a duchess.

He still held his snuffbox. Absently taking another pinch, he raised it to his nose and sniffed too vigorously, annoying himself further with an embarrassing sneeze.

A cheery hand clapped him on the back, and he turned to see a slightly inebriated gentleman laughing up at him.

"Rake!"

"Oh, hallo, Brookhurst."

"Watching over your charge, old man?" Brookhurst peered at the crowd around Marianna. "I'd say you had your hands full there. A lively miss, if I ever saw one."

Geoff's answering smile was a bit forced. "I never should have let Marianna come out so young, but she'll be sixteen before the Season closes, and as usual I yielded to her pleading. Devious, little minx." He shook his head, ruefully. "She can always manage to wrap me around her finger."

"The time has come to let another man cope with your problem, old boy." Brookhurst eyed that fetching damsel appreciatively. "You'll have no trouble getting her off."

"Indeed. I have received an offer from young Ault already."

As they watched, Sylvester, sixth Duke of Ault, claimed Marianna for the country dance. Other heads turned, eyes on the fair-haired young nobleman and his ravishing ebony-curled partner.

"A very handsome couple," Brookhurst remarked. "You'd go far before contracting a more advantageous marriage for her."

Geoff nodded. Yes, he thought, and they might suit very well. The duke was an extremely pretty young man. Too dandified by far, but he had a good height and an excellent figure, as well as classic features. He should appeal to a romantic miss, but could Ault curb Marianna's volatility? He had very serious doubts on that score.

"By the way," Brookhurst gave him a curious sidelong look, "I hear I'm to wish you happy as well."

"That is correct. Lady Charlotte has agreed to accept my offer."

Brookhurst shuffled his feet, looking hard at his gleaming evening pumps. "Your business, of course, old boy, but as a friend . . . why?" He glanced up at Geoff's stiffening face and then quickly looked away.

Years of friendship told. Sir Geoffrey relaxed, a touch of Rake Cole returning. "Must have an heir, you know," he said lightly. "My duty, since Charles is gone."

Brookhurst stuck out his hand. "Good luck, Rake. Name the first boy after me, and I'll stand godfather." He shook Geoff's hand warmly, punched him on the arm, and walked away.

Looking after him, Geoff felt no elation, no pleasure in receiving the well-wishes of his best friend. Brookhurst, he noted, had said good luck, not congratulations.

A movement of the dance brought Marianna and her partner into the vicinity of his betrothed. Lady Charlotte, eldest daughter of his godfather, the Earl of Langham, sat in quiet conversation with a purple-turbaned dowager. Geoff's contemplation shifted from his niece to his fiancee. Now there, he told himself, was a woman of superior gentility, one who knew what was due to her name. Like most formerly ramshackle gentlemen, he held firm ideas regarding utmost respectability in the woman who'd be his wife. No breath of scandal would dare blow in the vicinity of a female of Lady Charlotte's character. He had chosen her carefully.

Lady Charlotte had seen several Seasons, and long ceased to be considered on the Marriage Mart, when he inherited the title. Recognizing his responsibility to his family to contract an excellent marriage and produce an heir, he had immediately begun to look around for a lady of sufficiently good lineage to occupy the position of his wife and the mother to his future son. Lady Charlotte had duly come to his attention, and he deemed her suitable as much for her family's close ties with his, as for her breeding and lack of romantic notions. Lady Charlotte he believed to be a sensible woman who would grace her position, know her duty, demand little, and always be a credit to him. Her consequence would go far to counteracting his sad reputation, and would create a proper background for his brother's only child. And, after all, one did not look for beauty and passion in a wife.

Within a week of making his decision, he had presented himself at the home of the Earl of Langham, requesting that astonished peer's permission to pay his addresses to Lady Charlotte. He suspected the earl of having long since given up hope of marrying her eligibly—if at all—and therefore would eagerly accept the offer of a mere baronet. And an infamous here-and-thereian, at that. Geoff's lip curled, remembering. No doubt his not contemptible fortune had also biased the impoverished earl in his favor. Lady Charlotte, he absolved of any such mercenary thoughts.

He became aware, suddenly, of a footman hovering by his side trying to catch his attention, and gave him a testy glance. "Yes?"

"Your pardon, Sir Geoffrey, I bear a message from Lady Charlotte."

"Let's have it then," he snapped. Oh, the devil, had she also noted Marianna's return to the ballroom? He was tempted to suggest she mind her own business. Brookhurst's attitude toward his betrothal must have set his back up more than he realized.

"She requests your company, Sir Geoffrey, and asks that you bring her a glass of lemonade."

"A royal command, eh?" Geoff attempted to hide his ill humor behind a gracious smile, and headed toward the heavily laden refreshment table at the end of the hall. A few minutes later, he moved carefully along the edge of the ballroom, balancing two glasses, one of which contained champagne. Lemonade hardly suited his mood.

Heads turned again as he worked his way toward the place where his fiancee was seated, for Rake Cole made an imposing figure in his scrupulously correct evening attire. He was a handsome man, and arresting with his dark brows, slightly aquiline nose—and habitual frown, acquired since being saddled with the guardianship of his aggravating niece.

Lady Charlotte, as always, was perfectly gowned in orange blossom crepe with a demure décolletage, tiny puff sleeves of gauze and silver thread, and very long gloves. A hand-painted chicken skin fan completed her costume; she reached up to tap his hand with it.

"But you do not dance, Geoffrey!" She took him to task playfully. "Only see how many of us are seated."

She was right, of course, which annoyed him further. A gentleman should do his duty at a ball, particularly by his fiancee. He bowed, nearly decanting the lemonade into her lap.

"Forgive me, Charlotte. It is only that I have been trying to keep an eye on Marianna. Augusta is far too lax."

"I do not see your sister. Where can she be? Do give me that before you spill it." She took her glass from him and patted the empty seat beside her. "Pray sit down, Geoffrey. Since you have brought up the subject, I know you will not mind my speaking on a matter which must be of concern to us both."

Geoff sipped his champagne in silence, finding he minded very much.

She nodded toward the dancers. "I see Marianna is now partnered with Ault. A most charming couple, do you not agree? I believe him to have a definite *tendre* for her. I should very much prefer to have her settled before we are wed, but her behavior of late . . . ?" She raised delicate brows. "I am sure you deplore her excessive spirits as much as I."

"Yes," he replied shortly, preparing to endure the forthcoming lecture and obscurely resenting it on Marianna's behalf.

"Now there," Lady Charlotte went on, "she would be forming a most excellent connection. From the way he hovers about her, I feel it would not be wonderful if Ault should make her an offer. You must do whatever is necessary to throw them together. She is being forward to a fault, you must know, a thing quite unbecoming in a miss of her station. Should Ault approach you, you must close with him at once, before he changes his mind."

Geoff, driven to contrariness, finished his champagne in a gulp. "He already has and I turned him away."

Lady Charlotte gasped. "You are quizzing me, I make sure!"

"I told him she was too young." He shifted in his seat. "I may have erred," he conceded, "but he called on me in yellow pantaloons and a beehive hat. His collar points were so high and well starched that he couldn't turn his head. I'm afraid it put me off."

"Ah, nor do I approve of dandyism." She gave his knee a forgiving tap with her fan, and he moved away before he could stop himself.

"It both renders the person ridiculous and serves no practical purpose," she went on pedantically, "but in this case, my dear Geoffrey, I feel we must overlook such a minor foible. It is a pity his mother passed away last year. No doubt she must have influenced him for the better. This fancy for fashion came upon him only recently."

"Indeed. I remember her as a very determined female. Probably why Ault is such a milk-toast."

Lady Charlotte demurred. "He is not a sportsman, a type I realize you favor, but his manners and address are everything that is most amiable and obliging. His understanding I consider to be excellent, and he is not in the least high in the instep, never overconscious of his rank, nor above being pleased in superior company."

"Yes, no doubt." Geoff's attention had wandered, focused on the company present. The country dance completed, the couples were leaving the floor. Where was that dratted girl this time?

He came to a sudden decision, making up his mind to accept the offer of the Duke of Ault. His hesitation, he had to admit, had been in part pure snobbery. The duke's mother was French. As Rake Cole, he knew Frenchwomen. As Sir Geoffrey, he could not like that French blood.

"He may not have been in direct succession to the

title," Lady Charlotte was saying, "but his breeding is impeccable. His mother was the daughter of a marquis."

"His mother died insane," Geoff countered, his eyes scanning the room.

Lady Charlotte registered mild shock. "Oh, surely, not insane! A little queer towards the last, perhaps, but we must not hold that against the son."

"I beg you will excuse me." He rose suddenly and walked quickly away, but not before hearing the last of Lady Charlotte's measured speech urging him to encourage young Ault to hope for a happy conclusion to his suit. An uneasy feeling had begun to creep over Geoff that perhaps he had made *two* gross errors of late. *His* goose was cooked, but one mistake, at least, could be corrected. Marianna should become the Duchess of Ault.

The sixth duke stood alone in the center of the floor; a vague, perplexed expression on his handsome face, as though he had lost something. Geoff touched his arm.

"Ault, I wonder if I might have a word with Your Grace?"

On the carriage ride home, tucked between her flighty, golden-haired Aunt Augusta and prim Lady Charlotte, Marianna was informed of her great, good fortune.

She stared across the commodious coach at her uncle, struck dumb, her face vivid with horror.

"Ault!" her Aunt Augusta exclaimed in disbelief. "I had no idea he was hanging out for a wife."

"He also must have an heir," Geoff informed his sister somewhat stiffly, and suddenly became conscious of Lady Charlotte's presence.

Marianna found her tongue. "But why *me?* I do not wish to be married! This is my first Season, and I am not yet sixteen!"

"You will be in a month's time," he reminded her. "You needn't be wed until then."

"But, Uncle Geoff! Ault! He is of all things what I most dislike. A dandy! A fop! Why, Captain Fairfield took me right away from him in the rudest manner, and he never raised a hand! He is a—a coxcomb! A popinjay!"

Lady Charlotte shook an admonitory finger. "Really, Marianna, a lady of your quality does not use such words to describe a gentleman."

"Well, you know what I mean! Captain Fairfield is twice the man he is!"

Geoff's lips tightened. "Ah, the man behind the curtain? So you knew his name then?"

Marianna flushed and shrank back into the velvet squabs lining the carriage, and Augusta frowned at her brother.

"Now that was unkind in you, Geoff. Quite outside of enough."

In the semidarkness of the coach, Geoff caught Marianna's hurt sniffle and relented.

"I'll admit that jibe was unforgivable. You must hold me forever in contempt."

"We only took the air for a few moments," Marianna complained, sulky-voiced. "It was so very warm in the ballroom, and actually he is an old friend. Why, I have known him forever—ever since my first ball."

"I see," Geoff soothed. "My mistake entirely. A friend

of all of three weeks must be considered unexceptionable."

"Now you are roasting me, Uncle Geoff!"

"No. Merely trying to make you see the appearance of your actions to others. You can have no notion how many persons may have observed you coming back into the room, and the gentleman in scarlet following in a bare few minutes."

"He didn't!" Marianna exclaimed. "But that was stupid in him! He should have waited longer!"

Augusta nodded in the near-darkness. "I quite agree. It shows a lack of understanding that one must deplore. It is stupidly rash on your part, Marianna, to trust your reputation to anyone so nod-cocked."

Much struck by this bit of wisdom, Marianna subsided, only to spring forward again as she remembered the original argument.

"But I don't want to be married yet! I am having a very good time! You just want to be rid of me, because you are being wed yourself!"

This came so close to the truth that Geoff searched in vain for words to deny it. Before he could speak, Lady Charlotte threw fuel on the coals.

"You are being married," she said, "before you ruin yourself beyond recall."

Marianna collapsed in tears and Geoff came near to reprimanding his fiancee, a thing unheard-of in the gentleman he strove to be.

"Please, Charlotte, you are not helping. And you, Marianna, are making of this a Cheltenham tragedy."

"I'm not being ruined, Uncle Geoff! I'm not!" Marianna was fast working herself into a case of mild hysterics, a ploy that her uncle recognized and refused to countenance.

"Marianna, don't waste these high flights on me. You are behaving like a Bath miss!"

"And I don't want to marry someone you choose for me! I want to pick my own husband!"

"My dear girl," Lady Charlotte spoke with finality. "Persons of our order do not marry to please themselves."

About to advert on just those lines himself, Geoff checked. Was he right to force on Marianna a marriage of convenience, such as he was about to make for himself?

Augusta took the weeping girl into her arms. "Leave her alone, both of you. Marianna, do stop and think. Geoffrey is in the right. A girl has only her face to invest in her future. You must take all advantage of it now. You cannot hope for a better offer than this from Ault."

"He is a duke, Marianna," said Lady Charlotte, as if that settled the matter. "You will be a duchess."

Marianna chewed her lower lip thoughtfully. The idea of outranking Lady Charlotte suddenly dried the tears she was already having trouble maintaining. She'd be a duchess . . .

Three

The wedding of Madeleine and Guillaume Gagny took place immediately after the signing over of the deed to the cottage of Mlle. Celeste Moreau to her cousin, Mlle. Madeleine Martin.

Two weeks later as she landed on the quay in England, after a tempestuous passage of the Channel, the memory still brought sentimental tears to Celeste's soft brown eyes. The newlyweds were so happy. If only the Duke of Ault proved to be an amenable *parti,* she would be satisfied with half such happiness.

Still a bit pale and shaken from the rough crossing, she traveled by stagecoach to Ault-in-the-Vale, a mile from the castle, and was set down with her trunk before the only inn in the village. She eyed the ancient tavern doubtfully, for it seemed not at all a proper place for a lady. Several men, farmhands or drovers from their loutish appearance, lounged against the wall, watching her with an interest that rendered her extremely uncomfortable. Leaving her trunk at the doorstep, for she could not lift it, she walked into a gloomy miasma, redolent of mutton, cabbage, and beer.

Owing to narrow windows with panes that had not been cleaned in this century, it was dark in the tiny entry.

A flight of stairs rose directly in front of her. On the left, an archway led to a public bar, where more men sat about with tankards in their hands. They, too, stared at her, and she looked quickly away. On her right, a hall led past the stairs to the back premises. There were several doors, one of which stood open, and she saw tables and chairs within. A coffee room. She felt ravenous, for the coach had not stopped long enough all day for its passengers to manage a meal.

She clutched her reticule, mentally counting the few coins within. The trip had cost far more than she had anticipated, but she had arrived. Tomorrow, she would be with her uncle. Meanwhile it was evening, too late to visit the castle, and besides, she was sadly travel-stained. It would take the last of her capital, but she meant to engage a room for the night so that she might don a fresh gown and appear rested and at her best when she met him.

The innkeeper came out of the bar, wiping his hands on his apron. He looked past her, saw no companion, and looked back at her, his gaze taking in her disheveled, black bombazine. His expression of affable welcome changed to a frown. "What d'yer want, miss?"

"I desire a room for the night," she told him. "And also a meal. My trunk, it is outside, for I cannot lift it. Have it carried to my room, *s'il vous plaît.*"

"Y'er French," he accused.

She agreed that she was.

"What'cher doin' 'ere?"

Although she considered him rude in the extreme, she was about to reply when a woman, nearly as round as she was tall, came from the coffee room. The newcomer was enveloped from neck to feet in a voluminous, wrap-around apron. Clean, Celeste was pleased to see. A ruffled, white mobcap covered her hair.

" 'Oo's this?" the woman demanded. "If it's work she's wantin', we don't need no more maids."

"Sez she wants a room," explained the landlord.

They both looked at her with suspicion, and Celeste suddenly realized why. In this England, ladies did not travel alone. She hastened to explain herself to the round female, whom she presumed to be the innkeeper's wife.

"I am a governess," she said. "I have come from France to teach the children. Of a certainty, my good woman, I am of the most respectable. It is that my uncle is the priest of the Duchess of Ault. I go in the morning to call upon her."

The woman's suspicion increased. "That's as may be," she sneered. "A likely story."

Celeste stiffened. "It is the truth. She will tell you herself."

"Well, now," the man folded his arms across his broad chest, or the place his chest would have been had it not joined company with his belly. "I'm afraid that there won't be possible." He suddenly glanced behind him, uneasily.

"And why not?" Celeste demanded.

"Because that there duchess 'as been lyin' in 'er coffin in that big vault up to Aultmere for more'n a year."

Daunted, Celeste stared at him, her heart sinking. Then where was her uncle? Was he still at the castle? But he must be, where else would he go? She drew herself up.

"En fin, then I will visit his Grace, the Duke, for I must at once learn of my uncle. He is still there?"

"That I couldn't say, miss, not 'oldin' with these 'ere Catholics."

"Church of England, we are," said his wife. "Can you pay for this room yer wantin'?"

There didn't seem to be anything else she could do. Celeste inquired the amount and counted out the proper coins, studying each of them carefully so as not to make a mistake with the strange money.

"*Zut,* these English!" she muttered to herself, but was given an excellent, though plain, dinner and a room with dry sheets.

In the morning, she borrowed the gig belonging to the inn and the pot-boy to drive it, and set out for the castle known as Aultmere. The ill-fated black bombazine had seen its best days, having been, besides sat on by Madeleine, worn during the long journey by boat and stage. She discarded it, and donned her best dove gray carriage gown, her black gloves, and the black bonnet, now lined with pleated gray silk and decked with a cluster of gray ribbons. Her black cashmere shawl was looped over her elbows and allowed to hang stylishly down in back, disguising some of the creases impossible to prevent, even with her careful packing.

Arriving at Aultmere, she marched up the wide stone steps to the great oaken front door and plied a huge brass knocker, shaped like a heavy ring depending from the jaws of a scowling lion's head. She gave it an extra bang; no brass lion could intimidate her.

The door swung open, and she faced a footman, resplendent in silver-laced livery. He also scowled on perceiving a lone female on the castle steps, but after facing the door knocker, a mere footman was nothing.

"I wish to speak with M. the Duke of Ault," she said with great dignity.

The footman, who obviously had aspirations of becoming a butler, already boasted the high-arched nose. He looked down it in a disparaging manner. "His Grace is not in residence," he intoned.

Taken aback, Celeste demanded, "Where is he?" before she could stop herself.

"I could not say," the footman answered in a tone that implied it was none of her business.

Celeste rallied. "Then, if you please, I wish to speak with the priest of Madame the duchess, Father Francois Moreau."

"I am afraid that will be impossible."

He was not afraid at all. Well, neither was she. "Why is it impossible? He is my uncle, and I wish to see him at once."

The footman unbent; it was hard to maintain butlerian dignity for long. "Well, you can't. 'E ain't 'ere. 'E's gone back to France." He stepped back, and the great door shut with the hint of a slam.

Celeste stared at the blank portal, some of the starch going out of her spine. Then she straightened. It is of the greatest luck, she told herself, that I did not have my trunk brought here but left at the inn. But now what was she to do? She had only three English ha'pennies left in her reticule.

She looked up at the scowling brass lion on the solidly closed oaken door, and made a very French gesture.

Head held high, she turned and walked back to the gig.

* * *

Sylvester Francis Henri d'Aubergne Barfeld, sixth duke of Ault, was in London, for the Season was in full swing. Completely unaware of Mlle. Celeste Moreau, no thoughts of marrying a beautiful governess had entered his head. Not a great deal ever did.

Two weeks had gone by, and although he had received Sir Geoffrey's permission to pay court to Miss Marianna Cole, he had not yet worked up the nerve to put his fate to the test.

The girl seemed almost to avoid him, and there was one of those confounded lobster-backs in particular, a captain, on whom she lavished her brightest smiles. Suppose she refused him for a common soldier? Him, a duke! His ego would not survive such a blow. In desperation, he went to Sir Geoffrey.

Geoff, his eye also on the red-coated captain, was fast losing patience.

"Don't be such a gap-witted clodpole!" he said, completely forgetting the exalted rank of said clodpole. "Of course, she'll accept. I told her of your intentions weeks ago, and she agreed. She's just amusing herself while she can, and I do not wish her to be so amused. Come tomorrow, I guarantee she will be receptive."

Vastly encouraged, the Duke of Ault returned to his quarters and spent the next hours closeted with his man, selecting from his resplendent wardrobe the ideal raiment to enchant his future bride.

Promptly at eleven o'clock on the following morning, he presented himself on Sir Geoffrey's doorstep. Admitted by an interested butler, and observed from behind cracked doors by two footmen and no less than four maids and the housekeeper, he was led upstairs to the drawing room, where he was left to cool his heels.

Feeling rather nervous, he adjusted the intricate folds of his neckcloth in the mirror over the mantelpiece. His hair he didn't dare touch, its artless carelessness owed to the genius of his man, as did the shine of his impeccable Hessians. He froze for a moment in near-terror. Were his collar points beginning to wilt? How foolish of him to elect to walk the few blocks on so warm a day! He tested the stiffly starched edges with a cautious finger—and reflected behind him, he saw the face of Miss Marianna Cole, convulsed with laughter.

He whirled about, scarlet with embarrassment, but managed to make her an exquisite bow. She returned a dignified curtsy, almost straight-faced, and waited. As always in her presence, his usual haughty demeanor deserted him. In love with her he was not, but her undeniable beauty and vivacity intrigued him to a point where he was convinced that no other woman could fill the empty place in his life.

Since the death of his mother, Aultmere had become unbearably lonely. He missed having a female about to manage for him, and Marianna was quite the prettiest girl he had yet encountered. The fact never occurred to him that no one could appear less capable of managing a ducal estate than did this delightful young maiden.

Marianna remained standing just inside the door. She looked him over with a speculative eye, in a way that made him acutely self-conscious. This must be, he realized, because she was seriously considering his worth as a prospective mate. Why was he worried? He was a duke!

Mentally, he ran over his costume—pale fawn inexpressibles, all correct. His second best waistcoat—should he have worn the new silver-laced brocade?—he had just checked his neckcloth and the day being clement, there could be no mud on his beautifully polished boots.

His confidence restored, he stepped forward holding out his hand. Her fingers felt cold in his warm, slightly clammy grasp, as he raised them to his lips for a lingering kiss. Did she shrink back? Or did he imagine it? He looked up at her, but her face gave nothing away but the same speculative interest.

"I've spoken to your uncle," he began. "He has given his permission for me to pay my addresses to you." He hesitated. Why didn't she speak, or nod—or something? An awful thought came to him. "I say, he has told you, has he not? He said he did."

"Oh, yes." Her voice lacked enthusiasm, but seemed not at all forbidding. Encouraged, he dropped formally on one knee and raced on before he lost his nerve.

"Marianna, I beg you will do me the honor of accepting my hand in marriage." The speech poured out almost as one word, and the beastly girl looked like she struggled to control a giggle! Laughing at him again! He got to his feet in a hurry. "Well?"

Marianna stared at him, suddenly sobered. This was it. She had to commit herself, one way or the other. She would be a duchess—Lady Charlotte's words ran through her mind like racehorses coursing round and round upon a track. A duchess—a duchess—a duchess—you will be a duchess . . . she answered quickly before she could change her mind.

"Yes, I should very much like to be a duchess." She clapped a hand to her mouth as she heard her own incriminating statement, but Ault didn't seem to have noticed.

He dragged a huge, ugly signet ring from his finger and held it out. "This will have to do until I go back to the castle. At Aultmere there is an emerald that belonged in my mother's family. You shall have it as soon as possible."

Marianna let him slip the heavy ring onto her finger. It promptly slid underneath, too large and too bulky for her slender hand. She righted it and gazed down at it with revulsion. Belatedly recalling her manners, she murmured, "Thank you."

"Well, then."

She felt the relief flowing from the young man before her. Conscious of the irrevocable step she had just taken, she looked him over carefully. As a husband, he would not be a bad bargain. Besides the title. Tall, with fair hair casually disarranged by a master valet, he had good features, and his shoulders beneath the padded coat were broad enough. She need never be ashamed of his appearance, could she but get him to a respectable tailor. Handling him would be easily within her power, she judged, from the awkward way he now stood before her, shifting from one foot to the other. She decided to end the interview.

"Good-bye," she said simply, holding out her hand to be kissed once more.

He let out a long breath, apparently feeling he had gotten over rough ground more lightly than he had expected. A quick brush of his lips against her fingers, and he retired gratefully.

Through the open door, Marianna saw her Uncle Geoff

pounce on him as he went by. She returned to her room slowly, prey to mixed feelings.

When she met her uncle later over a light nuncheon of cold meats, fruit, and tea in the small morning salon, he greeted her with a smile of approval.

"Good girl."

Still dithering between triumphant dreams of lording it over Lady Charlotte as the Duchess of Ault and moments of ghastly reality, she didn't answer.

"Come now, life is not all bad," he rallied her. "You will be very happy as mistress of Aultmere. Magnificent place. Three times as large as ours. You'll see it tomorrow."

She raised her eyes at this. "Tomorrow?"

"Yes." He busied himself peeling a peach with a tiny, silver knife. "I've arranged with Ault to drive out there for the day. It's not too far, but will take all of two hours to get there, so we must be up and away betimes."

Marianna dropped a forkful of ham back onto her plate. "But I cannot go tomorrow! I have a fitting for my new ball gown, and then I go to tea at the Chisholms'."

"Cancel both."

"Uncle Geoff!"

"Ault will travel with us there and return. Lady Charlotte feels that the sooner you become familiar with your new status, the better. We will depart at ten in the morning, so you must be home early tonight in order to be ready."

"But, Uncle Geoff, you know I *hate* long carriage drives! I shall be ill from the jolting! I won't go—"

"You are never ill," he interrupted callously. "The

early rising and fresh air will do you a world of good after all this partying. You will go."

She went.

The journey indeed became tedious. Utterly wasted were her yellow muslin ruffles and charming chip straw hat, for beyond informing Marianna that she resembled a daffodil in spring and attempting to kiss her cheek, the sixth duke confined his conversation to her Uncle Geoffrey. She rapidly grew bored with accounts of the elegance of his town establishment as well as that of Aultmere, and the unfortunate turn of the cards at White's the previous evening.

She whiled away the time playing at a favorite game, fancying herself a captive princess. The traveling coach was closed and stuffy, owing to Ault's fear of contracting an inflammation of the lungs from a stray draft. This and the fact that for the last mile they had traveled through the darkness of a densely wooded area, gave credence to her daydream of being dragged by an ogre to his gloomy, bat-ridden castle. She particularly hated bats. Once arrived at the odious castle, she was to be wed to the ogre and then eaten. She shivered in rapturous anticipation.

Not of being eaten, of course. Before it came to that— probably while they were still on the road—she would be rescued by a handsome knight astride a gallant white charger. The stranger would hold them up at pistol point, wrest her from the arms of the hideous ogre, and carry her off over the bow of his saddle. His splendid steed would gallop them away across the fields, just such fields as they now approached.

She was rudely jerked back to the present by Ault,

who leaned over to touch the heavy signet ring Uncle Geoff had insisted she wear.

"Not much farther," he said. "We have nearly reached Aultmere, and you shall soon have your emerald."

Uncle Geoff prodded her with an elbow.

"Oh. Yes, thank you. I expect I shall prefer that."

"It is a signet ring also," the duke went on, dashing her hopes. "From the d'Aubergne side of my family. My grandfather was a marquis, you know."

"I didn't."

"Oh?" He sounded a bit dashed. "Well, he was."

How nice for you, Marianna thought, but you are still my ogre. Will I never be rescued?

Suddenly the carriage pulled to a stop, the horses rearing. The footman on the box behind squealed and ducked.

Marianna released the leather and dropped her window. A roughly dressed horseman on a piebald cob had ridden into the road directly in front of them, brandishing a huge, long-barreled pistol.

"Stand and deliver!" he demanded in a rather high-pitched voice. He tried again in a far gruffer tone. "I mean, your money or your lives!"

Four

"Oh, my God," said Geoff, disgusted. "Now what?"

"A highwayman!" Ault, who sat next to the other window, shrank back into the corner. "My purse! Where shall I hide my purse?"

"Shove it down between the cushions." Her uncle leaned casually across Marianna, whose eyes were wide more with interest than fear.

The road agent managed to get control of his voice. "Outside, all of you!" he yelled hoarsely.

Having had a clear view of their youthful bandit, Geoff sounded rather amused. "Perhaps we better obey him. That appears to be a serviceable pistol he holds."

Ault seemed unable to move. Reaching past him, Geoff released the latch on the door and pushed it open. Marianna scrambled up, and he gently put her back.

"Let me go first, my dear." He climbed over her feet and dropped to the ground.

The footman still crouched under his seat at the back of the carriage, while the coachman struggled to quiet his horses. Turning his back on the man with the gun, Geoff let down the steps and stretched up a hand to Marianna, already on her way out. A shaky duke followed and stood behind her.

Marianna gazed with fascination and not a little disappointment at her first highwayman. He seemed absurdly young, no older than herself. The upper part of his face he had hidden behind a bit of black cloth with eye holes, rather like a loo mask, and wisps of tawny gold hair stuck out from under his slouch hat. His pants were worn buckskins, and he wore herdsman's boots, strips of old blanketing tied in place with spirals of leather about his legs. An ancient frieze coat hung on his shoulders, being several sizes too large.

"I don't believe he is much to fear," she remarked disparagingly. "That's not my idea of a highwayman."

"However, he does hold a pistol." Geoff still sounded amused. "We'd best humor him for the moment."

"But only see his horse!"

Looking at it, it was impossible to tell if it was a white animal with patches of brown, or possibly a bay splashed with white. It stood splay-footed, motionless as a statue carved from stone, its head hanging and eyes closed, apparently asleep.

The highwayman seemed to be rather taken aback at the sight of Marianna. "Here now!" he exclaimed. "I didn't know there was a lady!"

"Get back in the carriage, Marianna." Geoff smiled. "You are upsetting our—er—captor."

"No! I want to see what happens."

"Nothing's going to happen to you, ma'am." The young highwayman sounded unhappy, but his pistol remained steady. "The rest of you, your money or your lives! Oh, no, I said that."

"Make up your mind," Geoff suggested mildly. "We are in somewhat of a hurry. Marianna, do get back in."

"I won't."

"Suit yourself." He shrugged his shoulders. "But nothing is going to happen. You heard him."

"Listen," the would-be bandit put in plaintively. "This is a robbery. I have a gun. Hand over your valuables."

"Oh!" Marianna squealed. "You can't have my pearls!" As her hand flew to her throat, the ugly ring on her finger flashed into her view, and she had an inspiration. "Here," she cried. "You can have this."

She pulled the ring from her finger and threw it at him. Instinctively, he caught it, and Ault bounded out of hiding.

"Here! No! You can't have that!"

The highwayman glanced down at him. "Well, actually, I don't want your gewgaws. What I want is three pounds ten."

"Well, you're not getting it." Geoff was becoming exasperated. "Come now, put that cannon away. Get back in the coach, Marianna."

She ignored him. Ault jumped up and down beside the color-splotched horse, trying to catch the young man's arm and grab back the ring. The pistol turned to aim at his face, and he retired suddenly.

"Enough of this prank. Give me the ring." Geoff held up an imperative hand, snapping his fingers. The highwayman started to hand it to him, then took a second look at it, and froze.

He stared at the ring, then at Ault, his mouth dropping open. Slowly, he tucked the ring into his pocket, still staring at the sixth duke. The atmosphere of the farcical holdup changed, and a new note entered the young man's voice as he spoke to Marianna.

"Ma'am, where did you get this?"

"Why, I—"

"Marianna, get back in the coach. And you, give me that ring." Geoff continued to stretch up his hand.

"No!" Both young people spoke at once. The piebald nag was jerked awake and turned sideways to them. His rider studied the group before him, and finally waved the pistol at Marianna.

"I think you'll suit me best, ma'am. I want answers to a number of questions, and I believe you will talk most readily."

"I will not!" Marianna shrank back.

"Then perhaps I shall shoot that pretty gentleman."

The pistol turned again towards Ault, and all at once it occurred to Marianna that this might be an acceptable solution to her problem.

"Go right ahead." She shrugged a delicate shoulder, while Ault gave a protesting cry.

"Oh, then the other is a better choice?" The gun shifted to Geoff.

Marianna, who by now didn't believe a word of his threat, gazed calmly up at the sky. "I couldn't care less. Shoot them both." The bandit stared at her helplessly.

Geoff was becoming thoroughly annoyed, and spoke unwisely. "Stop acting the little fool, Marianna. Get back in the carriage, we've wasted enough time."

Marianna paled with anger. "I am not a fool!" she cried. "And I won't get back in. I don't want to go to Aultmere, and I won't get married! I'd rather be abducted by this highwayman, so there!"

Her uncle glanced at her dispassionately. "You are behaving like a little idiot. You'll do as you are told, my girl. Get in."

"I will not!" Defiantly, she ran to the horse. "Give me a hand up, sir."

"Here now!" gasped the highwayman.

Geoff, white-lipped, spoke with an ominous calm. "Marianna, you—would—not—dare!"

His words ignited the already smoldering tinder of rebellion that had seethed within her for the last several hours. A grand gesture was clearly called for, and here was one to hand.

"I would dare anything!" she flared. "You! Take me up with you at once!"

The highwayman appeared to be regretting his rash proposal. "I don't think I should," he demurred. "No, really, miss, it wouldn't be the thing."

Marianna, who had formed an accurate, though unflattering, opinion of the danger posed by their bandit, stamped her foot. "Now!"

The young man hesitated. "Abducting a lady ain't what I had in mind."

"You're not abducting me." Marianna yanked at his leg impatiently. "You're taking me to the nearest inn, so I can hire a chaise to bring me back to London."

"Well," he pushed up his hat with the barrel of his pistol, then quickly lowered the gun to point at Ault, who had sidled forward. "Will you tell me about him—and this ring?"

"Yes, yes." Marianna yanked at his leg again. "Help me up."

Ault began to protest, but Geoff, now so angry he could hardly speak, held him back. He took a deep breath. "Careful, he might be fool enough to pull the trigger. They won't get far, and it will do that tiresome chit a world of good to get a scare!"

"I don't care about that!" Ault cried. "He's got my ring!"

Geoff turned his furious gaze on the duke, and then onto Marianna. "Oh, the devil! I wash my hands of this whole affair."

This, to Marianna, was the outside of enough. She gave the highwayman's leg an extra hard yank. "Help me up—*now!*"

"I can't help you, ma'am," he objected. "I have to hold this gun and my horse. My hands are full." He kicked one foot free. "Here, step in the stirrup and come up behind me."

"I can't reach!"

Muttering under his breath, the young highwayman moved his oddly colored horse over to a convenient milestone. "Step up on that and swing your leg over."

Marianna squeaked. "My skirts!"

"Dammit, this is no time to be prudish." He dropped his rein and reached down a free hand, managing to keep the pistol aimed steadily at the men by the carriage. One good heave, and he hauled Marianna up behind the saddle. She sat astride, revealing a regrettable expanse of her best silk hose and new lace-trimmed drawers.

The piebald cob started off down the road at a shambling trot, which his rider managed to maintain by kicking furiously with both feet.

The minute they headed away, Ault sprang up into the box, shoving aside the bemused coachman. He dragged a loaded musket from its rack by the driver's seat.

"Hold, you idiot!" Geoff shouted. "You can't shoot without hitting the girl!"

He was too late. Ault raised the musket and fired. The kick of the explosion knocked him backward into the box. Geoff, first horrified, then livid with rage, swung up and snatched the gun from his hands.

"Did I hit him?" Ault struggled to his feet, aided by the fascinated coachman. "Is he dead?"

"No, thank God!" said Geoff, his voice tight with wrath. "But you scared the devil out of the horse and it's running away with them. Of all the damn fool things to do!"

"I didn't get him?" Ault grabbed for the musket. "Just let me—"

"Oh, no, you don't! They're clean away."

"I'll get him—I'll see him hung at Tyburn!"

"That you won't. Calm down! If you don't stop dancing around up here, you'll fall off the carriage!" He turned to the coachman. "Quit gawking like a gapeseed, man. Come and help me unhitch one of these nags. I'll be up with them in five minutes."

"He's a thief!" howled Ault. "He must be hung—he stole my ring!"

"He did not," Geoff snapped. "Marianna gave it to him. For God's sake, Ault. He is only a boy—and from the sound of him, not a commoner." He climbed down from the box followed by the coachman, whose shoulders shook with silent guffaws. Between them, they managed to get the sixth duke to the ground.

The two men unhitched one of the leaders, and Geoff looped up the long driving reins. Clutching a handful of mane at the withers, he vaulted easily onto the horse.

He reckoned without his steed. The animal was well-trained as a carriage horse, used to working in tandem with his mates, but he had never been ridden. He took instant exception to the proceedings, bucking and rearing.

Geoff, ordinarily an excellent horseman, bounced and slid on the slippery bare back. He dropped the ends of the long reins, they entangled the horse's hooves, and both crashed to the earth.

The coachman, no longer silent, caught the excited horse and retrieved the reins. Geoff cursed freely, displaying Rake Cole's rich vocabulary and arousing the man's instant admiration. Snatching the reins from him, Geoff looped them over the horse's head and remounted.

This time, crow hopping and sidling, they got under way. The horse spun around twice and took off at a fast canter—in the wrong direction.

When the shot blasted behind them, the highwayman gave a startled oath. The cob shied violently and took off at a clumsy, bone-shaking gallop.

Marianna, who had been trying to pull the yellow ruffles of her skirt down over her legs, shrieked and threw both arms around the man's waist. Her chip straw hat, its ribbons flying, parted company with her head and sailed down the road.

"Lord, I'm glad he didn't hit the horse!" the boy shouted over his shoulder. "I've only borrowed him. Here," he passed the pistol back. "I can't shove this in my belt with you hanging around my middle like that, and I need both hands for this beast if we are to stay on."

Marianna freed one hand and took the gun gingerly. "Will it go off?"

"Oh, it's not loaded. I don't have any bullets. Try to fix this damned mask; it keeps slipping, and I can't see."

She rammed the gun into the back of his belt. It jabbed her in the stomach with every jarring step, the cob now having slowed to a trot that was far worse than his canter. Reaching up, she pulled off the highwayman's hat, releasing an untidy mass of straw-colored curls.

The knot in the strip of ancient black silk eluded her shaking fingers for several minutes, before she finally jerked it off over the top of his head.

"Whew! That's better." He tossed his hair from his eyes. "I don't see how Jed ever put up with that devilish thing. Hey!" he cried as he saw her hand reach out to toss the cloth into the road. "Don't throw that away! It belonged to Jed!"

Marianna poked it into his belt beside the pistol. "Who is Jed?"

"My stepfather. He was a highwayman. They hanged him last month on Tyburn Hill," he added airily.

"Oh, I'm sorry."

"It's all right, he quite expected it, and he'd had a good long life. He must have been every bit of forty." He kicked the horse, who showed signs of slowing. "By the way, I'm Charlie Makepeace—but don't you let that onto the Runners," he added sternly. "Remember that my life is in your hands."

"Oh, is it?" Marianna felt a shiver of delight at the thought. "You are quite secure with me, I assure you. Never shall your name pass my lips," she vowed.

"Oh, well, as to that—you can call me Charlie, that's safe enough. Who the devil are you?"

"M—Marianna," she stammered, a trifle shocked by his language.

He considered it. "Nice," he decided.

Although the cob had dropped to a walk, Marianna noticed that Charlie swayed unsteadily in the saddle.

"I say," he remarked after a short silence. "I don't think I can hold on with this leg much longer."

Marianna looked down over the horse's side and screamed. "You're all bloody! You were hit!"

"It's naught but a scratch," he reassured her. "But it hurts like the devil. If I hadn't stuck out my leg so far the better to kick this slug, they'd never have touched me."

"We must stop and take care of it! Oh, I'll never forgive Uncle Geoff—or Ault—whoever did it," she declared roundly. "How much farther do we have to go?"

"Only to the church. I have urgent need of the parson."

"You're going to die?" Marianna squeaked.

He threw back his head and laughed uproariously. "Lord, you are a goosecap! I told you it's only a scratch."

A bit miffed, she demanded, "Then why do you want a parson? You aren't abducting me, you know. I wanted to come. You don't have to marry me."

"Good god, no! Whatever gave you such an addle-brained notion?"

"Well," she explained meekly, "I was just being carried off to be wed to someone against my will, so it was sort of on my mind. You see, you look so much like him."

Charlie brushed this aside. Only one phrase caught his interest.

"Against your will? You mean you *were* really being abducted?"

"Yes, I was." Marianna became quite pleased with the

idea. It was just like her daydream. "I was being taken
to this castle—Aultmere, it's called—and they were going to marry me to this odious duke."

"Of all the dastardly schemes!" Charlie sounded highly
incensed. "Then I certainly shan't return you to their carriage, as I meant to do. But I can't keep you with me—"

"What are we going to do?" Marianna asked hopefully
after a few minutes of silence.

"I've been thinking on that," said Charlie. "I was going to take you to the inn where I'm staying, but I don't
think I should. It's rather a rough place. And there may
be a spot of trouble," he added naively. "I forgot to tell
them I borrowed the horse, and it will be awkward now
that I haven't the three pounds ten to pay for him and
my shot. We will go to the church, and that will kill two
birds with one stone. They will be obliged to give you
sanctuary, and I shall find my parson."

By now they were coming to the outskirts of the village
of Ault-in-the-Vale. He turned the cob off the road and
into the plowed fields behind a row of thatched cottages.

"The inn's on this end of town," he explained. "Best
we avoid it, until we are through with the horse."

Marianna could see the steeple of the church above
the roofs. As they neared it, Charlie squeezed the cob
through a break in a hedge just beyond the low buildings
and crossed over. It was a small church, made of rough
gray stones tinged here and there with brown and green
from ages of moss and damp. Its spirelike steeple held
only one bell, but on each side of the heavy oak double
doors, stained glass windows promised a comforting ka-
leidoscope of colored light within.

By its side, actually leaning against it, stood the vicarage, a two-story, thatched roof cottage rooted in turf. A tumbledown stone wall enclosed the vicarage yard.

"We'll have to go round," Charlie explained apologetically. "Old Dauntless can never jump that."

Thank goodness! Marianna thought. They traveled the length of the wall, entered a gate that hung by one hinge, and turned up the path to stop in front of the house.

Stretching back an arm, Charlie seized her by the elbow. "Lean toward me," he directed. "Swing your off leg over in back and slide down. That's the girl," he added as she followed his instructions.

He lost his grip on her arm, and she landed in a sprawling heap on the grass verge. "Well, you're down anyway." He dismounted more carefully, balancing on his good leg, and politely extended a hand to help her up before turning to bang on the vicarage door.

Mlle. Celeste Moreau, startled by the banging on the vicarage door, dropped the cloth with which she was drying the good vicar's china chocolate cup. She smoothed the patched apron protecting her dove gray muslin, patted her hair, and pulled the door open.

"Allo?" she said, raising delicate brows at a pair of bedraggled urchins. The girl, though somewhat in disarray, was expensively gowned and plainly a member of the English Quality. The fair-haired youth beside her, who stared belligerently, wore the common garb of a peasant, for all that his features were delicate and well formed. She looked past them at a gangly caricature of a horse, whose dam had been unable to decide whether to produce a brown or a white foal and had been caught

unprepared. The beast had discovered a patch of grass and showed signs of moving in indefinitely.

"*Sapristi!*" she murmured.

"I'll be damned," said the boy, by way of greeting. "A Frenchie!"

Celeste by now had noticed his blood-soaked legging. "*Ma foi!* You are wounded! Come inside, *mon pauvre,* but at once." She bestowed on him her most ravishing smile. He melted instantly and followed her into the vicarage.

The indignant young girl, left on the doorstep, hurried into the tiny entry hall after them. Celeste pushed the boy into a chair in the low-ceilinged combination kitchen and living area.

"*Laissez-moi vous debarrasser de votre chaussure.* The boot," she amended, remembering to speak English. "It is that we must take it off."

The girl ran to kneel at the bemused boy's side, trying to unwind the strips of leather that held his legging in place, scrambling them so that Celeste went after a kitchen knife to cut the wrapping from the wounded leg.

"*Tiens!* That is a bad hurt. How came you by it?"

He inspected his bared bloody leg with interest. The wound fortunately was not deep, the ball had torn away some flesh, but had not lodged inside, and he seemed no little relieved. "Thank God, we don't have to cut out the bullet."

Celeste noted with amusement that he had observed the knife with a bit of anxiety. But, a bullet? Had he then been shot?

"How is this?" she asked. "A bullet—?"

"My uncle shot him," the girl explained, looking carefully away. Not that the sight of blood bothered her, but she seemed to find a chair on the other side of the room of a most unique design. "At least, I think it was he. We were escaping from him," she added.

Celeste, still under the heady influence of the wedding of Madeleine and M. Gagny, clapped her hands. "Ah, but a delight, this! It is an elopement, *non?*"

"Good god, no!" cried the boy, thoroughly shocked.

The impropriety of their traveling together without a chaperone suddenly struck his companion. "Of course not. He—he is my brother!"

"Ho?" said the young man.

"Yes, yes." The girl pinched his arm, and he yelped. "Charlie came to my rescue when my wicked uncle abducted me! He saved me from—from a terrible fate. My uncle was taking me to the castle to be married to the Duke of Ault against my will—a man I scarcely knew!"

The Duke of Ault! Celeste's interest sharpened. "You were to be married to him? And you escaped?"

"My—my brother held them up with his pistol and wrested me from them."

The boy she called Charlie opened his mouth as though to argue this point, and she pinched him harder.

"Ow!"

"Ah, you are in pain!" Pretending she had not seen, Celeste rose and poured water into a bowl from a chipped pitcher on the dry sink. This girl must not marry her duke! She turned back to Charlie and tore off a section from a soft linen towel, soaking it with a brown liquid from a bottle she took from the cupboard.

Charlie eyed it with some trepidation. "Will that sting?"

She smiled at him. "But you are a man, no? You will not mind a little hurt."

"Of course not." He stiffened and watched her uneasily as she patted at his leg, first with clear water, then with the medication.

"Alors, it will be better, you will see. And you, *ma petite,* you will tell me more of these abductors while I work." Especially more of the Duke of Ault. "What is wrong with this duke that you do not wish to marry him?"

The girl seemed to struggle with her conscience. "Nothing, really. He is rather handsome, but he is a fop! A rattle!"

Celeste blinked at her. "I do not know these words. What is he?"

"I only meant he is a dandy—he thinks only of his clothes! But I do not wish to be married. I want to have fun and parties and beaux, before I must settle down and become an old lady!"

Celeste nodded, with a sense of relief. "I quite see. Of a truth, you are too young to become a matron." But *she* was not—and she had no objection to a man of fashion. *Au contraire!* She very much wished to meet this duke who rattled. "Tell me more of him."

The girl obviously had been thinking rapidly, concocting a tale. "They will come after us, I know," she began, "and they will probably try to say that Charlie was a highwayman, who robbed us on the road. But he didn't, as you can see." Her hand went to her throat. "I still have my pearls."

"She gave me the ring," Charlie put in, firmly.

"But of a certainty you did not steal," Celeste hastened to reassure him. "Do hold quiet the leg, while I wrap this."

"Not even my three pounds ten," he muttered.

Three pounds ten? That would be English money. Had he then lost his purse? Celeste was dying of curiosity, but first she must tend his wound, then she would have the truth.

She tied the ends of the linen cloth tight. "*Ça ira.* There, it is done. Your uncle should not have fired upon you. It is of the most infamous."

"Oh, yes, most," the girl agreed quickly, as though pleased to have settled it all so easily. "But it may not have been Sir Geoffrey—" she stopped and swallowed, "that is, my uncle, who shot Charlie."

Celeste caught the name—and the title. All was now clear. "He is a 'Sir,' then, your uncle? Ah, I understand." *En fin,* life in England was just as portrayed in the novels! "We have here the wicked, depraved baronet."

"Well, not really." The girl sounded doubtful, then went on in a firmer tone. "But he does kiss the housemaids. At least, I saw him kiss Betty. She is the pretty one, who giggles and acts silly whenever he is around. And I am determined not to go back to him—for awhile."

"But what do you do now?" Celeste sat back on her heels and looked up at her. "*Vous n'avez meme pas seize ans, je parie?*"

"What the devil was all that?" demanded Charlie, suspiciously. "Why can't she talk in plain English?"

The girl frowned. "I couldn't follow it all, but I think she believes me to be only sixteen years old. I will be going on seventeen, after my birthday next month."

"I am at least eighteen." Charlie considered a moment. "Maybe even nineteen."

Celeste stifled a giggle. *"Pardon,* excuse please! I see you both to be much older than I thought. And I will only speak English. I have been most rude, for I am quite fluent in your language. Now." She stood up, straightening her skirts, "How are you named, the two of you? You first."

"Charlie—Charlie Makepeace. But you must not tell anyone," he added.

"Ah, no?"

The girl shook her head. "No. His life is in your hands. You may only call him Charlie, and I am to be just Marianna. We—we do not wish the Runners or—or anyone to find us. This is a church and we claim sanctuary," she finished triumphantly. "That's why we are here."

"I am here to see the parson," Charlie corrected her.

"He is sleeping. He takes the nap, for he is an old one."

Charlie had been eyeing Celeste with growing curiosity. "Who the devil are you?"

This form of address did not faze her. "I am one Celeste Moreau. I am housekeeper for the Father—no, the Reverend—Brinkman."

"You don't look like any housekeeper."

"Well, I have not long been one. I am come to England from France these past two days to live with *mon oncle,* the elder brother of my dead father, only to find a tragedy. His employer, the Duchess of Ault, is also died, and since my uncle has therefore returned to France, the good vicar takes me in."

Her plight apparently appealed at once to Marianna.

"How like him not to await you here! Oh, you cannot trust an uncle!"

Celeste could not let this pass. "The fault was not his. The letter I wrote to him was never received. It is even now on the mantel, for the *pauvre* M. Brinkman did not know where to forward it. And, you must know, I have not the funds to return to my home—or even the home to return to—so here I stay."

"Have you no relatives who could send for you?"

"But no, Mademoiselle Makepeace, I am now an orphan, and my uncle, who is a priest, has returned to his church in France."

Marianna sat in silence, as though absorbing her new name, while Charlie began to burrow in the pockets of his oversized frieze coat.

"A French priest? Here in Ault'n'Vale? Listen, take a look at this." He fished out a crumpled sheet of closely written notepaper that was wrapped around a heavy iron key, carelessly throwing the paper on the floor. "This key was sent to me by a French priest!"

She took the key from him and glanced at it curiously. "But what is this?"

"Only look at the crest on the end—and then the one on here!" He held out the signet ring that Marianna had thrown to him. "You see? They are one and the same!"

Celeste looked from one crest to the other. "I think, me," she remarked thoughtfully, "it would be best to put this matter before *M. le Vicar.*"

Five

Nearly an hour later, after a somewhat difficult ride, Sir Geoffrey Cole arrived in Ault-in-the-Vale. Almost the first sight to greet his eyes was the piebald cob, grazing peacefully in the churchyard at the far end of the short village street.

Relief caused him, unwisely, to kick the carriage horse into a canter. Not being in complete agreement as yet on this new mode of travel, and accustomed only to the crack of a whip for signals, the horse took instant exception to this violent attack upon its ribs. Bucking and sidling, it danced the length of the street, much to the delight of the hangers-on holding up the front wall of the raffish tavern.

Consequently, Geoff was in no pleasant mood when he finally dismounted in the churchyard, leaving the insulted animal to join the cob in the grass. His face grim, his lips thin, he banged on the door of the vicarage. Minutes passed before the door opened, during which time his temper did not improve.

Then—an enchanting figure stood on the threshold. Geoff stared at soft brown eyes, edged in dark lashes, and a peach-bloom complexion. An abundance of glossy chestnut curls were tied on top of her head with a knot of ribbon matching the gray of her gown, the rest allowed to cascade to her shoulders. She was tall, slender, and moved with the grace and lightness of a floating bit of thistledown. She tightened her lips, causing an adorable dimple to appear in one delicate pink cheek.

"Bonjour," she said with a fascinating accent. "It is Sir Geoffrey, am I not correct?"

Geoff's mouth dropped open. He realized he was gaping like a fool and shut it with a snap. What was a country parson doing with a French maid? And such a lovely one!

On her part, Celeste perceived the epitome of the wicked baronet of her novels. A decidedly dashing man, though his highly fashionable garments were in a sad state of disarray. He had lost his hat and his dark hair was tousled, one curling lock hanging romantically over his brow. To top all, there was a savage spark in his eye and a dangerously rakish air about him, definitely the sort of villain to abduct an heiress and fire upon her brother as he rescued her. Or rather, she acknowledged on looking closer, he could be every inch a wrathful guardian bent on preventing an elopement. Never for a moment had she believed the tale of brother and sister. In any case, he was a Sir, a dastardly evil English baronet, and therefore not to be trusted an inch. She must be on her guard for the worst.

Putting on her most formal manner, she addressed him coldly. "If you are come to see M. le Vicar, you cannot. He takes the nap."

Still bemused, Geoff continued to stare. "Then he errs. He is missing a beautiful sight."

She drew herself up. "Sir, you shall not kiss me," she said.

Geoff had, by now, regained his senses. "Why would I do that? On second thought, since the coast is clear, why should I not?"

"Because I am the housekeeper here as you can see, and not a maid. You are therefore not to kiss me." She moved back a step at the expression on his face.

Was she being coy? This was a new and intriguing approach, tantamount to an invitation. Her gray gown and patched apron proclaimed her a maid of some sort. In the lexicon of Rake Cole, maids and Frenchwomen were fair game, and here were both in one enchanting package. It had been some time since he had kissed a housemaid so lovely. And never, could he recall, had he kissed a housekeeper. The novel idea appealed to Rake Cole. He wasted no more time. Stepping into the room, he swept the housekeeper-maid into his arms and kissed her soundly.

Celeste wrenched herself free, patting at her disordered curls. How right those English novels had been!

"Of a truth, you are the wicked baronet!" she scolded, removing herself to a safe distance. "You should not have done that. Have I not told you, I am the housekeeper?"

"You don't look like a housekeeper to me—you're far too pretty for such a matronly position." He studied her critically. "And you are too young."

She frowned at his apparent disapproval of her, drawing together her featherlike brows and becoming very French. It was for her to disapprove of him! *"Voyons,* M. Sir Geoffrey, I am a good age and of the most respectable. *Mon oncle* was the priest of Madame the Duchess of Ault."

"How came you to be working here?" he demanded.

"It is that I have arrive in England these two days past to join *mon oncle,* only to find him returned to France. *Le bon M. le* Vicar, he gives me a home and for him I now labor."

Geoff looked past her into a disordered room. In their haste to escape his coming, there hadn't been time to clear away the bowl of water and the soiled towels that hung from the dry sink. The pitcher, luckily empty, had tipped over on the stone-flagged floor, and the chair Charlie had leaped from at Sir Geoffrey's knock lay on its back.

Geoff glanced about significantly. "You do not labor very hard."

"But no," she agreed readily, the dimple peeping into view. "I cannot keep the house. I am of little use, only he, *le pauvre homme,* cannot afford any housekeeper, so I am better than none. I make him English tea and the hot chocolates, and I see that a woman comes from the village for the laundry. Already she teaches me to make meat pie and boil potatoes. Next I learn the peas and vegetable marrows."

Remembering that he was the villain, she changed the subject. "Tell me, M. Sir Geoffrey, was it you who put the bullet into M. Charlie?" She shook her head, setting the chestnut curls dancing. "I do not think you should have done that, either."

"Certainly not. I assure you, I do not shoot children. Although," he added bitterly, "I have been sorely tempted."

"Du vrais, they seem to have been very silly. I do not, me, know the right of it as yet. I have been told a tale of abduction, a forced marriage, and a dramatic rescue. Am I to understand, *en fin,* it is instead an elopement?"

Sudden humor dawned in the wicked baronet's eyes,

quite transforming his rather forbidding expression. "No. I am afraid, ma'am, that instead they may have very nearly told you the truth. I was taking her to the Castle of Aultmere, and perhaps against her will, though she had at first complied." He paused considering. "The boy I suspect to be a fortuitous complication, not one of her schemes."

Celeste's eyes widened. "Did he in truth hold up your carriage with that so monstrous pistol? Could it not have been for a lark?" she suggested hopefully. "A prank? For all he is garbed in the rough clothing, he is of gentle birth. His speech and features must preclude the role of a common thief."

Geoff took a turn about the disordered room. He paused by the gray stone fireplace and kicked a straying log back inside. "I could well imagine it to be for a wager, except that he made off with an extremely valuable ring. And my ward." He shook his head abruptly. "This has been highly entertaining, but it isn't getting us anywhere. Will you take me to them, or do I find them myself?"

Celeste had been eyeing him warily, uncertain of his actions. "May one ask, M. Sir Geoffrey, what it is that you intend to do?"

"Why, take her home, of course."

"And of M. Charlie?"

He shrugged his shoulders. "Do whatever you please with him. I only want my niece. And Ault's ring."

"Ault? *Le Duc?* That crest, it is his?"

Geoff glanced at her impatiently. "Of course, it is. He gave it to my niece as a symbol of their betrothal."

"Ault." She still seemed puzzled. "Then how comes that crest to be also on the key of M. Charlie? I do not understand."

His brows drew together. "Neither do I. What are you talking about?"

Before she could explain, an elderly clergyman, slight and stooped, his red-cheeked face blessed by a halo of wispy white hair, pottered into the room. He looked up at Geoff with unexpectedly sharp blue eyes. "What may I do for you, my dear sir?" he asked.

"I have come for my niece," Geoff explained. He threw the Frenchwoman a quick glance, suddenly feeling like a guilty schoolboy.

The old man considered him blandly and waited for him to continue.

He did so. "I am Sir Geoffrey Cole, and I want my niece."

"How do you do?" The clergyman inclined his head politely. "My name is Brinkman. I am the incumbent of this parish."

Reminded of his manners, Geoff promptly forgot them and exclaimed, "I know they are here! That—that horse is wandering around your yard."

A look of comical dismay passed over the lovely housemaid's face. *"Mon dieu,* I feared we would forget something."

Geoff clamped his teeth on a note of triumph. "So you *are* harboring them!"

The old man raised his nearly nonexistent eyebrows and attempted to straighten his back in a most austere manner.

"But of course," he replied. "This is a church, my dear sir. We have frequently been known to offer sanctuary in the past."

Geoff regarded him steadily for a few moments, and Mr. Brinkman returned his gaze with a spiritual calm.

Then the clergyman suddenly seemed to decide the best defense would be offense, for he drew himself up again and tried to glare.

"Sir, the young lady has told us how you abducted her and shot the brave young man when he came to her rescue."

"Oh, for god's sake!" Geoff began impatiently. "I mean, I beg your pardon, Reverend. It was not I who shot at him. It was—was—" He paused, not wanting to bring in the Duke of Ault. "It was a mistaken attempt by another to frighten them into stopping."

The aggravating prelate and his unlikely housekeeper waited, obviously unbelieving. Not wanting to accuse the youth of highway robbery, a hanging offense, Geoff searched his mind and decided to accept the lady's former suggestion. "They were eloping and my niece is a minor."

"Sir!" The reverend gentleman stepped back, shocked. "You try to deceive me! The boy is her brother!"

Geoff had had enough with subterfuge, especially since it didn't work. "I don't know what this talk is about a brother, but I intend to see my ward and that—that young highwayman!"

"I assure you, sir, the boy is no highwayman."

"I know that, but he certainly held up our carriage and ran off with my ward." His irritation got the better of him. "Oh, the devil! I mean—I beg your pardon. Just give me my niece and the duke's ring—I don't care about her—her brother."

The vicar primmed his mouth. "You should care, sir," he reproved. "The poor boy was wounded. That bullet creased his leg."

"Good," said Geoff, considering it to be a fitting punishment. "Now, where is my niece?"

"She is here, in the care of Mlle. Moreau, my housekeeper. Here, I feel most strongly, she should remain until this affair is properly explained to me." Mr. Brinkman spoke stiffly, as though he had rehearsed this speech.

Geoff shook his head. "I'll thank you to bring her to me at once. She goes home."

"No."

He eyed the stubborn old man with exasperation, aware of a stalemate. "Yes," he countered, and grew further annoyed as he realized he was being drawn into a childish argument. The housemaid, he suspected of trying not to giggle. She certainly appeared to be choking on something.

To his further annoyance, the vicar proved the more adult of the trio. "My housekeeper, sir," he said by way of casting soothing oil on the troubled waters, "is, I assure you, an adequate chaperone for the young lady, and you may be certain she will come to no harm in the sanctity of a church. I believe that she should remain here for the time being."

Celeste came to a decision and glanced at the vicar. "I think, M. Brinkman, it would be best for him to see them. I will take care of all. Do you go to finish the prepare of your sermon for the Sabbath." Taking a deep breath, she turned to face Sir Geoffrey as the old man wandered thankfully away. "We have here a mystery to be solved. It is that the signet on the ring and on M. Charlie's key are one and the same, to me a circumstance of the most interesting."

Geoff's black brows came down again. "To me also. I

would like an explanation of all this. Come, where are they?"

"One moment only."

Celeste left the room and returned several minutes later, pushing a rebellious Marianna before her. Geoff, however, stared not at his niece, but at the youth who limped in behind them. Even in his rough garments and with his fair hair uncombed and badly cut, Charlie's resemblance to Ault was startling.

Marianna spoke first. "Go away, Uncle Geoffrey!" She set her lips in a mutinous line and clung to Celeste's waist with both arms.

Geoff looked down at her then, his face stern. "Well, miss, and what have you to say for yourself?"

He received no answer other than a defiant sniff.

"Come, there's been enough of this foolishness," he went on. "I will admit, in light of your actions today, you are too young to marry, but it is high time you curbed your flights of fancy and learned to be more circumspect in your behavior. I am taking you back to Sussex for the rest of the Season."

Marianna shrank from the hand he extended and shrieked theatrically. This was enough for Charlie. Pulling the long-barreled pistol from his belt, he aimed it at Sir Geoffrey's chest.

"Unhand her, sir!" he declaimed. "You shall not force her to—to—" He turned to Marianna. "What should he not force you to do? He says you are not to be wed after all."

"He is not to force me to leave here," she prompted, *sotto voce*. "Tell him he must let me remain in the sanctuary of the church, where I shall become a nun."

"That won't fadge." Charlie sounded doubtful. "I think it is only for Catholics."

Geoff's patience was not his strong point. He reached out and caught Marianna by the arm, only to find the barrel of Charlie's pistol inches from his nose.

"Put that cannon away," he snapped, backing off.

"It's not loaded." Marianna massaged the arm he had released. "Charlie doesn't have any bullets for it."

"Well, that's one good thing, at least." Geoff straightened his neckcloth and sought to retrieve his lost dignity under the obvious amusement in the Frenchwoman's eyes.

"It belonged to Jed," Charlie explained with pride. "He was a real highwayman. This coat's his, and the mask, too."

"I'm almost afraid to ask how you acquired these— er-*accoutrements*."

"Why, he left them to me, when they hung him on Tyburn Hill last month."

"They hung him, did they?"

"Aye, he couldn't remember the neck verse."

"What's that?" Marianna demanded.

"A verse from the Fifty-first Psalm, of course," Charlie explained condescendingly. "Could he have recited it in Latin, they'd have thought him a parson, and he could have queered the old full-bottom."

"Fooled the judge," Geoff translated for Celeste, who was plainly puzzled. "How came you to know so unsavory a character?" he asked the boy.

"Old Jed?" Charlie grinned, unabashed. "He's—was— my stepfather."

"I see. Then you are—?"

"Charlie Makepeace, only don't let that on to any Runners. It's a real famous name," he added to Marianna with an insufferably smug air. "They'd give plenty to lay their hands on a Makepeace."

Geoff was unimpressed. "Only this Jed, surely. Not you."

Charlie's face fell. "Not yet, at any rate. This was my first try, and it didn't go too well. I'm still short three pounds ten," he added gloomily.

This was a point that had aroused Geoff's curiosity. "May one ask why you require that vast sum?"

Charlie explained readily. "I owe ten shillings to Bob Hawkins at the inn, and the three pounds was to buy Dauntless."

"Dauntless—?"

"The horse."

"The—the—three pounds for that circus animal?"

"Hawkins won't take a penny less, and I cannot go on the High Toby lay without a horse."

"Somehow I feel you are not cut out for a life on the high road." Geoff rubbed his chin, thoughtfully. "I fear, however, that the Duke of Ault takes your experiment seriously, and will put forward an immediate search for you. What on earth made you choose such a distinctive mount?"

"Well, sir," Charlie said candidly. "He was the only horse available."

"Naturally. I quite understand how it happened. Let's see if we can undo this tangle." He looked about for a seat and selected the edge of the table, perching on it while Charlie limped over to upright the tipped-over chair for Marianna. Celeste, who had decided to suspend judgment on this intriguing baronet, pulled up the only other. Marianna sat down, and Charlie took up a protective stance behind her. All three folded their hands and looked at Geoff hopefully.

Seeing that something of worth was expected of him, Geoff ran a hand through his hair to gain time for thought, then cleared his throat. "Now," he began. "First I must get to the bottom of this affair. Why did you take that ring, after saying you did not want our jewelry?"

"I didn't want it," said Charlie. "She gave it to me. I wanted three pounds ten to buy Dauntless and pay my shot at the inn. I only kept the ring because that man said it was his. I hadn't looked at him before, but when he yelled out, I took a good gander, and I says to myself, 'Charlie, you see that face when you shave.' "

"Which can't be often," amended Geoff. "All right, I, too, see the resemblance." He refrained from adding that there might be a simple explanation. "Where do you come from, lad?"

Charlie rolled his eyes upward. "Nigh onto a hundred leagues north of here. Well, actually, a bit over sixteen kilometers," he corrected himself. "The thing is, I was quite rolled up and couldn't pay my fare on the coach, so I had to walk."

Geoff nodded. Sixteen kilometers was no great distance. Charlie could well be a merry-begotten son of the fourth duke, and that would account for his startling resemblance to Ault. But Charlie seemed unaware of the possibility; why then did he want the ring?

"Miss—Mlle.—Moreau, is it? Yes. You said something about two crests. There is a matching ring?"

She shook her chestnut curls, arresting his eyes once more. *"Mais, non,* it is a key, the other."

Charlie dug into a capacious pocket and brought out

both key and ring. A bit hesitantly, he allowed Sir Geoffrey to compare them. The crests were identical.

Geoff looked up. "I collect this Jed stole the key?"

"That he did not!" Charlie flared. "That's my key!" He snatched back both and bestowed them once more in his pocket. "It was sent to me. Parson got it in the mail from a Frenchie here in Ault'n'vale, saying he was to give it to Charlie Makepeace and that's me. There was a letter with it, too, only Parson couldn't make out the words."

Geoff raised his eyebrows. "Let's see that letter."

"Oh, I haven't it anymore." Charlie shrugged cheerfully. "Wasn't any good to me, all in gibberish. I kept it for a while to wrap the key in, but what with one thing and another, I mislaid most of it. There was one piece left." He looked vaguely around on the floor. "I had it when I came in here."

Celeste swooped down upon a crumpled bit of paper, closely written, that had landed behind the hearth broom.

"Voilà, it is here. M. Charlie threw it down when he unwrapped the key for me to see." Her dimple deepened. "It is a very good thing, is it not, that I am a bad housekeeper and so did not toss it into the fire?" She handed the sheet to Geoff, who smoothed it out on his knee.

"This is only the last page, and it is in French. Mlle. Moreau, perhaps you will translate for us?"

She took the dog-eared sheet and moved away to hold it to the light by the mullioned window.

"Mais, je ne comprende pas!" she exclaimed. "It is that this is signed 'Fr. Francois Moreau!' The key was sent you by my uncle!"

Six

Celeste read through what remained of Charlie's missive quickly. "It begins in the middle of a sentence, but the meaning is that he wishes the enclosed letter to be delivered to the son of one Mary Makepeace, the wife of Jedediah Makepeace—"

"That's me," put in Charlie.

Marianna shushed him. "Quiet! I want to know what it says."

Celeste translated carefully. "It is written here 'to the son by adoption of Mary Makepeace, wife of Jedediah Makepeace, in order that he may ascertain the truth if he still be living—' "

"I am," whispered Charlie, and yelped as Marianna poked him in the ribs.

Celeste looked at them, a dawning wonder in her eyes. "He wrote of this matter to my father! I found his letter, and because of it, I came to England. *En fin,* of a surety it must be the same, for he mentioned a key to solve a great problem! Can it be that by this key, he meant not a solution, but an actual key? And this is it?"

"Go on!" cried Marianna, clapping her hands. "What else does it say?"

Celeste returned to the letter, her voice trembling. "

'—I find that in spite of my holy vows to keep sacred the confessional, I cannot go to my grave bearing this formidable secret, as such another one has already done. I go now to my native France, to my superior, to confess this terrible sin, but I go relieved of a heavy burden, and in the conviction that the good God will forgive me, for I have tried to right a great wrong.' And there it is signed by my uncle," she finished.

"What the deuce does all that mean?" demanded Charlie. "What has it to do with my key?"

Geoff coughed gently. "It would seem that chances are you may be in—ah—some way related to the former duke."

Charlie was not stupid. "But the key! If he should be my father, maybe he left me something that is locked up in the castle! And this Ault fellow is hiding it from me!"

"The rest of the letter! Oh, Charlie, but you are addlepated!" Marianna pounded him on the arm. "How could you lose it? It might have been a will leaving you great wealth!"

Geoff shook his head, his expression thoughtful. "Hardly that. If it had been a will, there would be no reason to send a key."

"A hidden treasure, then!" Marianna exclaimed. "Oh, Charlie, and if you have lost the map—!"

"There was no map. Only pages of that French gibberish." Charlie took out the key and examined it closely. "It is too big for a strong box or a chest. It must open some room."

This appealed to Geoff's rakish sense of humor. He grinned. "Obviously, it is the key to the cupboard containing the Ault family skeleton, and you, my boy, must be it."

"But perhaps we have here the treasure hunt!" Celeste's brown eyes sparkled.

Delicate pink flushed her cheeks, and Geoff decided suddenly that it might be rather pleasant to remain in Ault-in-the-Vale for a little longer and help to uncover this mystery. He discovered that though he had attempted to bury the reckless inclinations of his youth, the grave was shallow. Rake Cole had begun to resurface the moment this delightful housemaid entered a scene that had become unbearably dull. But much as he might enjoy so hazardous a gamble, he could not involve two delicately bred young misses in such a ticklish undertaking.

Marianna had other ideas. "Uncle Geoff," she ordered, "take us to Aultmere immediately."

"But yes!" Celeste chimed in. "I have the greatest desire to meet this duke of whom I hear so much."

"I'm afraid we can't do that," he told her with a touch of regret. "I really do not feel that we should include the duke in our search for Charlie's keyhole. It may be that he will not like the answer—and certainly, Charlie must go nowhere near there. Remember, Ault would put a price on his head. He was not pleased to lose that ring. Do give it to me, boy, and I'll see that it is returned."

"No," said Charlie.

Geoff's black brows descended. "You cannot keep it. He will have you hanged for a thief!"

Charlie set his mouth in a stubborn line. "She gave it to me. I'll keep it until I know what my key is for; it is the only clue I hold."

"Oh, no, you must not give it back!" Marianna cried. "He would try to make me wear it again, and I will not be betrothed to him! I will not!"

"Well, you need not be," Geoff soothed, "but we must return his ring, and we must get back to him. No doubt he is awaiting us at Aultmere this very moment."

"No!" Marianna clutched at Celeste, ready tears in her eyes. "I won't go! I want to stay here! I want to! I hate him—and I'll hate you, if you make me go near him!"

"Don't be ridiculous, Marianna. Come, we have had enough of this play-acting."

"I—will—not—go!"

Geoff gazed at her helplessly. He could see no way of removing her other than dragging her from the vicarage, kicking and screaming as she most assuredly would be doing. A vision of the delight of the hangers-on at the inn floated before him, and he remembered he had only the carriage horse and possibly Dauntless to convey them to Aultmere. He shrugged his shoulders in defeat. "So stay."

Unexpectedly, Charlie ranged on his side. "No," he said. "You have to go, Marianna. If I can't search the castle, you must."

Marianna brightened at once. "Of course! Do give me the key. I shall find where it goes easily."

"No."

"But, M. Charlie," Celeste turned to him, her lovely face anxious. "How is she to search for a keyhole without a key?"

"Yes!" Marianna added her pleas. "I shall stay at the castle. Ault will invite me, I know, for he is fond of me. When I am there, I can slip out of my room at night and try all the locked doors."

"That you won't." Geoff put his foot down firmly. "Besides the impropriety of sneaking about the castle at night, it would not be at all the thing for you to stay there. It is a bachelor establishment. There is no female in residence, and you are unchaperoned."

"Then I will stay here with Celeste, and you shall search. If I am here, Ault must let you visit him for a while."

Geoff was momentarily sidetracked on hearing her name. Celeste. A heavenly name for a heavenly creature.

Marianna seized her advantage. "You must go to him at once and beg to remain for a visit."

Geoff woke up. "I see. And what am I to tell him?"

Marianna thought for only a moment. "Tell him I intend to remain here in the village, for I wish to become better acquainted with him before we marry. Then he will invite me to visit the castle, and I will ask him to show me all over it, to see if I should like it. I can then tell you which doors are locked, and you can try the key in them during the night." She sat back, satisfied that she had found the answer. "We will find Charlie's cupboard in no time. Give Uncle Geoff the key, Charlie."

"No."

"Charlie!"

"No, I won't part with it. It is mine—all I have."

Celeste brought forth a solution. "It is but to make an impression of M. Charlie's key in wax, is it not? Then M. Sir Geoffrey can go down to the kitchen in the night and find the keyboard where all the keys for the castle are no doubt hung, and he will discover the one that matches. Of a certainty, it will be labeled, and we will then know what door to unlock."

This met with instant approbation from Charlie and Marianna. Geoff did not stand a chance. Over his objections, it was settled that Marianna would remain at the vicarage, and he was to opportune Ault for an invitation to visit indefinitely at the castle.

Geoff rapidly revised the good opinion he had begun to form of this Frenchwoman and sat back, frowning at all of them. That this mad scheme would land him up to his neck in the bouillion, he felt sure. They ignored him and the preparations went ahead.

Celeste rummaged in the cupboard below the dry sink and came up with a tallow candle. The key, first accidentally heated on the hearth to near red-hot, had to be cooled again before they pressed it into the candle, with a pad of cloth, making a clear impression. Celeste beamed with pride.

"Do you but see, M. Sir Geoffrey? It is of the simplest! Now you have only to find where the keys are kept, and to try each one into the pretty cavity we have produced!"

Somehow, Geoff complained, there would be unexpected difficulties, but he was again overruled. Marianna became very cheerful now that all seemed settled to her satisfaction.

"What about me?" Charlie demanded. "I can't go back to the inn. I have borrowed Bob Hawkins's horse, and he will in all probability say I have stolen it, for I cannot pay my shot. He will turn me over to this duke to be hung!"

Marianna looked at him, exasperated. "Uncle Geoff will pay your charge at the inn on his way back to the castle, and you shall slip Dauntless into his stall while he occupies Mr. Hawkins. Then you must return here to the sanctuary of the church, where you will be quite safe."

Charlie, Geoff noticed, had begun to appear haggard and worn. The boy had lost a good deal of blood from the looks of the towels, and the leg, he was sure, must pain him severely. He could be in no condition to do more today.

"No," he said, using Charlie's favorite word. "You both remain here. I see it is up to me to return the horse and see this Mr. Hawkins."

Charlie turned to him gratefully. "Thank you, sir. To tell truth, I'm beginning to feel queer as Dick's hatband, not at all in plump currant."

"Does he speak the English, this M. Charlie?" Celeste whispered to Marianna. "I find I do not always understand what he says."

Geoff, who had overheard, cuffed the boy lightly. "Less of the cant while you are here, young man. Remember you are in the company of ladies." He prepared to take his leave, but not before seeing Charlie laid down on a comfortable couch in the vicar's study across the tiny hall.

Celeste walked with him to the door. A glance back showed Geoff they were alone. Paying them no heed, Marianna had gone into the study with Charlie, and Geoff could hear their voices raised in a violent argument over who should hold the key. Two years of circumspect behavior had somewhat repaired Geoff's shady reputation, but one could not maintain so priestly an attitude forever. He turned to the lovely housemaid, and a devil danced in his eye.

Her eyes widened. "Stand back, *monsieur*. I shall call the good vicar!"

"Never mind," said Geoff. "No need to disturb the old gentleman. I can manage quite well by myself."

Before she could protest, he caught her in his arms and kissed her again. Her face flaming, Celeste slammed the vicarage door after him.

Marianna erupted from the study at the sound.

Her fists clenched at her sides, Celeste stormed at her. "That uncle of yours! *En effet,* he is in truth the wicked baronet of whom I have read! He kissed me when first we met, and now he kisses me once more!"

"Is that all?" Marianna nodded knowledgeably. "No doubt he will do it again. I told you he always kisses pretty maids, and you are French as well."

"I do not understand." Celeste wrinkled her nose, puzzled. "Of a certainty, I am French. But why then does he think he must at all times kiss me?"

"Oh, it is not only you. It is his opinion of French women in general. He believes them to be frivolous and fast, and therefore to be fair game."

"Fast?" Celeste frowned, her temper returning. "It means, does it not, that the so wicked baronet thinks *me* not *comme il faut?*"

"It is only that he is accustomed to ladies of the strictest reserve," Marianna explained, attempting to spread oil on the troubled waters. "And you are sometimes flippant. You see, he is betrothed to a highborn lady of the utmost gentility."

"Ah, so he is betrothed. And does he love this so respectable lady?"

"Oh, no. He means to marry her because her breeding will raise the social standing of our family. That is why he wishes to marry me to the duke."

Celeste wrinkled her nose. "Breeding is what one does to raise excellent pigs."

Marianna giggled. "Indeed, Lady Charlotte will produce splendid pigs. Insufferably starched and correct to the tips of their snouts! I shall hate them!" She sobered.

"And I shall hate to have her as my aunt. She is so full of her consequence, so top-lofty, so high in the instep! Her manners and behavior are impeccable, and she will insist that I be the same."

Celeste came to a decision. *"En fin,* we must separate him from this paragon of perfection. It is not good that you must live in this constrained manner. We must see what we can do."

Marianna gazed at her, hopefully. "Do you think we could make her cry off? Because Uncle Geoff is a man of honor, you know, and he will not."

"Of this honor of his, I have doubts, but of our ability to contrive, I have none." Celeste tried to look worldly wise. "A challenge, *n'est pas?* It will do him a world of good to be freed from this what-you-call high-stickler."

Outside, with the impressed candle heavy in his pocket, Geoff stood in the yard, still feeling Celeste's slender body in his arms, still tasting the heady flavor of the loveliest housemaid—he could not accept housekeeper—he had ever met. But gradually, a sense of foreboding crept over him. Rake Cole slid apologetically into the back of his mind where he belonged, and Sir Geoffrey shook his head, a head too easily turned by a pretty face. Oh, the devil! What had he let himself in for?

He stared resentfully at the piebald cob, who placidly ignored him and chewed grass in company with the carriage horse. Finally, not wishing to be seen riding the ridiculous animal, he led Dauntless out through the cemetery at the rear of the church and along to the inn by a back lane. As they walked, he noted with surprise that the towers of Aultmere could be seen across the fields behind the vicarage. He judged he must be less than a mile from the side gates, though the castle lay a good two miles away by the winding road.

When they reached the inn, they were met in the stable yard by Mr. Bob Hawkins himself.

"You be returning old Dauntless, eh?" The man shifted the straw he chewed to the other side of his mouth and looked Sir Geoffrey over with mild curiosity. " 'Ow came you by 'im?"

There seemed no need to tell other than the truth. "I found him grazing in the churchyard. They told me he was yours."

"Aye, a young gentleman stayin' 'ere was mindful of buyin' that nag." Mr. Hawkins spat out the straw with regret. "Mayhap 'e changed 'is mind. Saw 'im lopin' off with Dauntless this morning, and thought mebbe 'e was tryin' 'im out." He took the reins and tied Dauntless to a post, shaking his head. " 'Tis not a beast easy to get rid of. Well, thankee for your trouble, sir. I daresay the lad piked off, not 'avin' the ready to pay me."

Sir Geoffrey took out his purse. "You must not be out of pocket. Let me cover his shot and give me his baggage. I'll—I'll see that it is sent after him."

Hawkins blinked at him. "It queers me why you'd want to do that."

Geoff had an uncomfortable feeling he'd made an error. He tried to carry it off, hoping the man would think him an eccentric. "Let us say it is a whim." He tossed over a whole half-crown, the first coin he got his hand on, and knew for sure the innkeeper thought him insane, but it couldn't be helped.

Ten minutes later he was back at the vicarage, where he left Charlie's small bag on the doorstep. He felt no qualms at leaving Marianna. She could get into little trouble in a church. He knew her to be a romantic little puss and felt sure that though she now was glorying in having an adventure, she'd soon tire of village fare and beg him to take her home.

As there seemed to be no other mode of transportation, he sighed and remounted the carriage horse. Stuffed to satisfaction on fresh grass, it made no objection and accepted a rider willingly enough, for which Geoff was thankful—at first. Having adjusted to this new way of travel, it took off at the high, prancing trot with which it pulled the carriage. Geoff, attempting to post without stirrups, swore quietly and jerkily.

To his surprise, he had not gone far before he came upon his carriage, still sitting in the road, and he grinned as he realized the problem. Minus the right leader, the left horse had balked and refused to move.

His mount also recognized the familiar equipage and his stable mates. The neigh that shook through his torso nearly rattled Geoff from his back. The answering chorus from the other horses rang in his ears, while the remaining leader, trying to rejoin his partner, reared and plunged, setting off the two wheelers.

The coachman held them, but with the traces already off balance, the high-sprung carriage tilted. Ault, who had been standing on the lower step ready to enter, lost his footing and fell, face down, into the muddy ditch beside the road.

Feeling his rough ride more than compensated for, Geoff rode up to greet him with a cheery shout.

Seven

The Duke of Ault, sprawled on his stomach in the scum-covered ditch, slowly raised a mud-streaked face. Geoff, hastily swallowing his mirth, dismounted and ran to his aid.

"Oh, bad luck, old man!" he exclaimed, shaking his head with spurious sympathy. "My deepest apologies! I can't imagine what got into those idiotic horses."

The coachman had his hands full with his rearing and neighing team, but the footman scrambled down from the coach. With admirably straight features, he joined Geoff by the recumbent duke. Together, they fished his Grace from the stagnant ditch and planted him on his feet. He stood, dripping muddy water, slime, and defunct bits of vegetation, with only one thought.

"My ring!" he demanded in a voice that skidded an octave. "Have you brought back my ring?" He dragged a soaked handkerchief from one of his sleeves and mopped his face, spreading the mud more evenly. "Did you capture the thief?"

Geoff strove to keep his own voice in order. "Not exactly."

Ault dropped the handkerchief. "What do you mean, not exactly? Yes or no?"

"No."

"No!" Ault spluttered. "You've been gone forever! Did you find no trace of the misbegotten villain?"

The footman retrieved the soiled square of linen, and began to scrub ineffectually at the duke's coat front and splattered waistcoat. His exquisite inexpressibles were ruined beyond saving, and Ault slapped his hands away, looking ready to weep. "I want to go home," he declared.

Geoff frowned at the repellent figure before him. "Do you not wish to know what has become of your betrothed?"

"Marianna? She said she was going back to London." The mention of Marianna reminded him of his loss. "And she gave that thief my ring!" he exclaimed, highly incensed.

Out of patience, Geoff steered him into the carriage. "For your information, she is safe. She has decided to remain in Ault-in-the-Vale for a short time, visiting at the vicarage."

"Whatever for? Does she know what became of that highwayman and my ring?"

Geoff ignored this. "I intend to remain also, to keep an eye on her, and I beg you will grant me the hospitality of Aultmere for an extended stay, while I attempt to talk some sense into the confounded chit—that is, my young ward."

"But I came only for the day. I cannot stay here, my man is in London! I cannot cope without him."

Sir Geoffrey waved this aside ruthlessly. "Send for him. He will be here by nightfall, and you certainly cannot expect to be seen returning to London in your present condition." He shut the carriage door and leaned out of the window to shout at his coachman. "On, we go to Aultmere."

Ault seemed taken aback by the turn of events, but he granted Geoff's request to spend an extended visit at Aultmere and accepted the tale of a shy maiden's desire to know her intended husband better before the wedding night. He did not, however, accept Geoff's suggestion that he not call in the Runners, after Geoff told him he could not claim his ring was stolen. Marianna would swear he gave it to her, and she in turn gave it to the boy. They proceeded on their way in a strained silence.

The Castle of Aultmere sat in impressive grounds. Once through the massive iron gates, a mile of winding, oak-lined drive took them past the mere for which it was named, the broad waters glimmering in the sun. A yew alley led off to a rose garden and acres of lawn with a pattern of ornamental squares known as knots. Each square had dwarf box hedges outlining fancy geometric designs within, like miniature mazes. Rabbits and deer bounded away across the rolling greens as they trotted by. Swans floated placidly on the mere.

Looking past the line of trees on the far side, Geoff could see the stone building that was visible from the cemetery at the back of the vicarage, and he realized they must have come nearly full circle by following the road. Seen from this side, over the trees, the structure took on the aspect of a pillared Grecian temple, too large for a gazebo or pavilion.

Ault followed his gaze and gestured with a return of his pride. "The Ault family vault," he said. "My ancestors for near a dozen generations lie within. I shall join them one day."

Once inside the castle, Geoff found the prospect of identifying the key more difficult than he'd expected. The candle with the impression of Charlie's key made a weighty bulge in the pocket of his hitherto impeccably fitting coat, and a heavier one on his conscience, keeping him aware of what he must do. A task he thoroughly regretted assuming. Try as he might, he could think of no excuse to go into the kitchens where the castle keys must be hung, and he could not match his wax impression if he did not do so.

It remained only to sneak down at night and search with the aid of a candle, a far more formidable task than it had seemed in the admiring glow from those soft brown eyes. Mentally, he cursed himself for a bacon-brained sapskull, but there was no turning back. He could not lose face before those lovely eyes. He marshalled his thoughts.

First, he must explore Aultmere by day and locate the blasted kitchen premises. At his estate, the keyboard hung in the butler's pantry, which should be easy to find. Next, he'd have to observe the habits of the domestics to fix upon the best hour of the night at which to put his fate to the test.

He had no opportunity the first evening, owing to Ault having a passion for two-handed whist that equaled that of Lady Charlotte. It was nigh on cock's crow before he could break away and retire, too weary for adventure.

In the morning, he borrowed a horse from the Aultmere stable and rode over to the church. Marianna burst through the door, running headlong up to him as he dismounted in the vicarage front garden.

"Uncle Geoff! At last!" she cried, catching his sleeve

with eager hands. "I thought you'd never come. I've been watching from the upper window since dawn. Did you find the key? Did you locate the door? Where is it?"

Geoff scarcely heard her, accustomed to her importunate chatter. His eyes were on the girl who remained in the doorway, a vision in quiet gray, a fresh white apron, and chestnut curls escaping from her ruffled mobcap.

Marianna yanked at his sleeve. "Tell me!" she ordered.

"What? Oh no, there are difficulties."

Celeste came down the shallow steps and hurried to his side. "But what is this?" she asked. "You have not had the success?"

She looked up into his eyes and, had it not been for the presence of Marianna, he'd have kissed her on the spot. He smiled down at her, and tried to shake off his eager niece. The warmth of his smile brought a most becoming pink to the French girl's cheeks, and she stepped hastily back.

"Why, what can you mean?" Marianna demanded. "You had only to try the keys on their keyboard! Oh," she amended tragically, "do not say there was not one to match!"

"No, no. It is only that I could not think of an excuse to invade the kitchen premises by day and—"

"You could not think! Uncle Geoff—"

"It is only a temporary setback."

"But you have had all night to search. Why did you not sneak down in the dark?"

Feeling the Frenchwoman's questioning eyes upon him, Geoff lost some of his patience in spite of his perfectly good alibi. "Because the da—condemned place is a rabbit warren, and I have not yet found the way to the servants' quarters. I cannot try the keys until I find where the confounded keyboard is hung. You cannot expect me to find anything in the dark of night, before I have explored the lay of the land by daylight."

Marianna turned away, disgusted. "You cannot have tried. You may be sure I would not be such a slow-top!"

Celeste hastened to pour oil on the troubled water, succeeding instead in adding fuel to the fire. "But he is right, *ma chérie*. If he is to remain at the castle, he must not be suspect by our duke. It is for him only to discover the whereabouts of this keyboard. It is then for one of us to slip inside after all are abed. A matter of the simplest, if he will but see that a door is left off the bolt."

Geoff stared at her, dumbfounded. He might have expected so harebrained a scheme from Marianna, but he had thought Mlle. Moreau an intelligent woman. A lady would not even consider so wild a flight—but then she was not a lady, he reminded himself. She was a French housemaid, and the devil was in it, a demmed pretty one. Unconsciously, he straightened his neckcloth before delivering an ultimatum.

"You will do no such thing. Never have I heard a more nonsensical idea!"

Marianna, however, squealed with delight. "Oh, yes, that is it! I will go, for Charlie cannot. He can barely walk from his couch and could never reach the castle."

Geoff's black brows came down in a thundercloud. "Do not act the fool, Marianna. You know very well that I will not allow you to try so mad a trick."

Her lower lip came out in a pout, but she subsided, after a fashion. "But you are doing nothing," she muttered. "Charlie would do better."

He ignored her remark, knowing it was but a childish gesture. "I undertook this against my better judgment, and I will carry it through. You will remain quietly here and see to it that Charlie does not venture out of doors. Ault is determined to send for the Runners, and I am doing my best to dissuade him."

"Then let us move inside," Celeste advised, "before M. Charlie joins us, for he has a curiosity of the greatest and may have seen your arrival."

Charlie had not, being occupied with replenishing his wardrobe, but the sound of their voices in the room below brought him limping down the narrow stairs.

Dressed in respectable garments supplied by the Reverend Mr. Brinkman, Charlie was transformed. Marianna clapped her hands at the sight.

"Not only does his key have the crest of Ault," she exclaimed, "only see! He is the image of Ault himself."

It was true, confirming Geoff's belief in a somewhat shady relationship between Charlie and the present duke. Cleaned up, his unkempt hair combed and trimmed by Celeste, he was a very handsome young man, a youthful edition of Ault, taller, broader in the shoulders and, amazingly, with more classic features. Even his borrowed plumage being on the sober side and rather too small did not detract from the new Charlie being very well to pass.

Celeste eyed him with awakened interest. So, M. Charlie resembled closely her duke. Her desire to meet that nobleman increased pleasurably. He must be a well set-up gentleman indeed. Marianna's refusal of the duke's offer of marriage was not to be understood, but it was to be forwarded at all cost. The unappreciative Marianna must not marry this most desirable duke. Not, at least, until she had a chance to captivate him for herself.

"Have you found the lock for my key?" Charlie demanded as he reached the foot of the stairs. "Is that why you have come?"

All three speaking at once, they explained the delay, Marianna adding that her Uncle Geoff had failed miserably.

"I have not failed," he countered, offended. "I have not yet tried."

"I'd best go myself," Charlie announced. "I'll find it in short order."

"That you will not," said Geoff flatly.

"No, indeed," Marianna told him. "You cannot go anywhere. You can hardly take two steps without resting."

Insulted, Charlie staggered three to show her. "By tomorrow I'll be in plump currant, then I'll—"

"Do nothing," Geoff finished for him. "You keep out of sight. Ault threatens to call in the Runners and demands that you be hanged for highway robbery."

Incredulous awe spread over Charlie's features. "Hanged!" he gloated. "If only Jed were here to see. I'll wager he was older than I before a price was put on his head."

"If you expect to become much older yourself, do not set foot out the door," Geoff ordered.

Marianna had been studying Charlie, in light of his startling resemblance to Ault, and suddenly exclaimed, "I have it! I have solved the mystery. Charlie must be the real duke! He did not die, but was somehow spirited away, and an empty coffin sealed in the vault. The key is to open the coffin!"

Geoff put a stop to this foolishness. "Do not be a silly goose, child."

"I am not a child!" cried Marianna, thoroughly insulted. "And I am not a silly goose! You shall not call me so! It could very well have happened as I said!"

"But yes," Celeste agreed, delighted. "I have read of such doings in your English novels. It is an idea of the most romantic!"

If that was not just like a Frenchwoman, Geoff thought. "These Gothic novels do not reflect real life," he said aloud.

Celeste gazed at him, censure in her soft brown eyes. "Oh, do they not? Have we not here the innocent maiden, abducted to be forced into an unwanted marriage by a wicked baronet?"

Geoff, indignant, started to speak, but was interrupted by a contrite Marianna. "Not exactly, Celeste. I had stupidly agreed to marry, because I wished to be a duchess and outrank Lady Charlotte."

Celeste favored Sir Geoffrey with a forgiving smile. "Ah, not so very wicked perhaps, but of a certainty, insensitive to the dreams of a captive ward. One can understand a desire to rise above this Lady Charlotte, whoever she may be."

Charlie chose this moment to take an unfortunate hand in the discussion. He had no interest in Lady Charlottes, but he could not let a gross error pass uncorrected and made a disparaging remark. "Coffins do not have keys, hen-wit," he told Marianna. "Any idiot knows that."

She responded hotly. "How do you know this one does not? How many coffins have you seen?"

"There was Nana's, for I went to her funeral. I do not

know how they buried Jed, for Parson sent me home and I didn't get to see."

"Just as well," said Geoff, frowning at Marianna, who had exclaimed, "Ah ha!"

"But I am quite sure," he went on, "you'd find no keyhole in the casket of a duke."

"All the same," Marianna declared, "I'd give a deal to see inside that coffin."

Charlie guffawed. "A skeleton would look back up at you, and you'd faint dead away."

"I would not!"

"But of a certainty, she would not, M. Charlie!" admonished Celeste. "We are of the bravest, Mlle. Marianna and me. I would look also."

He did not say "Hah!" but it was clear on his face.

It was high time to nip these ridiculous fancies in the bud. "Enough," Geoff commanded. "There will be no more talk of peering into coffins or like nonsense."

Mr. Brinkman had entered quietly, seating himself on the settle by the hearth. He spoke, startling the combatants.

"Why," he asked, gently puzzled, "do you wish to disturb the slumber of that poor child?"

Marianna turned to him, eagerly. "Because I do not believe he is there to be disturbed. I am sure we would find the coffin empty."

The vicar shook his head, his fluffy white halo bobbing. "No, that you would not." He beamed kindly at them all. "You may rest as easily as I pray he does. I myself attended the funeral services for the little duke. I watched the sealing of his coffin, and saw the child inside." He pottered off, entering his study with the purposeful expression of a vicar with a sermon to prepare.

Marianna, sadly disappointed, began to pout. Her beautiful theory was ruined. But why then did Charlie resemble the Duke of Ault so closely?

Celeste also had a problem. "I do not understand," she said. "Is it that you believe this Ault is not the real duke?"

Geoff assured her that he was. Why, he wondered, did she look so relieved? "Sylvester was not in the direct line, but he is most certainly the rightful duke."

"How came he to be so?"

Patiently he explained, for he enjoyed the sensation of being appealed to by wide, brown eyes which now held only trust and interest in his every word. "The thing is that the fourth duke's wife died in childbirth, and he married the widowed French mother of the heir next in line, a cousin. He needed a female to care for his infant son, and felt that her boy, six years old at the time, would be a companion for him. A short time later, he himself died in a hunting accident. The baby then became the fifth duke, but it died of the plague three years later—"

"Ah, *le pauvre petit,*" interjected Celeste.

"—and then, Sylvester, the second wife's son, being the heir, became the sixth duke."

Marianna, who knew the story, had been worrying Charlie's problem. Like a little terrier after a rat, she refused to give up. "If the key does not open the coffin, perhaps it is to a secret room in the castle, containing a lost treasure! Or there may be a hidden will, an inheritance usurped. Perhaps Charlie is a poor relation, and the old duke wished to make all right for him."

Charlie liked this idea. "Then I must get into the castle and search for that will!"

"No, you won't," said Geoff.

"I believe you would be wasting your time," Marianna went on thoughtfully. "If there were such a will, surely Sylvester's mother would have burned it."

Celeste disagreed. "Not if someone—her priest, my uncle—heard her confession and knew of such a will."

"It could have been on the missing pages of your letter! Oh, Charlie, how could you be such a nodcock!"

"Mais non!" Celeste intervened before Charlie could come up with a suitably scathing reply. "Why then would my uncle send this so mysterious key?"

Geoff held out a hand. "Let me see it again."

Reluctantly, Charlie gave up his key, and Geoff examined it carefully. It was very old, heavy iron, and the huge crest on its end definitely belonged to the House of Ault.

"Too large for a safe box, it must be to a room," he mused. "Perhaps one of the oldest cellars?"

Celeste, from her vast experience with gothic novels, had another idea. "Or even, Sir Geoffrey, to a tower room containing the ancient bones of a victim of murder!"

"Oh, yes!" Marianna was also an avid reader. "Or it may be someone still living, hidden away because of some vile deformity."

This did not appeal to Charlie. "Then why send me the key? Am I to release the Monster of Ault upon the countryside?"

Once more Geoff attempted to call them to order. "Let us not be carried away by ridiculous flights of fancy, before I have even located the castle keyboard."

Marianna was not to be suppressed so easily. "I have been told that Ault's mother became insane. Perhaps she did not die, and is locked up in a tiny cell in the very top of the highest tower of Aultmere."

She applied to the vicar, who had wandered back in and was following their conversation with an expression of mild amusement on his benign countenance. He shook his head regretfully.

"No, my dear, again I disappoint you. Her Grace has been laid to rest. Although," he smiled at her crestfallen face, "the villagers claim the ghost of the duchess walks about the vault at night, moaning and crying out anguished words in French."

Marianna squealed and pretended to shudder.

"Ah," said Geoff. If anything was needed to deter the youngsters from sneaking about Aultmere in the wee hours of the night, this should do it. He reckoned without the intrepid Mlle. Moreau.

"Mon dieu!" she exclaimed. *"Un fantome veritable!* This I should like to see."

He threw up his hands in defeat. "Very well, exercise your imaginations as you will. I see I shall have to remain at Aultmere until this affair is in some way brought to a conclusion."

Much to Marianna's satisfaction, Sir Geoffrey announced that he planned to hire a post boy to carry a message to his sister, Augusta, Lady Kent, asking her to cancel his engagements, because he meant to remain at Aultmere for a while. He would also send for his valet, his clothes, his groom, a trunk for Marianna, and his curricle. This augured well for their quest.

Having settled his plans, Sir Geoffrey took his formal leave of the good vicar, and Celeste innocently accompanied him to the door. He pushed her through and shut it firmly behind him. A quick glance up the road showed no one in sight. They were quite unobserved. Excellent.

With no further hesitation, Rake Cole swept the delectable French housemaid into his arms and kissed her in the proper manner for a gentleman on the loose.

She gasped—when she could—and would have shoved him away, but he had already released her. He removed his reluctant horse from the best grazing spot in the overgrown yard and mounted in a single, fluid move. A cheery wave and he cantered away.

Celeste stared after him, collecting her scattered wits. She had now much to think about, for she was finding wicked baronets were dangerous. Dangerously attractive. All her reading had convinced her that "Sirs" were not to be trusted, and so far, this one lived up to her expectations and more. And to top all, he had intended to marry the child Marianna to the Duke of Ault, a *parti* she had earmarked for herself.

But what of the key and the ring that bore his crest? What was the connection between Charlie, her uncle, and the Duke of Ault?

She was not about to give up so promising a mystery, one that would bring her in contact with her quarry. She had not yet met Ault. It was of the first importance that this be somehow arranged.

Eight

The great hall clock at the castle struck noon. The sixth duke of Ault stood by a window in his elegant bedchamber, waiting in nightcap and brocade dressing gown for his man Prouty to bring his morning tea.

Sylvester was not happy. He should have been, or at least smugly pleased by the view before him as he looked out over the spacious grounds of Aultmere. Lawns and gardens stretched before him to the shores of the mere, which lay shimmering in the heat of the midday sun. Swans floated on the water like puffs of whipped cream on a silver custard, disrupting the reflection of the grove of trees and the Grecian facade of the vault that sheltered his ancestors—somewhat removed. In lineage, that was. Totally removed from this earth in spirit. He shuffled his slippered feet uneasily, hoping they were. Tales of his mother's ghost had reached his ears by way of Prouty, a most talkative man.

His eye was caught by a figure on horseback skirting the far side of the mere. That chestnut was one of his! He came to attention, then relaxed. It was only his unexpected guest, out for a morning canter.

He watched as Sir Geoffrey Cole approached the Grecian temple and passed on by, disappearing into the grove. Where was he going? Ah, Sylvester remembered the vicarage. He could see the steeple of the church rising above the trees in the distance. Cole had promised to talk sense into his wayward ward, and was taking the shortcut to the village.

The whole affair of Marianna's debunking with that blasted thief who stole his ring and Sir Geoffrey allowing her to remain at the vicarage, had roused his curiosity. He began to grow uneasy. He had heard rumors of a Frenchwoman staying there from Prouty, who had already visited the local tavern. His mother had been French, and so was her priest. Could there be a connection? His mother became so very odd before she died, growing more and more depressed, as though she harbored some guilty secret. And the confounded priest went back to France . . . so quickly after her death . . . after hearing her last confession. . . . While otherwise not quick-witted, Sylvester had an active imagination where his own interests were concerned.

Prouty entered behind him, interrupting his unpleasant reverie. Sylvester was mildly attached to Prouty, his confidant and adviser on many subjects. The man was the son of a purveyor of fish on London's seamier side, and preferred to ignore that stigma. He had taught himself to speak proper English, except for an occasional problem with an *H,* as he climbed steadily to his present position. Feeling he had reached the pinnacle as gentleman's gentleman to a duke, albeit not one of the royals, he intended to stay there. Neither hell nor high water would budge him from his master's favor. The most faithful of hounds could take lessons in loyalty from Prouty.

He set the tea tray he carried upon a table beside Sylvester, and gave a meaningful cough.

"If your Grace pleases, Bagley, Sir Geoffrey Cole's coachman, is without, requesting an audience."

Sylvester raised his eyebrows. "What on earth for?"

Prouty realigned the spoons, teacup, and jam pot to his satisfaction, and unfolded the linen napkin covering a basket of hot muffins. "He declined to divulge that information to me, your Grace. Should I tell 'im—him— to depart?"

"No, no." Sylvester gestured impatiently. "Let us see what he wants."

The coachman already stood outside the open door, turning his cap over and over in his hands. Sylvester frowned. "Yes?" he demanded.

Bagley took three steps forward, tugging his forelock. He bobbed his head and spoke up bravely. "I was, wonderin', your Grace, iffen you was about offerin' a reward for the capture of that there miscreant."

Hope burgeoned in Sylvester's chest. Could the man know something that would lead to the recovery of his precious ring? And to the hanging of the thief!

The coachman mangled his hat, hopeful himself at the changing expressions on the face of the duke. "Do your Grace want that gallows bird traced, I knows where to start."

"Then tell me, fellow! Speed is of the essence, if he is to be run to earth."

For answer, Bagley held out his hand, suggestively rubbing his thumb across his callused fingertips.

The sheer impertinence! But there was nothing for it. Ault thrust his hand into the pocket of a coat hanging in his wardrobe, and yanked out a clinking pouch. He withdrew a silver crown, holding it just out of the man's reach.

"Well?"

The coachman licked his lips, but stood his ground, itching palm still outstretched.

Sylvester hesitated. But it was his ring—and he wanted that highwayman caught and hung! He added a second crown. Bagley paled, but his thumb moved again across fingers that now shook. Recklessly, Sylvester added a third coin and the dam was breached. The coachman's greedy eyes glittered and he capitulated, his story tumbling out.

"I were gone to the tavern in the village for an early pint, and 'ad reason to go to the necessary in the rear. I stopped to 'ave a word w' the 'ostlers, and yer'll never guess what I seen in one o' them stalls."

"Get on with it!" Sylvester ordered, losing patience. "Cut line, clodpole!" He waved the enticing coins, and the man finished in a hurry.

"That there piebald 'orse is what I seen. There can't be no two like that 'un, and it belongs to Bob Hawkins what owns the place. That's where yer'll find yer robber."

Ault tried to give him the coins with fingers trembling so with anticipation that he dropped the silver pieces on the floor. In his eagerness, he so far forgot himself as to bend and pick them up with his own hands. He dribbled them into the outstretched grimy palm.

Ault emulated his guest and rode out after breakfast for a breath of fresh country air, purposely going past the inn in the village. He was not sure he could entirely trust the coachman's word. After all, he was Sir Geof-

frey's man, not his. He was unable to think of an excuse
to ride through the stables in back of the tavern, and was
reluctant to go inside. The Duke of Ault was not in the
habit of mingling with his peasants.

But Prouty could.

He cantered back to Aultmere and sent his valet to the
inn, with orders to stand the innkeeper to a few pints of
ale and try to discover the existence of a piebald cob.

Bob Hawkins talked freely to Prouty, having known
him several years while the duke summered at Aultmere.
"Ah yus, I 'as such a odd-colored animal. Loaned it out
to a young gentleman 'oo was stayin' 'ere a few days
back. I doubts me that's 'ow yer come to see it."

"Perhaps." Prouty downed his ale and pushed the mug
toward the innkeeper. "Another, and one for yourself.
This young man, what did he look like?"

"Why, thankee." Hawkins drew two more pints. "Queer
thing, I couldn't 'elp noticin' 'e looked very much like
your master, but 'e 'ad more a look about 'im of the old
duke. Thought 'e might be a by-blow come to look over
the village."

"Cheers," said Prouty, and demonstrated his low beginnings by his ability to drain the tankard in one long
gulp. "This young chap, is he still in residence?"

" 'E ain't 'ere, if that be what yer mean. 'E piked orf
'cause 'e didn't 'ave the blunt to buy old Dauntless like
'e wanted."

Prouty fished a few shillings from his pouch. Ault had
given him a plentiful supply, remembering the avaricious
coachman, but the valet could see no point in wasting
good silver that might as well line his own pocket. He

plunked the coins down on the bar. "I have a fancy to see such a strangely colored horse, is it here now?"

"Yus, it be queer that. A gentleman returned old Dauntless the same day. A regular swell, 'e was. One o' the nobs. 'E paid the shot what was owed, and took the bag that there young'un left."

Queer indeed. Prouty wiped the foam from his upper lip thoughtfully. This bit of information should please the duke. He thanked Hawkins and almost left an extra shilling on the bartop, prompted by the guilty weight in his pocket. He recollected himself in time. No need to rouse suspicion; let the man believe his questions were innocent curiosity. After all, the strange piebald horse was excuse enough.

He wandered out to the stables where he found the particolored cob to be well worth the seeing, and once seen, not easily forgotten. It was not wonderful that Sir Geoffrey's coachman had recognized the blighted animal. After exchanging pleasantries with the stable hands and basing a few ribald jokes on the heritage of the poor beast, he made his way back to Aultmere to report to his master.

Sylvester now had much to think about. So the highwayman had an accomplice. No doubt the ringleader of a league of thieves on the High Toby. And where could his highwayman be—and his signet ring? Was it even now on its way to London, to Rat's Castle in the thieves' rookery known as the Holy Land, included in a bag of loot to be sold on the back streets? He might as well give it up for lost—but the thief who took it should pay—with his life!

His mind still occupied with these thoughts, Sylvester was retiring for the night when Prouty, who liked to en-

liven their time together with any trifle of gossip that
came his way, startled him with a casual remark.

"A bit of interest this afternoon, your Grace," the valet
began. "I daresay your Grace would be amazed to know
your Grace has a double."

His mind miles away in a London slum, Sylvester
blinked. "A what?"

"A double, your Grace. A man who looks enough like
your Grace so as how he might be your Grace's twin."

Prouty was an excellent valet, but Sylvester shrugged
into his nightshirt with an irritable jerk. Sometimes—no,
all the time—the man pretended to be so damned hum-
ble. His constant "Your Graces" got on the duke's nerves;
he might almost suspect the man mocked him, if he
weren't convinced Prouty wouldn't dare. He shoved his
head through the neck hole of the garment and spoke
sharply.

"What the devil are you on about?"

"This man, your Grace, as could be your Grace's double."

There the blasted valet went again. Sylvester winced,
but held his head still while Prouty rearranged his nightcap, reminding himself of the man's phenomenal hand
with a neckcloth. No one tied an Oriental or a *Trône
d'amour* like Prouty.

"It was like this, your Grace," Prouty went on, unconscious of giving offense. "When I took the shortcut home
from the village, I chanced to pass round the back of the
vicarage just as a man left the necessary house. I was
astounded to think at first it was your Grace, using a
stick and limping badly. I thought your Grace had been
injured, and ran to your aid. I hailed the man before I

realized he was a stranger, and very young at that. Your Grace may be sure I begged pardon for mistaking him."

He seemed to sense Ault was not happy to be thought the likes of a commoner, and hastened on. "And now I beg your Grace's forgiveness for being so addlepated, but I quite took leave of my senses in meeting a person so like your Grace as to be your double."

Sylvester merely grunted. But finally tucked into bed by Prouty, and alone in the dark except for his unfortunate imagination, Sylvester began a disturbing line of fanciful thinking. What if the young man who looked like him was his highwayman? He thought the thief had gone, but suppose he was this man who was his double and still at the vicarage . . . Marianna was there . . . with a Frenchwoman. Had this female a connection with his mother's priest?

He went over Prouty's words once more, trying to make sense of this sudden upset in his normally placid life. He almost wished the valet had not seen that blasted horse and the man who looked like himself. It had to be the highwayman. Now that he thought back on the scene, he became convinced that the youth with the fair hair under that disreputable hat had a familiar look about him . . . his seat on the cob, the mouth and chin that were visible . . . the set of his shoulders . . . it was all too easy to assume a resemblance.

Sir Geoffrey Cole went to the vicarage to demand his ward—but allowed her to remain there, and a gentleman returned the cob and picked up the baggage. This new thought disturbed Sylvester more. Sir Geoffrey? No, he was surely furious at his ward's abduction by the highwayman. But if the thief left the horse, Cole might have returned it. And took the man's bag? That didn't make sense. Did Sir Geoffrey intend to pursue a search of his own?

Sylvester gave up trying to sleep. He got out of bed, wandered to the window, and stared out into the night. The moon was full, and through the trees he could make out the top of the marble vault where his ducal ancestors lay— where his mother had joined them. And now two of his own servants claimed to have seen her floating before the vault at night, moaning words in French and wringing her hands. He shuddered, feeling a sudden draft. But it was pure fustian! He tried to shake off an eerie sensation.

The men were tap-hackled; they had to be. A pair of gibble-gabbling paper skulls with more earwax than brain, blathering about in the tavern to make themselves interesting.

All gammon, of course, like the rumors that started when his little cousin died, rumors that he had been murdered, only squelched by the doctor swearing that he died of the plague. No, why would his mother's ghost walk? She died peacefully at the last, in her right mind after confessing to her priest and receiving the final sacrament. Confessing . . . to what? His scalp began to crawl.

Looking past the vault roof, down the valley toward the village, he could see the steeple of the church. Who could that young highwayman be? The belief was growing on him that the man who took his ring, and his double at the vicarage, were one and the same. Other thoughts came unbidden, and would not be shrugged off. Moonlit nights made one overly fanciful. Suppose that man was a relation—a half brother—or he could even be the little duke still alive . . . Sylvester swallowed hard. A sudden lump had bounded up into his throat. From where had *that* idiotic thought come?

He knew from where. He had been only nine years old when his little cousin became ill with the plague. His governess and the duke's nursemaid both fled, overcome by fear of contagion. Shoved aside by all the hubbub surrounding the duke, Sylvester had been relegated to the care of whatever domestic happened to be available— and he had listened to their talk, not understanding. The innuendoes and suppositions were suddenly silenced when they saw him near, but he gathered they all thought something was not right, some foul deed was suspected. He had been forbidden to go to the village, and had instinctively avoided it since. The uneasiness he felt then had taken root in his child-mind, not forgotten, but suppressed until this.

Could his cousin be still alive? That was ridiculous, he couldn't be! The vicar and the doctor both saw the boy dead—but the thought of his stolen ring began to lose its importance in the light of a new terror.

There was a way he might find out if there had been a misbegotten son of his uncle, the fourth duke. He knew there was a record book in the village church in which all births and deaths in Ault-in-the-Vale were recorded, but how was he to get a look at the vital pages without arousing the curiosity of the vicar and his parishioners? By slipping silently in by night, of course. Once he found the record of an illegitimate child with reason to resemble himself, he would sleep easy.

Sylvester was not known for his bravery, being ornamental rather than valorous. Such wild imaginings as now plagued him, however, could not be trusted to Prouty. He'd have to handle this by himself.

The moon was bright, and it was not yet much after midnight. The castle lay silent; all were abed. The church would be empty, and church doors were never locked. He lighted his bedstand candle and searched for his clothes, donning them higgledy-piggledy without Prouty's aid, but no one was going to see him if he could help it.

He paused, his hand almost on the bellpull. The thought of the sensation caused by his demanding a horse to be saddled at this hour of the night brought him to a standstill. Every tongue belowstairs at Aultmere would be running like a fiddlestick by morning. He'd best slip out and go round to the stable himself.

Not daring to light a candle, lest some domestic be still about, he made his way down the curved central staircase and across the great hall, moving silently as a mouse. But in no way as quickly. Mice had no trouble avoiding heavy furniture in the pitch-black interior of an ostentatiously provided castle. Why had he never paid more attention to the placement of his own chairs and tables? He bit back a cry and rubbed a severely barked shin, at the same time backing into a tall pedestal bearing a tremendous Chinese urn. He wrapped both arms around the vase, barely catching it before it crashed to the floor. A suit of armor seemed to walk into him as he turned, but he managed to steady it. Sweat dewed his forehead, and he wiped it with his coat sleeve. By now, he had become totally disoriented. Where, oh where, was the way outside? He felt like sitting down on the cold stone paving and swearing with frustration.

Then, like a benediction from above, he saw a dim glow

ahead. All was not lost. The full moon, finding a crack between the drawing room draperies, shed a faint beam of guiding light. He crawled toward it, his spirits rising as though uplifted by the stiff brandy he so sorely needed.

The ever conscientious butler, for which he'd ordinarily be grateful, had secured the latch on the mullioned casement. It took a few minutes of desperate struggle—while the duke cursed the efficient Wapshott—to work it clear. Another minute, and he had stepped over the sill and out into the moonlit night. A cool breeze soothed his overheated brow, and his wits returned enough to allow him to leave off the catch and brace the window open with a handy flowerpot for his return. This was not a time to worry about burglars.

Rounding the side terraces at a trot, he headed for the stables. Would the stable hands be asleep? All at once, he wasn't certain he could take out a horse, saddle and bridle it—let alone mount—all by himself. He had never been an outdoor type, preferring when he went abroad to be driven comfortably in a carriage. Confound it, would he have to rouse at least one man?

That would be all it would take to spread the story of this escapade far and wide, no doubt to be accounted for by ribald tales of village maidens. He drew himself up, not wholly displeased by this idea. Better that sort of speculation than the truth. He'd now and then suspected his lower servants of holding his manhood in doubt, because he did not frequent the abodes of the more willing wenches well known to Prouty and his footmen. Let them talk.

The stables loomed before him. He turned the corner and stopped at the sight of several of his men casting dice by the light of a lantern. Their voices were low, but broken by raucous laughter after each remark. What amused them so? A sudden sinking held him still as he caught a few words—about that afternoon's holdup and his missing ring. How much had that coachman of Sir Geoffrey's babbled into every eager ear? From their merriment, he gathered they felt he had not shown to advantage in that encounter. He knew how they would react to seeing him now—the stifled sniggers, the sidelong glances. He shuddered. Having no desire to further appear a figure of fun to his inferiors, he decided to pass up riding to the village. He could easily walk, taking the half-mile shortcut past the mere and out the side gate, where a path used by his servants led to the back of the tavern.

He started off, his spirits somewhat soothed by the beauty of his grounds in the moonlight. A light drizzle earlier in the evening had left a sparkling dew on grass and shrubs. The dampness enhanced the fresh odors of newly turned earth in the garden beds, the delicate fragrance of roses and flowering trees quite charming him as he hurried along toward the grove that bordered the shore of the mere. How different the way looked at night—and on foot instead of horseback. Not at all what he had expected when he walked into the grove. For one thing, he hadn't realized how dark it would be under the trees.

Cut off from the moonlight by the thick covering over his head, he lost the path within minutes and found himself pushing through wet branches that snapped back, catching him in the face, nearly blinding him and dribbling odd bits of debris down his neck. He banged into a stout tree trunk, and fought his way free of a grasping net of sharp twigs and damp leaves that glued themselves to his person.

Once loose, he stood still, attempting to orient himself. The black night closed about him, and he became aware that he was not alone. Twigs crackled, bushes rustled, and small animals scuttered away through the fallen leaves about his feet. Crickets chirped, falling eerily silent as he began to feel his way, forcing one foot ahead of the other. But this was his own grove! In the daylight he knew every inch like the back of his hand. Rabbits and other tiny denizens of his domain were harmless, and he could not become lost in only a few acres of trees.

Brushing off his disarrayed garments, he stepped boldly forward—into a puddle left by the light rain. He muttered a phrase he had overheard when one of the footmen ran into old Wapshott and spilled a plate of salmon mayonnaise down the butler's front. Those were his newly polished Hessians he had grabbed when dressing in such a hurry. Prouty would have a fit of the vapors. In the next instant, the duke had one himself, for an ancient spiderweb—probably filled with captured, struggling bugs—wrapped itself stickily about his head.

Sylvester had an innate horror of spiders, and he struggled frantically to escape from the clinging strands. Imagining fat, black bodies with eight horrid legs caught in his hair, crawling down his neck and under his garments, he panicked. Tearing off his coat and shirt, he flapped them wildly to dislodge the beastly things. He had room to flap. He had scrambled out from under the trees and into a clearing. The Ault family vault loomed pale and silent before him.

A sudden draft touched his bare back, and he shuddered. But a cold breeze was quite normal of an evening, he told himself firmly, and gave his shirt a final flap before putting it back on. He repeated the process with his coat, and was plunging his second arm into the sleeve when he could have sworn a shadow moved behind the Grecian pillars. He froze, playing dead with a wild animal's instinct for self-preservation, the servants' tales of his mother's ghost whirling inside his head. Surely it wouldn't harm her son. . . . Maybe it didn't know he was there. He waited, trying not to breathe, for an interminable length of time—probably all of two minutes—before he broke. He ran for the side gate as though pursued by devils, more afraid of finding out there truly were such things as wraiths and specters than of actually seeing one, for that knowledge would haunt him for eternity, coloring his entire life.

Diving through the open gate at a staggering gallop, he reached the fallow field behind the village and pelted in a straight line toward the church steeple, gasping for breath, for he was no athlete. Tall grasses whipped about his legs, staining his once pristine inexpressibles, and he didn't care. A haven lay ahead. Scarcely noticing, he stumbled and fell, measuring his length in the weeds, but he had arrived. He circled around the cemetery at the back of the church, having had enough of ghosts. He had reached his goal without coming to a horrendous end and, a ray of comfort, he remembered that though it was nearly two miles farther than by that condemned shortcut, he could go back to Aultmere by the open road.

The doors of the church were unlocked, as he was certain they would be. Sylvester shoved one open and collapsed inside, sitting on the stone paved floor of the

nave, catching his breath. He choked on a sob of relief
and discovered his cheeks were wet. He scrubbed at them
with a filthy sleeve and looked about. The moonlight
shone through a stained glass window, throwing a kalei-
doscope of color in a path leading to the altar, past black
shadows on either side. In his shaken state it almost
seemed a sending. No ghost would dare follow him inside these sacred walls. Surely this place was as holy as
the Catholic church of his mother. Crossing himself, he
prayed her wraith would not think his entering a Church
of England chapel a sacrilege.

The village records of birth, death, and marriage for
the past two hundred years were kept in huge volumes
on a stand in the chancel behind the clergyman's pulpit.
He found them almost at once. Lighting a taper from a
sconce on the end of one of the pews, Sylvester approached the heavy books in some awe. His hand trembled as he turned yellowed pages to the year of the little
duke's birth. He found no extra entries or any that seemed
disguised. He checked several years back and ahead, and
found no trace of an illegitimate son of his uncle. He
was sweating, a drop trickling down his spine. Suppose . . . again he checked the essential entry, the one
recording the death of the fifth duke.

Candlewax dropped on the page, but in his preoccupation, he failed to notice the cream-colored spot.

Nine

While the Duke of Ault, unbeknownst to his sleeping household, fled one ghost and raised another, Sir Geoffrey Cole traversed a nightmare of his own. Stung by Marianna's remarks about his being useless, spoken in the presence of the French housemaid—though that should certainly not bother him!—he was determined to find the board on which hung the keys to the castle of Aultmere.

He waited until after midnight, when the castle at last fell silent, before he picked up his lighted chamberstick and eased open his bedroom door. Checking his pocket for Celeste's tallow impression of Charlie's key, he peered up and down the empty, black corridor. It seemed safe to start. Sir Geoffrey had taken up the candle, but it was Rake Cole who slipped stealthily out, relishing the aura of danger with a pleasurable tingle of excitement. Off on an adventure. Unconsciously, his rakish swagger returned to his stride.

A good part of his day had been spent in attempting to memorize the terrain of what he'd come to believe was one of the more labyrinthine castles in Great Britain. Of the original fifteenth-century building, only the Great Hall remained intact. The rest had been built up, torn, or fallen down and built up again in a bewildering variety of tastes by a succession of Aults, the result being that no two consecutive rooms appeared to be on the same level or of the same construction. He had but a vague idea of the whereabouts of the kitchens, having only located the double baize doors through which the bearers of viands had entered and exited during a long and overly bountiful dinner. Now, as his nerves began to churn inside him, he wished he had not eaten so much.

He began, naturally, by being quite turned around in the unfamiliar surroundings, and headed off in the wrong direction. Not that he noticed the change at once. He was too occupied with keeping his footing, interrupted continually by single steps up or down, no doubt an effort on the builders' part to accommodate the changing levels of the floor. The walls of the long corridor were hung with ancient paintings of Ault ancestors considered too unimportant for places in the Grand Portrait Gallery on the third floor. Even within the tiny pool of light from his candle, he could sense all those haughty, disapproving eyes staring at him from the black shadows, and he shielded his light to keep from seeing them.

It seemed a long time before he came to the head of a staircase that plunged away into darkness and climbed into a deeper black above. Keeping a hand on the banister beside him, he crept down into the unknown below him, one step at a time. It struck him as he went that the stairs wound round in shorter flights and more landings than he remembered. Surely this was not the way he had come up to his room. When he reached the ground floor, he stepped out on wood, not stone flags. Raising his candle revealed the *accoutrements* of a private chapel. He had missed the Great Hall entirely, and it was only from there that he knew his way into the realm of the domestics.

Realizing wherein lay his error, Rake Cole reverted to Sir Geoffrey and intelligently did the only logical and sensible thing. Instead of exploring further, he back-tracked. Up the stairs, counting the three landings he'd passed, and—he hoped—turning in the right direction. He did. He soon recognized his corridor by the repulsive portraits that seemed to mock him as he passed.

He walked toward his bedchamber and, with an awful sinking, discovered that all the doors looked alike. He'd never be able to regain his own room except by a course of trial and error, but he needn't worry about that yet. He still had that keyboard to find. Rake Cole took over once more. No doubt when he returned with the key properly identified, he'd remember how many doors Wapshott had passed before throwing one open for him. Even remember on which side of the hall.

It took longer than he expected to reach another stair head, but this one was so wide and gently curved that he knew he was on the right track, a premise confirmed by the pervasive odors of age, mold, and damp that as-sailed his nostrils as he started down.

The reassuring chill of damp stone crept up through his boot soles as he reached ground level. He held his candle aloft, creating a pale, glowing circle in which to find his way across the black and white checkerboard of the marble paving. The light flickered on polished suits of armor guarding the newel posts at the foot of the stairs and each side of a cavernous hearth, taller than his head and reach-ing back into the dark of a subterranean cave. His candle glimmered over silver trays and brass urns on huge carved tables and black oak chests. Great tapestries, gray and colorless in the faint light, stretched across the stone walls in a vain effort to control the fitful drafts that set the gonfalons above him to swaying as his candle played over them. At least Geoff hoped they were drafts.

Something eerie about the walls and ceiling fading away into black nothingness around his pitiful pool of candlelight roused uncomfortable thoughts of earth-bound spirits. Too many tormented souls must have passed this way, as witnessed by the assembly of bloodthirsty weapons hung among the moth-eaten stag heads between the tapestries.

Geoff paused, getting his bearings, and sudden horror froze him to the spot. Hollow echoes of measured footsteps thudded along the passage that opened beyond the gigantic hearth. Where to hide? His wildly swinging candle passed over a door beneath the staircase. He doused his light, dove inside, and stepped into an empty bucket. Mops, brooms and feather dusters, dislodged from their corners, rained blows on his head and shoulders. A storage cupboard for housemaids' supplies? It would do to store him, as well. He cracked open the door enough to peek out.

A luminescent glow approached through the black shadows, and he half-expected to see a wavering, translucent monk or beheaded courtier drift by. What he saw was far more substantial. The portly figure of Wapshott the butler, carrying a taper, trod purposefully across the hall toward the dining room—a room, Geoff remembered, that contained several sideboards replete with lifesaving decanters. He licked his dry lips.

The butler came out almost immediately, his taper in

one hand and in the other, an ornate crystal decanter sloshing with a dark liquid. His private bottle must be drained and, Geoff surmised, Wapshott had no more desire to go down into the ancient cellars after midnight than Geoff had himself. If Aultmere were haunted, it would surely be by former residents of the dark dungeons below. And if that blasted key of Charlie's did not fit a lock above ground, he'd only explore underground by daylight.

Meanwhile, Wapshott had reached the baize doors, and Geoff, once more Rake Cole, slipped out of the cupboard and trailed him. That keyboard might well be in the butler's pantry. He crept silently along, his eyes on the sparkle of Wapshott's candlelight on the decanter. If one had to be a wage earner, it must be a pleasant life being a butler, as Wapshott's girth attested.

Ahead, the butler entered his pantry and shut the door, leaving Geoff in total darkness, holding his snuffed candle. He had forgotten his pocket luminary and had no way to relight. He cursed freely, borrowing Rake Cole's vocabulary while that spirit deserted him. His only course was to carry on, feeling his way along the stone passage until he could find a kitchen with a banked fire he could blow into flame. After peering through door-less stone arches into several sprawling rooms, he discovered a cooking area with a red glow beneath one of the ovens.

Fooled by the hollow feel of an empty space, he stepped boldly in, up to the beckoning hearth, and onto the tail of a sleeping cat.

An indignant yowl split the air. Throwing caution aside, Geoff scrambled under a vast table that occupied the center of the room and pretended with all his heart to be an insignificant mouse. Already, Wapshott's measured tread sounded in the stone passage without. Entering with his candle, the butler set it on top of the table, shrouding Geoff in deeper shadows. He held his breath.

Wapshott addressed the cat. " 'Ere, old moggy, where you been 'iding? Yer should be out, 'are-brained little beast."

Geoff shrank back as the butler bent, a difficult feat for one of Wapshott's figure. As he watched, the butler tickled the insulted cat under the chin.

"Come along then, old puss." He gave a coaxing chirp and the cat purred an answer.

From his hiding place, Geoff listened to this exchange with interest. So, butlers were human beings and talked in the language of the rest of the domestics, when not on duty.

Wapshott scooped up the cat and grunted with the effort, wafting a breathful of excellent port under the table. He bore the cat off, an iron latch rattled somewhere, a heavy door creaked open and slammed. Wapshott's footsteps faded away.

Geoff crawled out and lighted his chamberstick from the fire. There was no way he could search the butler's pantry until Wapshott retired. He had ascertained that the servants slept on the third floor above this wing, and if that blasted cat had not alerted anyone else, he felt reasonably safe except for the butler. Wapshott remained in his pantry, drinking that tempting port, and Geoff began thinking longingly of a stiff glass to while away the time until the butler retired.

He had a light now. It would be easy enough to slip back along the passage, and seize a decanter of his own to sustain him while he searched through the keys on the butler's keyboard.

To think was to act. By the time he made his way back to the dining room, his nerves were tingling, and he snatched the first reasonably full bottle he saw, half-expecting to meet Wapshott in the passage on his return trip. The butler, however, proved a slow drinker, and Geoff huddled in one of the archways waiting for the coast to clear. He took a large swig from his decanter and choked, strangling, his throat on fire. That was smuggled French brandy, not wine, he had helped himself to. He gasped and swallowed repeatedly to clear his airway, not all that displeased. This night would not be a total waste, finding the keyboard or no.

He settled down to wait, sitting on the cold stone floor and sipping with care to soothe his discomfort, while he ruminated on the wiles of a certain hurly-burly French-woman and her unladylike ideas. Whatever madness had come over him to undertake this ridiculous assignment? He had thought himself above succumbing to soft brown eyes and a dimpled smile, but there was more to Miss Celeste Moreau than her lovely face. She was a challenge he could not resist. To his manhood? Or his spirit of adventure? He had kissed many a housemaid, but never one who appealed to him like this. Ah, but she was not a maid. She was a housekeeper, and a new experience. He sipped his brandy and grinned. A housekeeper he'd like to have himself. He let his mind dwell on the—he hoped available—charms of Mlle. Celeste. He was almost sorry when Wapshott finally came out of his pantry to make his stately way toward the back stairs.

Geoff shrank back into the chamber behind him,

crouching over his candle in a corner, blocking its glow
with his body until the butler had vanished. He rose to
his feet too quickly and staggered. That French brandy
had an unexpected potency. Holding up his decanter, he
swirled the dark liquor in the light from the candle, surprised to see how far the level had dropped. He leaned
a steadying hand against the damp stone passage wall
until his head cleared, before entering the butler's empty
pantry.

Not only empty of butlers. No keyboard, either. Remembering the ousting of the cat, Geoff tracked down
the huge back door of the kitchens. No keyboard hung
there, handy to use. For some reason, this lack of forethought seemed unaccountable. Keys were necessary and
should be kept at hand. He felt heartily annoyed at such
a careless way to run an estate. Time someone took
proper charge of the household! The castle badly needed
a mistress—he tried to imagine Marianna in that position
and shook his head, an ill-considered action that caused
him to clutch his temples.

Rake Cole might be a trifle foxed, but he could see
them all out, and he was not so much as half-sprung.
Confidently, he carried the brandy along as he conducted
a steady, purposeful search of each room he came to,
finally hitting the jackpot in the housekeeper's parlor.
Close to a hundred keys hung on the board, most were
tagged, many older ones rusted and obviously no longer
used. The decanter beside him, he settled down to matching keys to his wax impression.

After nearly an hour, his decanter drained and no
longer supplying encouragement, he gave up the job as
hopeless. None of the keys were the right shape or size,

and Charlie's was far older, larger, and more ornate. He faced a dilemma, for he shrank from going to the vicarage and reporting failure again. Not, of course, that he cared what a French housemaid might think. At least, at this hour of the night, he convinced himself he didn't. Leaving the empty decanter in the housekeeper's parlor— let them make of it what they would—he wandered back to the Great Hall, wearily climbed the stairs and, amazingly, remembered how many doors from the landing they had hidden his room. He even traveled in the right direction.

Mlle. Celeste Moreau sat on the lower step of the vicarage porch, idly listening to Marianna and Charlie squabbling about the reordering of the overgrown front yard. It was well after luncheon, and she nearly despaired of the coming of the wicked baronet. Had he not found a matching key? Did he think her—them—unimportant, and therefore felt it unnecessary to report another failure? Was it that he would not come at all this day?

It was not disappointment she felt, for he was of the most reprehensible. Only disillusion, for she had begun to think him quite *compatisant,* despite his regrettable tendency to kiss . . . mounting color heated her cheeks. Indeed, she did not want him to come, for he would surely insult her by kissing her again. Such unconscionable behavior was only to be expected from one of his ilk.

Her hands flew to her hot face, but no one observed her. Marianna had been trying to make a daisy chain of the dandelions that grew in profusion in the overgrown vicarage front yard. She had given up and now watched Charlie and offered useless advice, as he worked at repairing the broken gate. A peaceful bucolic scene, all of the most pleasant. Why, then, this depression possessing her?

Her heart gave a sudden bound. Hooves clattered on the hard-packed roadway, and a shining black curricle, drawn by a splendid pair of matched grays, hove into view around the corner of the tavern.

Marianna shrieked with delight, flinging her lapful of discarded dandelions to the winds.

"Uncle Geoff!"

Charlie dropped his hammer into the long grass, where it disappeared completely, and joined her. The curricle pulled up with a stylish flourish.

Tiens, he was here! In a flutter, Celeste patted at the burnished curls she had not covered with her demure mobcap. She had chosen not to wear it today, *certainement* not because she wished to appear at her best for so dangerous a man.

The youngsters clamored at the side of the carriage, startling his horses, and it took him but a moment to settle them. He had excellent hands, she noted, only to be expected of a—Corinthian, was it?—as such a rakish baronet was bound to be. She saw him shake his head at Marianna and Charlie, holding up a hand for silence.

"But Uncle Geoff," wailed Marianna. "Have you failed again?"

"You mean my key doesn't fit anything?" Charlie demanded. "Could you not find the castle keyboard?"

"No, no, it is not that. I found the board, but if there is a duplicate for your key, it does not hang with the rest." He shushed a rising howl. "That does not mean it lacks a keyhole somewhere. All is not yet lost."

He handed the ribbons to the groom who sat beside him, enjoying the scene. "Take them back to the stable at the tavern, Jobbs. I shall be here awhile." He dug out a handful of coins. "I hear their home-brewed ale is excellent. Wait for me there, I'll walk over and join you later."

"Yus, sir." The man grinned and pocketed the money.

Sir Geoffrey's answering grin went slightly askew. "Better you than me today." He turned to Charlie and Marianna, who clung to the side of his curricle. "Back off, you young romps, and let me come down."

Celeste had waited by the porch, cooling her cheeks. He had not yet greeted her, but the look he now sent in her direction brought the flood of pink once more. She noted that his face seemed preternaturally pale, his eyes bloodshot, and he dismounted with exaggerated care, setting his boots gently on the ground as if his head ached unbearably. Of course, he and her duke must have made a night of it. Her maternal instincts came to the fore. Poor man! A *tisane* was needed immediately to put him aright.

She left Marianna and Charlie upbraiding him unmercifully for not searching for a locked room, and hurried into the vicarage to check her herbal supplies. By the time they all trooped inside, she had a pan boiling on the hearth grate. She poured a greenish-brown liquid from it into a mug.

"Here, sir, you must drink this down. It will calm your stomach, and the head will also cease to ache. It is a recipe of my papa and never failed to bring him ease."

His warm smile turned rueful. "Am I then in that bad shape? I thought I concealed it rather well."

The glow in his eyes, though somewhat dimmed, caused the steaming mug of herbal tea to tremble, and she almost dropped it. Quickly, she put it into his hands.

"It is without doubt," she said, her dimple deepening, "only that the jouncing of your vehicle has given you the *mal de tête.*"

"Touché." He eyed the strange beverage askance and sipped at it with suspicion, then emptied the mug. The color began to return to his face almost at once. He gave her a grateful glance, tinged with surprise.

Marianna, this while, had been staring at Charlie, and Celeste caught a speculative expression on her face. Now what notion, she wondered, was forming in the mind of that impetuous damsel? She knew a tingle of anticipation—or was it apprehension?—whatever—and decided to second the suggestion she saw coming, if only for the amusement in seeing Sir Geoffrey's reaction. It began innocently enough.

"Uncle Geoff, even you now believe Charlie's key opens a lock within the castle."

Her eyelids fluttered innocently, and Sir Geoffrey stopped smiling. Suspicion tinged his voice. "And so?"

"You cannot test every door by yourself; you will need help."

Ah, thought Celeste. Here it comes.

"You have only to see to it," Marianna continued with a becoming naivete, "that a door or window is left unlatched, as we once talked of. Charlie and I can then slip in and help you."

In spite of herself, Celeste exclaimed, "You can not leave me out!"

"No!" Sir Geoffrey thundered. The word came down

like a boot stamping on the floor, and Celeste jumped. "Absolutely not!" He went on more calmly. "And you know you have no such intention, so put it out of your mind. You will run no ridiculous risks. Should you be caught, Marianna, I might get you off—though I doubt it—but Charlie would lose his life. All of you, keep far away from Aultmere. And Charlie is not to step foot out of this house."

"But I must," Charlie argued. "At least, out back. The necessary—"

"All right," Sir Geoffrey interrupted. "But be quick coming and going, and be sure no one sees you. Remember, boy, Ault means you no good."

Charlie sucked in a dreamy breath. "Aye," he said, his tone smug. "A price on my head! Jed'd be that proud."

Sir Geoffrey did not grin, but it must have cost him some effort. Celeste caught a glint of humor in his eye.

"Be that as it may, young man," he said. "You'll not profit from the infamy, if he sees you hung. And speaking of searches, if I am to spend my nights trying door locks in Aultmere, you must let me take your key."

Charlie stuck out his chin. "No."

"No," Marianna agreed. "You see, you must leave open a window."

Sir Geoffrey ignored her. Celeste took the empty mug from his hands and helped things along. "But, of course, Sir Geoffrey. The children must be kept safe. It is the obvious thing that *I* should be the one to climb into the window of the Duke of Ault. Me, he does not know, and should I be seen," she smoothed her apron, *"voilà,* we have here the new housemaid who has lost her way among these numerous halls." She beamed at him, radiating a Marianna-like innocence.

He looked down at her, an appreciative glint—and something warmer—in his eyes. "Lost you soon would be. There are no guide posts, and the confounded place is a veritable maze. I'll do the hunting alone. I, at least, have a legitimate reason for being there, and may become lost if I please."

Marianna had been thinking, a dangerous occupation for her. "Celeste, let us go over your letter from your uncle again. There may be some clue we have missed."

Charlie looked doubtful. "It's all in gibberish, like mine."

"It is not as you say gibberish to *me*." Celeste retrieved it from under the mantel clock, where she had placed it with Charlie's for safekeeping. She carried both letters to the settle and Marianna and Sir Geoffrey seated themselves, one on each side of her, while Charlie inspected the cool box for a leftover bun.

Sitting so close to Sir Geoffrey that his muscled thigh rested against her knee, caused a nervous thrill to run up inside her. She began to read her letter, striving to keep a tremor from her voice when his shoulder brushed hers. Had he moved closer—or was it she who leaned his way? She pulled hastily back, glanced at him, and encountered so blatant an invitation in his eyes that she dropped one of the sheets. They both bent to pick it up, their hands met, she felt a pleasurable tingle—and with it came an unsettling thought. Could she have dropped that page, unconsciously wanting his touch—and did he think she did it on purpose? Inviting further advances? The betraying color mounted in her cheeks once more.

Her glance at him flicked quick and away, but it was long enough for his hot eyes to burn into her very being.

One should not play with fire. He meant no good, this wicked baronet! She shifted as far from him as she could, pressing against Marianna, who whispered in her ear.

"Well done, Celeste," came on a delighted breath. "You will lure him from Lady Charlotte yet!"

Le bon dieu! How much had that girl noticed? Taken aback, Celeste realized she had quite forgotten this Lady Charlotte and Sir Geoffrey's unfortunate betrothal. And she had been flirting with him—yes, tossing the handkerchief as the English novelists put it—to a man as good as married! And he was picking it up! Truly, he was the wicked baronet to the core!

To cover her confusion, she folded up both letters and rose, shoving them back beneath the clock. "I think we find nothing new in these."

"But we have," exclaimed Marianna. "Charlie, this letter and key were sent you in Meadowcum. Were you born there?"

Charlie swallowed the last of the bun he had found. "Come to think of it, I don't know."

"No, of course, you were not!" She turned to Sir Geoffrey. "If Charlie is the real duke, he would have been born here in Ault-in-the-Vale, and his name will be in the great recording book in the church!"

"Fustian," said her uncle.

Charlie agreed. "You've more hair than wit, nickninny. Just because I have a key with a crest on it doesn't make me a duke. A relative, perhaps." He mused. "That would be interesting to discover."

This idea appealed immediately to Marianna. "Indeed,

Uncle Geoff, let us go at once and see. The record books are no doubt open to all, and Charlie may be in there!"

Sir Geoffrey, studying Charlie's features, nodded slowly. "Perhaps we might learn who he is." He looked at Celeste. Carefully, she avoided meeting his eyes. "Should we not ask permission of the Reverend Mr. Brinkman?" he asked. "Where is he?"

A safe question to answer, she smiled at him. "As always, after the luncheon he sleeps."

"Let us go!" Marianna was on her feet. "Celeste should be the one to ask."

Sir Geoffrey frowned her down. "He is an old man. We must not wake him."

"Then we shall not. Come on." Catching her uncle's hand, she pulled him toward the door. "If this church is like ours at home, the proper book will be easily found, for it is used almost every day."

Eyebrows raised, the wicked baronet looked to Celeste for confirmation. If it would keep him here— "M. Brinkman would not object," she said. "He, too, would be pleased to know the true identity of Charlie."

Charlie himself was all in favor of checking for his birth and was already at the door, idly twirling his key about with one finger hooked through a cut-out in the crest. It fell to the floor with a clatter, and he retrieved it.

"Here, now," said Sir Geoffrey. "You must not go about carrying that thing in your hand. I know you, you'll set it down or drop it somewhere. If you will not let me take it to Aultmere, you'd best hide it securely here."

Celeste knew the very place. "Put it inside the clock on the mantel. It is there I often hid small things when a child. No one looks into the inside of a clock."

Charlie held back. "Suppose it stops."

"It does so often. I give it the good shake, and it marches once more. For the time, we listen to the case clock in M. Brinkman's study which strikes every hour, day and night."

He acquiesced, but reluctantly. The precious key was hidden away for safekeeping, and they all trooped into the church next door. Celeste, whose duties included the sweeping of the chapel, led them to the huge book, and Sir Geoffrey turned the yellowed pages back to the approximate year of Charlie's birth. He checked through several years, but Charlie's name did not appear, although they found that of the fifth duke.

Nevertheless, Sir Geoffrey kept turning the pages. When they came in, the book had been lying open to the section some three years ahead, where the pages bore grim black borders, recording the deaths in the village from the plague. Among the names, the letters of his title scrolled and ornamented, was listed the death of the little duke. And near the bottom of that page was a fresh dripping of candlewax.

Geoff touched a finger to the wax lightly. "So, someone else is interested in the passing of the fifth duke," he remarked. "Now, why?" he wondered. "And why did that person need a candle, unless he came in the night?"

"In secret!" Marianna exclaimed. "We have a real mystery! Only think, perhaps Charlie did not die, and he is the real duke."

"Of course, I'm not dead! And I'm no duke, either, no matter what that book says."

Sir Geoffrey closed the volume, leaving the wax in place. "Don't be nonsensical," he told Marianna. "The real duke is accounted for. We must find Charlie's birth elsewhere."

That young gentleman nodded. "In Meadowcum. You're a bird-witted chit," he informed Marianna. "Leading me on a wild-goose chase."

Celeste put an arm around the insulted girl. "Come, we go home and have tea while we devise some other scheme."

Sir Geoffrey, much to her disappointment, excused himself. There would be, after all, no chance for him to kiss her with the children in constant attendance. For that, she was most thankful. She told herself so.

Geoff picked up his groom and curricle for the drive back to the castle. His thoughts centered on the charms of a pair of laughing brown eyes, and a face and figure far too lovely to be wasted on a housemaid. On reaching the front entrance to Aultmere, he had a rude awakening. A coach waited, the crest on its door that of the Earl of Langham.

Lady Charlotte had arrived.

"Hell and the devil confound it!" he muttered. What in blazes is *she* doing here?"

Ten

Throwing the reins to Jobbs, Sir Geoffrey jumped down onto the gravel drive. The headache eased by Mlle. Moreau's herbal tea came back with a vengeance. This had to be Lady Charlotte. Her father, the earl, would not have come by traveling coach. Geoff eyed that coach with foreboding.

Cursing fluently under his breath, he strode up the wide semicircle of steps to the tall double doors at the entrance to Aultmere. He gave the bell rope a yank that jangled through the Great Hall.

Wapshott himself opened the door and Geoff handed him his gloves and hat, jerking a thumb toward the waiting carriage. "Lady Charlotte?"

The butler inclined his stately head. "That is the lady's name."

"Damn," said Geoff. Ignoring Wapshott's raised eyebrows, he walked across the hall to the door of the front drawing room from which came the murmur of voices. He paused, looking in, startled again by Sylvester's resemblance to Charlie.

Lady Charlotte, correctly garbed in a conservative puce carriage gown and with a matching bonnet still on her head, sat sipping a glass of sherry. Her host, very much the Duke of Ault, nibbled a biscuit and gazed at her with a touch of awe. Geoff knew how he felt. Charlotte, on her company behavior, created an impressive presence. He, himself, had been quite cowed on first being presented to her. It was no wonder he had thought her the ideal woman to bear his heir.

Her very dignity brought to mind one who was her near opposite. He envisioned tumbled, chestnut curls, falling free, in place of the ordered coils of fair hair pinned tightly to Lady Charlotte's head; pink cheeks that flushed too easily, compared to cool, pale features; warm, laughing, brown eyes to cold, gray ice—enough. This was unfair. Their positions in life were poles apart, and Lady Charlotte was well suited to Sir Geoffrey. But Rake Cole's preference was for a certain French housemaid/housekeeper. Never, until he now observed Lady Charlotte again, had this dawned on him. Shock held him on the threshold.

Lady Charlotte was speaking in her deliberate, condescending—even to a duke!—manner.

"I find Aultmere very drafty and over large," she decreed. "Do you not prefer living in Town, your Grace?"

Ault agreed fervently. "Indeed, yes. I spend most of the year in my London establishment. Only the heat of summer drives me to the country."

"I cannot bear heat," said Charlotte. "But I prefer to reside closer to town." She turned her head slightly, saw Geoff in the doorway, and beckoned with her fan. "Geoffrey, my dear. You must join us."

There being nothing for it, he walked in. Bowing over her extended hand, he allowed his lips to brush lightly over her cool fingertips. One must preserve the niceties.

"What a surprise, Charlotte," he managed. "How do

you go on?" And what the devil are you doing here? he added peevishly to himself.

She tapped his hand with the ubiquitous fan, this one of everyday ivory and chicken skin, adorned simply with the Langham crest. "Surprise? Surely, Geoffrey, you could expect little else of one who has your interests at heart. I am determined to do all in my power to prevent the scandal I foresee."

"Scandal? What scandal?"

"I should think that obvious, my dear. When your sister Augusta informed me that you and Marianna were staying at the castle with Ault, I ventured to suggest to her that she should go at once to chaperone Marianna, for Aultmere is known as a bachelor establishment."

"I collect she has not followed your excellent advice."

Lady Charlotte frowned. "She informed me she was promised to the Crandalls for their ball on Thursday, and to a rout party on Friday. So, of course, seeing my duty, I came at once."

"Your duty?"

She favored him with a complacent smile. "Even you must be cognizant of the fact that a betrothed woman stands above an unmarried girl, and therefore my consequence is all the protection Marianna will need. We must give out at once that I have been with her all along."

"Highly commendable," agreed Sylvester.

"And highly unnecessary." Geoff glared at him. "Have you not explained to Lady Charlotte that Marianna is not here?" He thought rapidly, creating a story that even Marianna could not have bettered. "She is lodging at the vicarage. She—ah, wished to remain in the neighborhood

for a short time. To become better acquainted wit
Sylvester before their marriage, you must understand."

Lady Charlotte nodded. "Ah, I see. Quite correc
Boarding with a vicar rather than at an inn is mos
suitable. The reverend gentleman is married?"

"Er—no, but he has a female housekeeper."

Lady Charlotte perceived the flaw. "Will it not caus
talk in the village? I feel it would be best for her t
reside at Aultmere in my charge, now that I have come.

Best! Geoff recoiled inwardly. Best for whom? H
could imagine what Marianna would say to being place
in Charlotte's care! He was struck by a foreboding o
impending doom. If Marianna gained entrance to the cas
tle, nothing he could do would prevent that enterprisin
maiden from sneaking out at night to try every door an
cupboard—if Charlie would give her his key. Worse, i
he refused to part with it, she would be bound to some
how let Charlie in, and that careless young man woul
knock over suits of armor, step on cats, alert butlers an
footmen, and then how could he get the children out o
their mess? Marianna must stay where she was!

He had reckoned without Sylvester. That gentlema
spoke up at once, eager to kowtow to the elegant Lady
Charlotte.

"An excellent suggestion," he exclaimed. "I shall sen
a carriage for her at once. Indeed, I will go myself."

Geoff swallowed an urge to strangle him. Sylvester ha
to be forestalled—he must not see Charlie! He put on hi
loftiest Sir Geoffrey manner and turned to Lady Charlotte
"I fear I do not deem it proper for Marianna to reside
under the same roof with Ault, even with your presence."

She gazed at him in some astonishment. "This from *ou,* Geoffrey?"

"You must realize, Charlotte, this is a time of some delicacy for so young a maiden. I do not feel she should be pressured in any way. She is quite well where she is, and has developed a fondness for the vicarage housekeeper." He savored that title. How very respectable the term now sounded. Just so Charlotte never met that housekeeper.

His luck had run out.

"This housekeeper," she asked, frowning slightly, "is she a widow of respectable age?"

Here it came. "Ah, not exactly. I believe she is unmarried."

"I heard she is French," Ault put in, quite unnecessarily. Geoff frowned at him, wishing he could kick him in the shin.

Lady Charlotte rose, shaking out her puce skirt. "Geoffrey, I wish to visit the vicarage for myself. I cannot feel an unmarried Frenchwoman to be an adequate chaperone for so flighty a damsel as Marianna. You must know, I am against frivolity in any form, and I consider all French women to be frivolous."

Geoff strove to keep a desperate note from his voice. "I am surprised at you, Charlotte. I abhor generalities, and I assure you, Marianna can come to no harm in a vicarage."

She went on as though he had not spoken. "My carriage yet awaits, for I knew not but what I might depart at once for home with Miss Marianna. Geoffrey, you will accompany me to this vicarage, and we shall see."

Nothing would do but she must be off at once, and Sylvester, who for some reason seemed very eager to join the inspection tour, insisted on going along. Geoff felt ready to tear out his hair, there being no way to warn the vicarage of this raid by the enemy. Then Sylvester saved the day.

"Pray be seated, Lady Charlotte, for a few moments more. I must change my coat, if I am to go out. I'll not be above five minutes. Excuse me, please, dear lady." He scurried out into the hall and they heard him shouting for Prouty.

"In this case," said Lady Charlotte, "may I suggest dear Geoffrey, that you must drive your curricle. You will then be able to take his Grace back to Aultmere, as no doubt Marianna will wish to return to London with me."

Geoff, dizzy with relief, heartily applauded her forethought. "I shall go on ahead," he said, with admirable aplomb, "and await your coming. No doubt the vicar's good housekeeper will wish to put on a kettle for tea." At least, she knows how to boil water, he thought. Not that it mattered. Just so she knew of a safe place to hide Mr. Charlie Makepeace.

When the Langham traveling coach duly lumbered up to the vicarage at the sedate pace Lady Charlotte believed due her dignity, Geoff was dismounting from his curricle as though he had just arrived. He turned an innocent face toward the carriage, and hurried to beat her footman to the task of lowering the steps.

Celeste, standing on the low porch, quickly checked her companions. She herself wore her plainest mobcap and her most demure expression. Marianna stood beside her, looking impossibly angelic. The Reverend Mr. Brinkman had no need for subterfuge. Fresh up from his nap, he had taken his place behind the girls, his benign face beaming and ruddy, his fringe of white hair gilded to a halo by the lowering sun. A tableau designed to disarm the strictest critic, Celeste hoped it would even impress the daughter of an earl. Earls, she knew from her novels, were high-sticklers, the top-loftiest noblemen in the *ton*.

Charlie was nowhere in sight, and she sent a stern thought his way, cautioning him to remain so.

The carriage door was opening, and it seemed a gentleman would be the first to appear. A flush of anticipation tingled through Celeste. She held her breath, agog for her initial glimpse of her duke. A brief holdup ensued. His tall, beehive hat caught on the top of the low carriage door and was knocked askew. She could barely contain the suspense, but the wait was worth it.

For this meeting with his reluctant fiancée, Sylvester had donned a bottle-green velvet coat, padded in the shoulders and sharply nipped in at his waist. Yellow pantaloons set it off. His neckcloth, owing to Prouty's ministrations, was a miracle of convoluted creases, and his starched collar points, touching his cheekbones, were so stiff he would be unable to look sideways without turning his whole body. A diamond sparkled in a pouter-pigeon ruff on his shirtfront, and his waistcoat, of rose and lavender brocade, glittered with silver thread embroidery, competing with a dazzling array of rings and fobs.

Next to this magnificence, Sir Geoffrey was quite cast into shade in his simple country garb of sober blue coat and fawn buckskins tucked into white-topped boots.

Marianna's lip curled as she eyed Sylvester. "Popinjay!" she hissed in Celeste's ear.

Celeste stared at her, surprised. Ault was a duke, to

her a godlike being, and anything less than the marvelous sight he presented would have been a dire disappointment. She was equally impressed by the regal character of the lady who descended after him, resting a glove on Sir Geoffrey's arm. She was not fooled by the apparent restraint of Lady Charlotte's carriage attire. The cost of the puce material for her gown alone would have kept a thrifty French miss in garments for a year.

Remembering she was the housekeeper, she hung back while M. Brinkman stepped forward to greet his guests. To her amazement, he seemed not at all in awe of Ault or the lady, calmly ushering them inside and into the seldom-used parlor at the front of the vicarage. The kettle already steamed on the kitchen hearth, and she set about arranging a tray of cups and a plate of biscuits. As she carried it into the parlor, she caught the tail of a speech by Lady Charlotte.

"—now that I have seen your housekeeper, my dear vicar, I feel most strongly that Marianna cannot stay with so young a woman as chaperone. I have decided she must leave at once and return to London with me."

"No," said Marianna.

Lady Charlotte shook an admonishing finger. "My dear Marianna, surely you must realize—"

"No," repeated Marianna, a flat refusal reminiscent of Charlie.

Celeste, pouring the tea, ducked her head to hide a smile. M. Charlie had the contagion. How long, she wondered, before they all balked like stubborn donkeys and said only no, refusing to budge? Until meeting that young man, she had not before appreciated the efficacy of the simple word.

"But Marianna," began Lady Charlotte, somewhat taken aback.

"No. I shall stay here."

Celeste looked at Sir Geoffrey and saw the corners of his mouth twitch. He compressed his lips in a firm line, but a devil danced in his eyes as he returned her glance.

Lady Charlotte, nonplussed, turned to him. "Geoffrey, you must reason with her!"

"Why? She may remain here if she wishes."

Outrage stirred the most proper Lady Charlotte into nearly losing her monumental dignity. Spots of bright color flamed in her pale cheeks, making her almost pretty. *"Why?* You are being derelict in your duty, Geoffrey. Really, at times I quite despair of you!"

This statement, Celeste noted, did not perturb Sir Geoffrey at all. She remembered suddenly that she had told Marianna they should separate her uncle from this woman, and her determination took on new meaning. So beautiful a man—even though he was a wicked baronet—should not be wasted on this unfeeling female without appreciation for his worth. And she could not allow poor Marianna to come under the thumb of this strict and humorless person. Catching the girl's eye, she gave her a brisk, encouraging nod.

The Duke of Ault sat silent through all this, his eyes roaming the room as though searching for something. Celeste peeked at him from under lowered lids. Did he suspect Charlie's presence? Was he looking for evidence to pass on to the Runners he threatened to call? She scanned the room, anxious, looking for any telltale scrap that might betray him. But that was foolish of her! Charlie, to her knowledge, had never entered the parlor. His cot was in the vicar's study.

"Do you not agree, your Grace?" Lady Charlotte unexpectedly appealed to him.

Ault did not appear to hear. He was studying the staircase that began just inside the front door and separated the parlor from the rest of the house. Luckily, Lady Charlotte did not wait for an answer, aiming her argument instead at the bland vicar, who placidly agreed with whoever addressed him.

Celeste now had the opportunity to study Ault's features at close hand, and she was amazed at his resemblance to M. Charlie. And how insignificant he appeared next to Sir Geoffrey, in spite of his glorious raiment. For the first time, she realized that she stood in grave danger of becoming far too attracted to the wrong man. But Ault was a duke! And Sir Geoffrey, as well as being a wicked baronet, was betrothed to Lady Charlotte.

Scheming to separate Sir Geoffrey from his fiancée seemed impossible. Lady Charlotte was so perfect, so absolutely a lady, that Celeste felt quite gauche. A cloud of depression settled over her. Now that she had met the determined Charlotte, she could never imagine that lady crying off.

Lady Charlotte continued to speak as though Celeste, a mere domestic, was invisible and deaf. "I cannot quite approve of Frenchwomen," she informed Sir Geoffrey. "I have told you before that I consider their attitude to be flighty, and they cannot be trusted not to go beyond the line."

Geoff, relieved, saw Celeste quietly set down the teapot

and retire to the room beyond the stairs. Not, he noticed with amusement, so far away that she could not hear.

Charlotte, seeing she received no response, tried a new tack. "Perhaps," she suggested, "it will be best if we move up our own wedding date, giving me the right to properly execute the duty of chaperone for Marianna until her marriage to Ault."

Marianna leaped to her feet, but Geoff, as revolted as she, put a restraining hand on her arm. She looked from him to Lady Charlotte and on to Sylvester, who beamed back at her. Geoff pulled at her arm and she sat down again, her face mutinous. "No," she said.

Lady Charlotte next tried reasoning with her. "You must see, Marianna, that returning to London with me at once is the only solution."

"No."

"If you will not, and you remain here, I shall not be able to function as your chaperone, for I cannot stay at Aultmere, as no other female of Quality is in residence."

Good, thought Geoff. Perhaps she will go home. The next moment, the vicar innocently blasted his hopes.

"My dear Lady Charlotte, I believe I have the solution. If it will ease your mind about your young charge—though I assure you, your concern is unnecessary—may I offer you the hospitality of my vicarage? You may then remain here in Ault-in-the-Vale, and protect the name of Miss Marianna from any breath of scandal."

He sat back, beaming at them all, totally unconscious of the consternation in the faces of Sir Geoffrey and Marianna. Even Lady Charlotte, staring at him, seemed to realize her aristocratic mouth hung open. Slowly she shut it.

"Do you mean, my good man, that I should lodge here in the vicarage?"

Mr. Brinkman inclined his noble head. "It would give me great pleasure, and I am sure both Miss Marianna and Mr. Cha—" he stopped, aghast at his *faux pas*.

Lady Charlotte, absorbing this new idea, had paid him no heed. "I shall have to send my carriage back to London for my trunk. Geoffrey, do go out at once and tell my footman he is to fetch it for me immediately. Where is my room?" She rose to her feet, unaware of the thundercloud of dismay that loomed over her listeners.

What could they do about Charlie?

During the chaos that ensued over the settling in of Lady Charlotte, he was their main concern. He had been hiding in the attic, a cramped area without much air or light, and could not be left there indefinitely. While Marianna and Celeste bustled about, distracting Lady Charlotte, Geoff smuggled Charlie down the stairs and into the vicar's study, to be locked in despite his complaints.

"I have to get *out!*" he whispered fiercely. "I need to go back to the necess—"

Geoff silenced him with a hand over his mouth. "Climb in and out the window," he ordered. "And for god's sake, do not be seen. Ault is still here."

"I cannot stay hidden forever!"

"For a short time, you must," Geoff told him, his face grim. "There is a comfortable couch in here, the vicar will have to nap in his bedchamber."

"Food," said Charlie. "I shall have to come out at dinner time—or do I go over to Hawkins's tavern for my meal?"

"Someone will hand you a tray through the window. Believe me, we'll sort out this mess as quickly as may be. She cannot wish to remain too long. Just be silent and go to ground for a while."

Poor Mr. Brinkman, only too aware of having thrown all to the wind, puttered unhappily about getting in everyone's way, while his beloved home was reorganized from attic to cellar.

The lack of bedrooms in the small vicarage proved to be a brief problem. Marianna refused to share with Lady Charlotte, and moved in with Celeste. Charlie, who had slept on a cot in the vicar's bedchamber, was now on the couch in the study, a danger to them all. He objected to being locked away whenever Lady Charlotte was downstairs, which seemed to be always, and his presence disrupted the gentle vicar's work and nap schedule.

Geoff blamed himself for the bumblebroth. It was his fault for not putting a stop to the whole affair in the first instance, by removing Marianna from the vicarage the minute he found her there. He did his best to make all easier. Conferring with the vicar, he insisted on paying all the bills incurred by the influx of so many guests. Before he left, he ordered in food supplies and hired the church charwoman to cook and clean, much to the relief of Celeste.

For one entire day, all went well.

Then the Reverend Mr. Brinkman, working on next Sunday's sermon, went into his study for some papers. He left the door open behind him.

"Who is that?" demanded Lady Charlotte, peering in at Charlie.

The vicar, struck dumb, gaped at her.

Marianna gave a tiny shriek of dismay. "Oh, no! Please, Lady Charlotte, do not let Sylvester know he is here!"

"Whyever not? Who is he?" Charlotte displayed merely a mild interest.

"A—a student of Mr. Brinkman's," explained the needle-witted Marianna, hastily concocting a story as usual. "On a reading tutorial."

Charlotte put her finger on the salient point. "Why should Ault not know he is here?"

Celeste stepped in. "It is a matter of a stupid prank which has put him in some trouble with his Grace."

"Yes," agreed Marianna. "Sylvester wanted him dismissed, but Mr. Brinkman has kindly kept him on, for he must complete his studies before the next term. It is of the utmost importance that Sylvester not know."

They waited with bated breath, the vicar holding Charlie, who had headed for the window, by his coat tail.

Importunate young boys were no concern of Charlotte's. Of far more importance was coaxing an invitation from Ault for Marianna and herself to come to the castle for tea. When Geoff came the next afternoon, she asked him to suggest this to the duke.

Good god, this could not happen! Marianna, once inside Aultmere, would surely upset the applecart by snooping about and rousing Sylvester's suspicion. Geoff took Charlotte aside.

"I feel it best to keep Marianna and Ault apart for a while. Until she is more willing to accept him."

"I shall speak to her," said Charlotte.

"No, no, please. Let me handle this," he exclaimed hastily. "It is only that she considers him a dandy. Here in the country, he may appear in a better light."

Lady Charlotte considered this, and then agreed. "I have quite changed my mind about Ault," she told him.

"I find him most gentlemanly, not disagreeably foppish after all. He will do very well for Marianna."

During the following day, Charlie had to study with the vicar because Lady Charlotte, a natural busybody, took it upon herself to oversee his work. He already could read and write, having been taught by the parson in Meadowcum, who had taken an interest in the lad. To everyone's surprise—except that of Lady Charlotte—Charlie became fascinated with the classics and mythology in which he was to be tutored by the vicar.

Awestruck, he ran his hands over the leather-bound volumes on the shelves in the study. "You mean all these books have stories in them?"

Mr. Brinkman, delighted, produced English translations, and together they began to read of Ulysses' voyages. Unconsciously, Charlie played the part of a conscientious scholar.

Now that Charlie was dressed in respectable garments, lent to him by the vicar and Sir Geoffrey, his resemblance to the Duke of Ault dawned on Lady Charlotte.

"Is he a relation?" she asked Marianna. "A close one?"

Rattled by the sudden question, Marianna committed an error. "He's—he's a cousin," she exclaimed.

"Ah," said Charlotte, nodding in a thoughtful manner.

Marianna eyed her nervously. "You must remember, Ault is not supposed to know he is still here."

"Ah," said Charlotte again.

Charlie's supposed relationship to Sylvester was not mentioned again until the duke arrived in his carriage, proposing to take the ladies for a drive.

At the sound of his coach wheels, Celeste and Marianna had disappeared into the passage leading to the church with Charlie in tow, leaving Lady Charlotte to entertain Ault. She was delighted at the prospect of a drive, for she wished to have a talk with him alone.

As she settled back against the velvet squabs, she casually remarked, "What a lovely carriage," and embarked at once on the subject foremost in her thoughts.

"I am sure," she informed the duke, "the honest pursuit of knowledge must mitigate for an occasional schoolboy escapade that you must now forgive and forget. Allow me to congratulate you on the dedication and scholarship displayed at the vicarage by your young cousin."

Being in the act of rearranging her skirts to cover her ankles, she failed to perceive that Sylvester's features had congealed in frozen horror.

Eleven

Sylvester had invited Sir Geoffrey to go along, but his invitation had been refused.

"I have no wish to dawdle about the countryside making banal conversation," Geoff told him. "If you will pardon me, I shall instead drive by myself, for my pair are in need of some brisk exercise." Which, of course, would include a stop at the vicarage.

In a very short time he left his curricle and groom at the tavern, where Jobbs could relax over a few tankards of ale. With a swinging gait, Geoff strode toward the vicarage, grimacing at the thought of the probable cup of hot chocolate. But he would not exchange. His chocolate would be sweetened by a pair of laughing, brown eyes.

There were entirely too many people about the vicarage these days. One in particular, but for the next hour, she would be away. Lady Charlotte's presence somewhat impeded his plans for the vicar's lovely French housemaid, and it would not do for Celeste to think he had lost interest.

But she seemed in an odd mood. "Ah, Sir Geoffrey," she greeted him, her manner strangely cool. "I fear you have made this journey in vain. Your fiancée, Lady Charlotte, is not here. The carriage from Aultmere carried her away not a half hour past."

"Indeed?" he said, and his warm eyes brought a most becoming blush to her cheeks. "What a pity I have missed her." He stretched out a hand, but she moved out of reach.

"M. Charlie and Miss Marianna are seated on the back steps," she informed a spot above his left ear. "The sun shines, and they enjoy the fresh air. One moment and I shall call them."

This time he managed to catch her arm. "Pray do not disturb them. I would far rather talk to you."

She pulled away. "I am just at the making of hot chocolate for M. the vicar. Will you not join us?"

Resigned, Geoff hung his hat on the stand by the door and dropped onto the settle by the hearth. "Thank you. You can't think how I've been looking forward to this."

Her dimple appeared in spite of herself, and she became very busy at the table with mugs and a gently steaming pan of milk as the Reverend Mr. Brinkman wandered into the room from his study.

"I thought I heard voices." He held out his hand to Geoff. "How are you, sir? I am very glad to see you. Any news? Have you found a lock for young Charlie's key?"

Geoff had sprung to his feet, and he shook the old man's hand with every sign of pleasure he could muster. It bode fair to be one of those days.

"No," he admitted. "I am sorry to say I have as yet had no luck." He turned to Celeste and said in a firm tone, "I came by because I have a fancy—" though not a fancy to confide to a vicar "—a fancy to see Charlie's key once more," he substituted, sure from her quickly lowered eyelids that she knew exactly what he fancied. "Perhaps," he continued to Mr. Brinkman, "there will be in its size and shape a clue we have missed. Is it still in the clock?"

"It is." She finished pouring the chocolate and set three chairs at the table before she went to the mantel. Opening the back of the clock, she extracted Charlie's mysterious key and laid it before him.

Mr. Brinkman bent his head, studying the key over the rims of his spectacles. "Why, that is my key to the Ault mausoleum! How came you by it?"

Geoff and Celeste stared at him. They spoke as one. "But this is Charlie's key."

"Really?" The vicar picked it up and looked at it closely. "Yes, this one shows far less rust, it is much cleaner than mine. How very odd. Let us examine both. One moment." He pottered back to his study and fetched his key from a drawer in his desk. They compared his with Charlie's, and found the two exactly alike.

"Good god!" exclaimed Geoff.

"Indeed," said the vicar. "I understood there to be only one other key, and it is kept by the duke himself, but you say this is not it."

"No wonder I couldn't find one on the castle keyboard to match our impression. Sylvester had it hidden away," Geoffrey complained. "Had I known, I would have been spared a harrowing evening and the castle cat could have spent the night in comfort in front of the kitchen hearth, instead of nursing a sore tail out in the cold."

"Cat? What is this of cats?" asked Celeste, mystified. "And we no longer have need of kitchens, for we know where the key fits." She brushed the cat aside with a gesture. "Is it not now obvious, Sir Geoffrey? The treasure sought by M. Charlie is to be found in this vault. We must tell him at once!"

"Good god, no!" Geoff shook his head. "Charlie must

not set foot on Ault land—or even outside this vicarage. If that idiot Sylvester catches sight of him, it will be bellows to mend with us all. He'll have the Runners upon him before the cat can lick her whiskers," he added, some part of his mind still on cats and black kitchens.

"Why do you talk of cats?" Celeste demanded. "And you must not call *le duc* the idiot!"

"I beg your pardon." He patted her shoulder with a placating hand. "I was wrong. Some cats have very quick tongues. I should have said, before sundown."

Celeste appeared uncertain, but let the matter drop. *"En effet,"* she agreed, "I quite see that it must be we who make this search, and in secret. If M. Charlie gets this from the wind, we could not keep him away."

Geoff unscrambled her speech with ease. "And say nothing to Marianna. She could not keep such news to herself, and we do not want them along. We had best not be seen, and that means going in the night. Marianna would surely be terrified of the dark. She would betray us by screaming, and Charlie is not exactly cautious. He would be bound to get us caught."

"I regret," said the vicar suddenly, from the settle where he had taken his mug of chocolate. They both jumped for they had quite forgotten he was there. "I must tender my apologies," he went on, "but I fear I cannot go along with this expedition."

They gazed at him in some dismay.

"I am no longer as spry as I was," he continued, spreading his hands. "I fear I could not keep up with you youngsters, and would prove even more a detriment than our lame Charlie. You must go without me."

Geoff felt his stomach return to place, while Celeste

jumped up to hug Mr. Brinkman. "You will be sorely missed," she told him seriously, "for your advice must always be of the most admirable, but I see that you will be better off remaining here, to make the excuses should any of the others awake and wonder at my absence."

Seeing no reason to waste more time, they decided to go that very night, and Celeste walked with Geoff as far as the gate. He reached for her, clearly intending to kiss her again. She held up her face—and over her shoulder, he saw the old vicar, smiling and benign, watching them from the doorway.

"Damn," Geoff muttered under his breath. He squeezed her hand in a most meaning manner. "When the clock strikes twelve," he whispered. "In the lane in back of the cemetery."

She nodded, swallowing a gulp of disappointment.

After an evening of playing backgammon and spillikins, the vicarage retired early. Long after Marianna ceased to chatter, Celeste lay awake in a fever of anticipation. At last, the sound of even breathing came from the other cot, and she dared to slide from under her quilt and gather up the pile of clothing she had concealed beneath the bed.

Outside in the hall, she dressed quickly, donning the warmest of her gray gowns and a white wool shawl under her dark, hooded cloak. Her half-boots she carried downstairs to put on when she reached the tiny back porch. In the kitchen she paused, listening. Not a sound but the ticking of the clock on the mantel. The clock with Charlie's key. Suppose he awoke and remembered he had left it there? Tiptoeing into the study—thank heavens Charlie had returned to his palette in the vicar's bedchamber!— she took M. Brinkman's key instead, stuffing it into her reticule along with her tinder box and several stub ends of candle. One never knew what might be needed in such an escapade. The reticule itself she secured about her waist with the drawstring pulled from her cloak hood. She was ready, as ready as she could be.

The back door creaked when she opened it, and she froze, holding her breath. Nothing happened. No one shouted, "Who is there?" She let out the breath and slipped outside, leaving the door ajar. It would surely creak again if she shut it—and would announce her arrival when she returned. She stepped off the porch and through the roofed lych gate into the graveyard beyond.

How different the cemetery looked by night, all in deep shadow, for the moon was hidden behind the border of immense yew trees, some being part of the original Saxon planting, well over a thousand years old. She made her way past ancient stones and carved angels, whispering her thanks to those guardians for keeping the wraiths at bay. Were there any at the Ault mausoleum? But here was the lane and she paused, half-hidden under one of the spreading trees.

It was not yet midnight, but she had not long to wait. A tall shadow, broad-shouldered and confident, a silhouette she'd have recognized among a hundred, strode toward her across the fallow field. She had told herself she was not nervous or afraid of the dark, but before she could stop herself, she ran into his arms.

"Now that is how I like to be greeted," he whispered against her hooded ear, and would have kissed her had she not quickly disengaged herself.

"Sir Geoffrey, you must not!" she exclaimed. Then realizing where the fault lay, she apologized. "I do beg your pardon, it is just that here so close to the dead, I was grateful for the sight of one alive."

"Very alive." His arm went about her waist.

She removed it. "No, no. This is no rendezvous. We attend only to the business this evening."

"If you say so." Agreeably, he moved a pace away, and they began the walk across the field. But the damage was done.

Alone in the moonlight, each grew blindingly aware of the other, and tension mounted between them. Celeste felt it trembling within her, while Geoff was shocked to find how much he wanted to kiss the lovely girl so close beside him in the darkness. Once their arms touched and they jumped hastily apart.

Rake Cole faced a dilemma. It was one thing to kiss a girl inside a house containing other people, or even on a balcony at a ball, but a chivalry he hadn't known he possessed kept him from taking advantage of her, alone and unprotected, in the middle of the night. But had not this been his intention? The opportunity for which he'd been yearning? She was a housemaid, was she not? And his for the taking—his breath caught in his throat. Good God, he thought, I am a gentleman of honor after all!

He had come to realize that Mlle. Celeste Moreau was no ordinary maid—housekeeper—but was of gentle birth, despite her present circumstances. Though more free in her speech than an English lady—but then, was not his own niece?—Celeste's very Frenchness added a piquant touch that appealed to him strongly. Or could it be her very difference from Lady Charlotte . . .

She stumbled on a more than usually exuberant weed and clutched his arm. He put his hand on hers, and she made no attempt to pull free.

"It is very dark, is it not?" Her voice sounded subdued. "Even though we have the moon."

He stole a glance at her, but the hood covered her face. Her hand under his might have trembled; he couldn't tell. His grip tightened involuntarily; he fancied he felt an answering pressure, and his pulse began a faster beat.

All too soon, the side gate to the grounds of Aultmere stood before them, left slightly ajar for the free passage of the castle servants to the tavern in the village. Geoff wondered if Sylvester knew.

Ahead, they could already see the marble pediment and Grecian columns of the Ault mausoleum, gleaming palely through the trees on the upper side of the path. Celeste pressed close to his side.

"Afraid of the ghost?" he asked. "I'll protect you."

She became indignant at once and, to his regret, removed her hand from his arm. "Of a certainty I do not fear what cannot touch me."

Then her hand was on his arm again, but this time to pull him forward. They almost ran to the great vault. It loomed in the moonlight, deep-shadowed behind the four pillars at the entrance. There was no door, but more ornamental, wrought-iron double gates, locked in the center. Geoff had brought a small lantern, borrowed from the kitchen where the cat once more dozed by the banked oven. He struck it alight and held it high. Beyond the iron gates, they could dimly make out the beginnings of several rows of stone sarcophagi, some topped with life-size images of their inhabitants.

Celeste already had the vicar's key out. She shoved it into his hand. "Try, Sir Geoffrey. See does it work!"

Work it did. It took strength to turn the huge key in the ancient lock. If the ghost that had been seen was substantial, say, a prankster, it was no wonder she—it—roamed about outside. Geoff was sure no frail female could get in. But the one who accompanied him could hardly wait. She pushed past him and set one of her candle ends on the nearest coffin while she took out her tinder box.

"Do you take that side," she suggested. "I will hunt on this."

They began a thorough search for secret hiding holes, loose stones, or projecting carvings that might turn or press in to release the mechanism of a drawer or trapdoor. At the end of nearly an hour, they met at the back of the vault, having found no treasure hidden among the dozen coffins. Only dust, dead leaves blown in by the wind, and tattered cobwebs; even the spiders had departed.

"Nothing is here. Why then do they lock this place?" Celeste demanded, snuffing her candlewick with wet finger and thumb.

He grinned down at her in the dim glow from his lantern. "To keep the occupants in?" he suggested.

"Then it does not work, for I am told it is the mother of Ault who walks without."

Geoff pretended to shiver. "Let us hope she stays outside, while we are within." He set his lantern on the floor and reached to take her in his arms.

Clumping footsteps sounded on the front portico, too heavy for a wraith. Geoff doused their light, but it was too late.

"Who's there?" called a quavering voice. Someone

swung a lantern by the iron doors, the hulking figure of a castle workman.

"Oh, the devil," whispered Geoff, inadequately. "We should have pulled those shut when we came in." His arms went round her again, drawing her down to crouch behind the nearest sarcophagus.

His arms remained around her. When she turned her face up to his, it seemed the most natural thing in the world for him to kiss her and for her to respond, as though the whole evening had led up to this one moment. Shaken, they clung together, and almost forgot the man at the door until he called out again.

"You in there—come out!"

Geoff swore quietly, but Celeste literally rose to the occasion. She was wearing a light-colored gown under her dark cloak. She dropped the cloak and crawled around the coffin.

"Where the deuce are you going?" Geoff demanded in a stage whisper.

"Quiet, I have thought what to do. Stay you here, keep low," she ordered almost soundlessly. "Now, when I raise the arms, you must moan, as eerily as you can."

Before he could catch at her skirts to stop her, she came slowly to her feet, as though rising from the dead. In the dim light from the man's far-off lantern, her gray gown glowed pale. The man gave a gargled gasp and froze, rooted to the stone floor.

With her arms stretched before her, Celeste glided out into the aisle, wailing a few words in French. She raised her arms, and Geoff did his best to produce an unearthly groan. She moved forward, but in the dark she stubbed her toe on one of the low coffin pedestals, and gave a real moan. Always one to take advantage of an opportunity, she stepped up on the pedestal, rising smoothly, at the same time catching the ends of her shawl and raising her arms so as to appear as if she'd spread wings. Seemingly, she floated off the floor. Seeing his cue once more, Geoff produced another agonized moan, building to a crescendo.

This did it. The man shrieked in terror and fled from the vault. They heard him crashing away through the trees.

Celeste stepped down. "There now, was it not a matter of the simplest?"

There was nothing for it but to kiss her again, this time a resounding smack on her cheek, that somehow ended on her lips and remained there until she pulled away.

"Right," he said. "We'd best get out of here while we can, before—before something else happens." He caught up his dark lantern, and led her back to the entrance. He had left the key in the lock. He turned it again and gave it back to her.

As they slipped out through the side gate, a man approached along the field path, one of the stable hands who had been drinking at the tavern. Once more they hid, this time in the bushes, and Geoff, feeling a bit drunk himself, kissed her again.

"M. Sir Geoffrey, you must not!"

Not? Suddenly, years of Lady Charlotte stretched interminably before him. He crushed Celeste in hungry arms.

"I'm afraid I must." His words came husky, ragged. "This night may never come again."

With a strangled cry, she tore herself from him and ran headlong back across the field. The approaching man stopped and stared as she went by. He had seen them.

"Damn," muttered Geoff. "And damn again."

Twelve

It seemed to Sylvester, at breakfast the next morning, that the servants were whispering and sneaking glances at him. He called Prouty to his bedchamber after the meal, and demanded an explanation.

Prouty looked uncomfortable and shuffled his neatly shod feet. "They—ah—that is, your Grace, they are discussing her late Grace, the duchess."

Sylvester felt his toes curl. Now what? "Tell me at once, what are they saying about my mother?"

"It is Mott, your Grace, one of your Grace's footmen."

"Go on, man." But Sylvester had a premonition. He knew what was coming.

" 'E 'appened—happened to be walking in the grounds, your Grace, like as if he couldn't sleep, and 'e says 'e saw a light like, in the vault." Warming up to his tale, Prouty let his H's go. " 'E looked in, your Grace, and 'e saw 'er!"

The blood had drained from Sylvester's cheeks, and he grabbed a chair for support. "Go—go on."

Prouty gabbled out the rest with relish. "Rose up out of 'er coffin, she did, your Grace. Weeping and wailing in French. And she come at 'im, stretching out 'er wings and flying through the air. 'E was 'most paralyzed by 'er 'orrible groans and cries, but 'e managed to run. She chased 'im, your Grace, clear to the castle door. 'E's still that upset, your Grace, shaking like the ague. Wapshott 'as told 'im to stay in 'is bed."

Sylvester was not in much better shape. If his mother walked again, surely it was an omen, a warning of coming disaster.

Prouty eyed him anxiously and felt moved to utter words of comfort, or at least to distract his master's mind from the ghost of his mother. He sought a more agreeable subject and hit on one.

"A bit of choice gossip going about this morning, your Grace, regarding your Grace's guest."

"Umm?" Sylvester muttered, unclenching his fingers, one by one, from the back of the chair.

"A hand from the stables is spreading a story, your Grace. About our Sir Geoffrey Cole. Living up to his reputation, he is. Meeting that Frenchwoman from the vicarage in the middle of the night."

Sylvester turned on him so attentive an expression that Prouty bloomed. In command of his slipping H's, he continued. "Saw them out by the side gate, he did, your Grace. Hugging and kissing they were, until the wench ran off."

He awaited the result of his news and was rewarded. The Duke of Ault straightened, color flooding back to his face, and speculation gleaming in his eyes.

"Thank you, Prouty," he said, his words coming as though from a distance. "That will be all."

After Prouty bowed himself from the room, Sylvester remained by the window, immersed in deep thought. He looked out over the mere, past the pale roof of the vault to the steeple of the village church showing above the trees.

He was not stupid. Discounting the obvious embellishments, he put together the footman's story of a French ghost in the vault and Sir Geoffrey seen by the side gate with the Frenchwoman. An interrupted rendezvous, and a childish trick to frighten off the observer. He almost laughed. Then his first relief began to fade, replaced by a growing unease.

Ever since Lady Charlotte's revelation the afternoon before, he had known he had to discover the mystery of his ring, the bandit who was his double, and the unaccountable collusion at the vicarage. Skulduggery, for certain, and connivance, somehow all aimed at himself. He had not been able to make up his mind what to do before, but now he had a target of sorts. The Ault mausoleum. What had really been happening there last night? There was only one way to find out. Going to his desk, he opened a drawer, took out an ancient ornate key, and put it into his pocket.

He wandered outside, ostensibly taking the air along the shore of the mere in case anyone, Sir Geoffrey for instance, watched from a window. He drifted aimlessly into the grove—and ran toward the vault. He had to get a grip on himself before turning the key in the heavy lock. He knew it had been Sir Geoffrey and the Frenchwoman in there last night, but that didn't mean they—and now he—were not being watched by the spirits of the long-gone Aults whose bones crumbled within those stone sarcophagi.

Taking a very deep breath, he went in and at once took heart. No specters had scuffed the dust on the marble floor and left such clear footprints. A man, and the smaller prints of a woman. But how did they get in? He had the only key. Then he remembered. The vicar must have one, for prior to the advent of his Catholic mother, all Ault funerals were conducted from the village church. But why had they come here? An assignation only?

True, it might have seemed a secure and private place. The marks in the dust at the very back certainly pointed to bodies lying on the floor. He tried to be merely angry at this desecration of the sacred resting place of his ancestors—particularly of his mother who just might be walking because of it—but he couldn't rid himself of the feeling there was more to this than a clandestine meeting. Why so much activity? Footprints were left all over the floor, around every coffin and down along the walls. In some way, he was sure, this was all connected with his ring and that highwayman.

Back in the castle, he called on Prouty once more. "I want you to go to the tavern and speak with the innkeeper again about this young man who looks like me. I have thought he might be a by-blow of my uncle's, and I should like to know his name."

Bob Hawkins's ale being excellent, Prouty went with a will and was gone for two hours. He returned with news that caused Sylvester's scalp to crawl.

"Makepeace," reported Prouty. "Charles Makepeace. He said he came from Meadowcum."

Makepeace. When the little duke's mother died of the birthing, it was one Nana Makepeace, from the village of Meadowcum, who had a newborn of her own and served as his wet nurse. When the duke became ill of the plague three years later, it was Nana again who came to nurse him. He remembered all too clearly the sudden departure of the Makepeace family after the death of the little duke. He had heard from kitchen gossip that they went back to Meadowcum and took with them a son named Charlie. The resemblance—oh, God! WHAT CHILD DID THEY TAKE?

Sylvester's active imagination overrode his senses. Could his mother have paid them to abduct his little cousin to secure the dukedom for her own son? But the funeral. He had not attended, being too young. Was the coffin open—or closed? Wapshott might know, or Cook, but he dared not ask. None of the other servants were there so long ago. With the rampant fear of the plague, it must have been closed. On what? Suppose there was no body in the little duke's fancy coffin!

It was like an obsession. He had to know. And that involved opening the coffin. Could he do it? He *had* to, or never rest easy again.

Even Prouty could not be included in this. Sylvester went quietly out to the gardeners' shed in back, and provided himself with a long, pointed steel bar of great weight, one used to break ground for the setting of fence posts. Just the thing for prying the heavy stone lid of a sarcophagus to one side. He dragged it back to the vault. It proved to be the exact tool he needed. By using the pointed end like a battering ram, he managed to knock loose a chip large enough to insert his bar and lever the lid nearly a foot sideways, uncovering one end of the ornate coffin within. Now, he would see.

The casket was nailed shut, but he managed to jam the pointed end of his bar under the lip. With so much of the heavy stone cover still in place, he could only raise the lid a few inches, but it was plenty.

A stench of moldering bones wafted into his face, and he forced himself to peer into the crack. Resting on a rotting satin pillow and still topped with straggles of lank, dark hair, a small, yellow brown skull leered up at him from empty eye sockets.

It was all Sylvester could do to slam the coffin lid down, beat the nails back in with the end of his bar, and pry the stone cover back in place. That grinning yellow skull with its wisps of dark hair would float before his closed eyes forever. He'd never sleep again. But . . . there was a body in the little duke's coffin.

Outside the vault, he paused only to be humiliatingly sick behind a bush before he pelted back to the castle. Up in his bedchamber, he slammed his door shut and leaned against it until his pounding heart slowed to normal. Gradually, into the relief that enveloped him, crept a sense of horror. There *was* a skeleton in the duke's coffin, true, but its grinning skull had locks of straight, dark hair.

His knees buckled beneath him as the memory of his cousin rose before him . . . the little duke . . . with a headful of golden curls.

As his sanity returned, Sylvester's mind began to work. Had his handiwork left noticeable chip marks on the stone lid? Of course it had. He strove to control pure panic and think. If *he* had discovered the secret of the coffin, might not Sir Geoffrey and his Frenchwoman soon do the same? He dared not let anyone find what lay inside. They had a key to the vault, they would be back, it would not be long before one of them wondered at the marks on the little duke's sarcophagus. His first instinct was to order Sir Geoffrey from his premises, but that would intensify their suspicions.

Suppose they didn't see the marks, would it not all blow over, if he played the innocent? If no proof could be found, he would still be the legal Duke of Ault. If that incriminating evidence in the casket were destroyed . . . but he could not destroy the body for fear of rousing another ghost, nor could he open that coffin and stare again into those blank, accusing eye sockets. The only thing to do was remove and hide the entire coffin. If anyone looked in the sarcophagus and found it empty, why, he was but a child when it was put in place. How would he know anything about it?

He spent a half hour exploring the woods behind the mausoleum and found the perfect place. Thick bushes screened the border of the grove where it neared the kitchen gardens, and right at the edge was the plank cover of an abandoned well. If he could get the coffin to its vicinity, he could remove the well cover, tip the coffin in, replace the planks, and none would ever be the wiser.

But he needed an accomplice. He could not manage alone, and Prouty would not do. The man had by far too loose a tongue. Pensive, he stared out his window and his answer came into view. Out on his vast lawns, patiently scything the grass, was Thomas, the undergardener's slow-witted son. A hulking specimen with the intelligence of a toddler, he would neither question nor understand. Ten minutes later, while seated on the side terrace, Sylvester had a sudden urge to inspect a lilac bush just as Thomas slowly approached. He had heard the gardeners address the man as Tom-Tom, no doubt because the first mention of his name drew no response. The use of the familiar appellation should put the poor creature at ease.

"I have a job for you, Tom-Tom," he began.

"Duh!" Confronted by the duke in person, the simpleton gaped.

It took a few minutes and several more "Duhs" for Sylvester to get through.

"The weeds about the portico of the vault have grown too high," he explained carefully. "They have become an eyesore, and we have need of your scythe."

Tom-Tom looked at his tool blankly.

"To cut the weeds," Sylvester went on patiently. "You use the scythe to cut the weeds."

Ah, now Tom-Tom had it. He grinned, baring white teeth that gave Sylvester a moment of envy. "Yus. Tom-Tom cut weeds."

"And a compost barrow. You have a large barrow?"

"Yus."

"Then go fetch the barrow, and do you see the vault over there beyond the trees?"

A shadow crossed his companion's face. "Ghost," he said.

Sylvester nodded. "We will stop the ghost. Get rid of it."

"In the barrow?"

"Yes, yes. Hurry and fetch it from the shed. I will meet you at the vault." Tom-Tom hesitated and Sylvester reassured him. "I will protect you from the ghost."

To Tom-Tom, as at a lesser extent to Celeste, the Duke of Ault was a godlike being. If he said he would grant protection, he would. Tom-Tom nodded, tugged at his forelock, and ambled off toward the garden sheds, carrying his scythe.

Some twenty minutes later, as Sylvester paced, nervous

and impatient, in front of the vault, Tom-Tom appeared, complete with scythe and oversized barrow. Sylvester let out a long breath. Now for the hard part.

"I have changed my mind," he informed the vacant-faced, young giant. "The weeds are not as high as I thought. I have a different job for you."

Tom-Tom let his jaw drop. "Cut no weeds?" The jaw stayed down and the scythe joined it, landing with a clatter on the steps to the vault portico, clipping the duke on the shin.

"Not today," said Sylvester, hopping aside. "Today we send the ghost away."

Tom-Tom blinked, but his faith was strong. He did not run, though he hung back. "Ghost?"

Sylvester clutched at his patience. "Ghosts do not walk in broad daylight. You have nothing to fear. Did I not say I'd protect you?" Tom-Tom nodded, and he went on. "It is one of the coffins inside that holds our ghost earthbound. It must be taken out of the vault and carried away into the woods, where we shall hide it. You can do that if I help." He feared for a minute that Tom-Tom would refuse, but the jaw came up, the mouth closed, and he received a mute nod. "Then bring the barrow and come along."

Mystified but obedient, Tom-Tom trundled the barrow into the vault after his duke. They stopped at the sarcophagus bearing the crest of the fifth duke, but enclosing an unknown tenant. To his horror, Sylvester found the steel pry bar lying on the stone floor where he'd forgotten it. Sweat broke out on his forehead and trickled down his back. What if someone had come along? With the haste and strength of desperation, he instructed Tom-Tom in prying the stone lid aside so that they could pull the small coffin out one end of the sarcophagus. They decanted the brass-trimmed casket into the barrow and slid the stone cover back in place.

It was essential that even a thimble-wit like Tom-Tom should not know the final resting place he had chosen for the coffin. Sylvester stopped him when they reached the thick border of bushes near the old well.

Much as he hated the thought, he would have to sneak out at night to drag the coffin over, for the well was in clear view from the vegetable garden. Then if Tom-Tom talked, it would be a duke's word against that of one with no wits. He could deny everything. There would be no evidence.

"We can hide it here," he told Tom-Tom, "far back under these shrubs. The ghost will never find it, but you must never tell *anyone,* because ghosts can hear what you say."

Tom-Tom's eyes bulged and he began to shake, staring about him. "We are quite safe unless you speak. Ghosts cannot see by day." He hoped this was true, and he had not made it up. This odd fact had just leaped into his mind. "Only remember, you must never speak of this aloud. No one must know but you. If the ghost learns of this, it will surely haunt you forever."

His companion turned so pale that he feared the clodhead would faint. Sylvester knew only one solution to nearly everything. He dug into his pocket, drew out a handful of silver coins, and pressed them into the shaking hands. Tom-Tom's face glowed as though from a vision of Paradise. Clutching his wealth, he set off at a lope for the tavern in the village, leaving Sylvester standing beside the empty barrow.

He couldn't leave it, pointing as it did to the carrying

of a large object. He remembered suddenly that he had forgotten other incriminating evidence. The scythe lay on the vault steps, the wrought-iron doors stood open, and the pry bar lay on the floor inside. How could he have been so stupid? Catching up the handles of the barrow, he wheeled it clumsily through the trees back the way they had come. All lay as they had left it. He dumped the tools into the barrow and turned his iron key in the ancient lock, securing the vault. No, he realized, he merely held up unwelcome snoopers for the time it took to use their own key. Something more must be done about the everpresent menace of what he was coming to think of as the league of conspirators in, of all places, the village vicarage.

He hauled the loaded barrow a short way down the path toward the side gate, and left it where it would seem Tom-Tom had abandoned it on his flight to the village. He debated telling Prouty the coins had been stolen from him, in case the servants wanted to know where the fuddle-brained Tom-Tom had found so much money. He decided, however, honesty being the best policy when it could be used safely, that he would say he felt sorry for the slack-witted dolt and gave him some silver that was weighting down his pocket and spoiling the set of his coat.

There was still the matter—the hideously looming matter—of the young man who called himself Charlie Makepeace. He hung over Sylvester's head, a sword of Damocles on the slenderest of hairs. Golden blond hairs. Time was running out, he sensed fate closing in. His double at the vicarage must be removed, and for all time. He sopped his conscience with the knowledge that if society were to continue, thieves must be hung, and Makepeace was a thief who had made off with a most valuable ring.

He was very busy at his writing desk for some time after he came back to the castle, and one of the grooms was dispatched with a carefully written message to Bow Street. It contained an account—his version—of the holdup, a description of the highwayman, and the present whereabouts of that highwayman. That would take care of Mr. Charlie Makepeace.

Up in the ducal bedchamber, Prouty waited to freshen Sylvester's attire. As usual, he chattered as he combed and brushed his Grace's fair hair.

"I believe we have not 'eard the last of our ghost, your Grace."

Sylvester gripped the arms of his chair. "What do you mean?"

"Why, as I was returning from the village, your Grace, 'aving 'ad a few errands, you understand, 'oo should I meet in the field, running, your Grace, as if the devil 'imself pursued 'im?"

"Well? Who?"

"That empty-skulled son of one of the gardeners, your Grace. Ah, says I to 'im, joking like, I see the ghost from the vault is at your 'eels."

Sylvester tried to swallow, but his throat was too dry. "And was it?"

"Of course not, your Grace, but you should 'ave seen 'is face. White as linen, it was, I looked back and saw 'im go right by the tavern. 'E ran straight into the church. I collect as 'e 'as gone to be exorcized, as they say, your Grace."

Pinning carefully disordered curls on the top of his

Grace's head, he failed to notice the duke's startled reaction.

Sylvester sat stunned. Tom-Tom had gone to the
church. To the vicar. Had he been betrayed?

Thirteen

The Duke of Ault sat at nuncheon, covertly watching Sir Geoffrey, who lavished butter and jam on a muffin with an annoying air of complete unconcern. But then, Sylvester conceded, he could not know that his midnight rendezvous had been observed. It occurred to him, as he peeled a hothouse peach, that while the conspirators at the vicarage had managed to plant an undercover agent in his household, he could count on having a friend in the enemy camp. One whom he was certain had no knowledge of the duplicity behind her back. He absolved Lady Charlotte of any part in the nefarious doings of Sir Geoffrey and that Frenchwoman.

He had to know what had occurred at the vicarage after the arrival of Tom-Tom. Had fear of the ghost held his babbling tongue in check? If there were some way he could separate Lady Charlotte from the rest, she might in all innocence tell him what he needed to know. An invitation to Aultmere . . . but she would not come alone; the amenities must be observed. Marianna must be invited as well. While he believed in the integrity of Lady Charlotte, he had no such trust in Marianna.

From what he had seen of that impetuous damsel, he was sure she had espoused the highwayman's cause and was instrumental in hiding him at the vicarage. Young ladies were notoriously romantic, softhearted, and totally lacking in principle. Prouty said the man he saw limped and walked with a stick. Sylvester's chest swelled. That shot he fired after the runaways who had escaped with his ring must have hit him. Not bad marksmanship for one not noted for his actions in the field. It would be just like a chit of Marianna's type to insist the thief be nursed back to health. A health Sylvester meant to terminate. Or rather, have the Bow Street Runners do so. He shuddered, having no stomach for physical violence. Indeed, only the real terror of losing his dukedom drove him on.

Letting his mind wander through Aultmere, he sought a suitable attraction to lure the ladies. He needed one that might enthrall Lady Charlotte, but, he suspected, bore Marianna into letting the others wander at a distance, out of her earshot. Ah, he had it.

He cleared his throat and spoke loudly, for Sir Geoffrey, seated at the other end of the table, was a good twenty feet away.

"Do you go to the vicarage this afternoon to—ah—visit your niece?" he asked.

Sir Geoffrey coughed over a bite of muffin that had gone down the wrong way. His eyes glinted as he looked back at Sylvester.

"You may be sure," he said. "Can you doubt my desire to see how they all go on?"

Sylvester didn't doubt at all. The man's desire must almost equal his own. "I have a message for Lady Charlotte and Marianna," he told him. "An invitation, actually. Would you be so kind as to deliver it for me?"

This time the glint in Sir Geoffrey's eyes increased in intensity. It flared briefly, before being hidden under drooping lids as he pursued a forkful of ham round his plate.

"Certainly, your Grace. I should be delighted," was all he said, but Sylvester had seen that gleam. The sooner he could pump Lady Charlotte for information, the better.

Geoff arrived at the vicarage expecting an awkward meeting with Celeste, but it was Marianna who met him at the door. Her cheeks were pink with fury.

"How could you, Uncle Geoff! How could you go without us?" She stamped her foot. "Celeste has told us all!"

"All?" He cast a devilish look at the French girl, who shrank behind Marianna, flushing scarlet. Of course she had not told all. Far too much had happened between them last night for innocent ears.

Fortunately, Marianna was so incensed she saw nothing but her own grievance. "How could you?" she demanded again.

She was seconded by Charlie, who limped into the room from the study, as wrathful as she. "And not tell me you knew what my key opened! You shall not use it again, for I've taken it out of the clock. I should never have let it out of my hands!"

"I see," said Geoff, with another teasing glance at Celeste. "She has not told you all."

"M. Sir Geoffrey!" The flaming of her cheeks brought out the beauty of her clear gray eyes, and he nodded a compliment that lengthened the blush. He drew his own eyes away with some reluctance.

"We had no need of your key, Charlie," he explained. "We used Mr. Brinkman's. He has the duplicate of yours and knew what it was for. It was he who told us where to go."

Marianna and Charlie turned on the vicar, who sat placidly by the hearth, weathering the edges of the storm.

"He has one?"

"Like mine?" Charlie dug his key from his pocket. "Let me see it. I don't believe it."

Ever good-natured, Mr. Brinkman heaved himself up from his seat and pottered into the study. He returned with his key and held it out. Charlie snatched it from him to compare the two.

"I don't understand," he muttered, in a tone of wonder. "They *are* the same. Why did Celeste's uncle send me a key to a graveyard?"

"A mausoleum," said Marianna.

"What's that?"

"A vault, silly."

Geoff stepped in, heading off another squabble. "It is a building, in which coffins are stored above ground instead of being buried."

Charlie looked up from the keys. "What a heathenish idea!"

"It has been done since classical times," the vicar put in. "Indeed, the ancient Romans lined their principal avenues with sarcophagi containing important deceased, as a form of perpetuating their glory."

"Oh. Well, then," said Charlie, "it must be all right. I

want to see this place. Let's go at once!" He started for the door.

"No, you don't." Geoff caught his coat tails. "You are not going anywhere."

"But my treasure must be inside!"

"It will do you no good, if you are dead," Marianna informed him. "And do not think, Uncle Geoff, that you will leave *me* behind this time. I can play ghost as well as Celeste!"

"I'm not thinking it, for I know you will not go. Marianna," he added, shushing her clamor. "You know very well I cannot let you go into danger. After last night, there may be a man posted with a gun."

"After last night and Celeste's lovely play-acting, there will be no one near that vault. It will be perfectly safe!"

"Aha," said Charlie. "Then there is no reason why I cannot go also!"

Geoff sighed. "There is every reason. Should you be seen here in the village, en route to the vault, Ault will be down on you in minutes. As Marianna pointed out, whatever is hidden there will do you no good if you dangle from a rope."

Charlie subsided, uncertain, and Marianna patted his arm. "We will bring it straight to you," she said.

"You shall have it at once," Geoff assured him, hoping at least to keep him hidden awhile longer.

"See that you do! I will give you one more chance, Sir Geoffrey, but then it will be up to me."

Marianna hopped about clapping her hands. "You will see, we will find your treasure!"

Charlie eyed her, his expression sour. "I'd rather find it myself."

"You can't," said Geoff.

Lady Charlotte, who had been walking in the cemetery, came in at that moment and he turned to her. "I
am come with a message from Ault, an invitation to the
castle. He wishes to show you and Marianna the picture
gallery with the portraits of his ancestors. He feels the
impressive display will go far toward bringing her to her
senses."

"I should be pleased." Indeed, Charlotte's face lighted
with her pleasure. "It will be a most informative experience for Marianna. She should learn of the heritage of
her future family."

"Pictures," sneered that young lady, who no longer
had any desire to search the castle, now that she knew
it did not hold Charlie's secret. "And it is not my future
family. You go if you wish, Lady Charlotte, I will not. I
only want to explore that vault."

Geoff shook his head. "In time, child, in time. Meanwhile I think you should show some interest in Aultmere
while I am Sylvester's guest, if only for politeness' sake."

"Politeness! How can I be polite to a man who plans
to have Charlie hung?"

"Now, now," said Charlie. "It would be a proper gesture toward one who recognizes my worth. A price on
my head already!" He polished his nails on the lapel of
the expensive coat lent him by Sir Geoffrey, his expression unbearably smug. Marianna tried to box his ear, but
he ducked away, grinning.

"I'd advise you to take the duke seriously, young man,"
Geoff admonished. "One in his influential position is not
to be trifled with." He addressed his fiancée. "Charlotte,
I think it would be wise for you, at least, to see him.

You may be able to discover any plans he may have. He will do something. I know from hints he has dropped, he has learned that Charlie remained in the vicinity and his suspicions are centered here at the vicarage. He had the audacity this morning to ask me to look about for evidence of Charlie's presence."

Lady Charlotte stared, her hand at her mouth. But Ault *knew* Charlie was there. She herself had told him. But surely, a schoolboy prank was no cause for talk of hanging! Marianna must be bamming—but Geoffrey looked so serious. What had she done? She felt the blood drain from her cheeks. Before she could speak, a carriage rattled up to the front gate and stopped, amid much stamping of hooves and creakings of leather and springs.

She rose hastily. "If that is the coach from Aultmere, have them wait but a few minutes while I don my bonnet and pelisse. I will do my best to learn what I can." She hurried up the stairs. This difficulty between the duke and Charles had begun to trouble her seriously, for she had become fond of the studious young man.

When his carriage returned from the vicarage, containing only Lady Charlotte and not his future bride, Sylvester quite forgot to act disappointed. Really, they would get on much better without Marianna. He hurried out to meet Charlotte as the footman let down the steps, and offered his ducal arm to aid her in dismounting.

"Your Grace," she began at once. "I come only to bring Marianna's deepest apologies. She fears she is about to be laid upon her couch by the headache. I thought I'd best come in person to explain."

"Another time, then," he replied, seeing her safely on her feet. "But you must not run away now that you are come. Take pity on a homesick Londoner and sit with me awhile."

"Oh, but, your Grace!" She struck him lightly on the arm with her fan. "I should not come inside. I am not accompanied." She hesitated, for her almost coy. "But since you ask . . . such lovely rooms in Aultmere . . . I declare, it is a banquet for the eyes to walk your halls."

"The library, then, for you have not seen it, and it is quite my favorite room. Wapshott," he called to the hovering butler, "sherry and biscuits in the library." He took her elbow and steered her into the Great Hall. "The portrait gallery can wait until Marianna can join us. I'll not bruise your proper sensibilities by proposing a prolonged private tour and, do not doubt, the library doors will remain open that we may be easily observed, thus maintaining the proprieties."

As he spoke, a footman jumped to throw wide the doors he had mentioned. He led her in, seating her on a purple and gold brocade sofa within sight of the doors, and sat himself a fair distance away in a bottle-green velvet wing chair. "There, we may now have a comfortable coze."

She gazed about the book-lined room, appreciating the glowing oak paneling, the wine-colored plush of the drapes at the tall windows, and the Aubusson carpet beneath her feet. "Lovely," she breathed.

Sylvester breathed as well, a sigh of relief. She seemed quite pleased to sit and talk rather than pace the third-floor gallery. He had looked forward to showing off the portraits of his ancestors, but it was Marianna he meant to impress, not Lady Charlotte. From her, he only wished information. But how to lead up to his subject?

For a while, as they awaited the refreshments, the two expatriates from London discussed mutual friends to their detriment. It wasn't until Wapshott retired after bringing the tray, that Sylvester brought up the subject on his mind.

"I trust," he began, pouring her a glass of sherry, "that my young scapegrace of a cousin is still at the vicarage."

"Indeed, I have not seen him for some time."

For days, or only for the half hour spent in his carriage? Sylvester eyed her placid countenance speculatively, as she raised her glass to her lips. Did she sidestep neatly? But such a thought was most unhandsome. One had only to observe Lady Charlotte to know such a straight-laced paragon would take no hand in duplicity.

But the Makepeace youth must be there. It seemed safe to continue the subject and gain any information she might have. Perhaps, if he stressed the seriousness of the charge—

"He has run off with my signet ring and refuses to return it," he said, watching her closely. "I am in constant fear that he may mislay it, placing it beyond recovery. A well-known signet ring could not be sold, but it could be melted down for the gold. It is a family treasure, worn by five dukes before me, and it must be retrieved."

Lady Charlotte selected a meringue from the plate Wapshott had set by her side. "I did not know that is what he did," she said with indifference. "You have an excellent cook. These are delicious."

Sylvester plowed on, digging for a reaction. "I have concluded that a simple jobation will not do. His actions call for a severe wigging. This escapade has been carried too far. I have even thought of calling in the Runners. In fact," he went on as she continued calm, nibbling her meringue, "I sent a message to Bow Street this very morning."

She looked up at this with a disapproving frown. "Surely, your Grace, that is somewhat extreme for a schoolboy prank."

"Oh, only to come and frighten the lad, you understand," he explained glibly. "Teach the whelp a bit of a lesson."

She continued to frown. Had he gone too far and been goaded by her complacency into revealing his hand too soon? No, her forehead cleared. She sipped at her sherry and selected another meringue. Did her fingers hover an extra second over the plate? Or did she only hesitate in choosing the larger?

He'd never know. The proper half hour for a visit had passed, and she finished her sherry. On taking her leave, she smiled most graciously and thanked him for a pleasant talk.

"Perhaps," she said, "Miss Marianna will be able to come tomorrow. Such a treat for her, to see your family portraits."

His carriage still waited, his coachman being well versed in the length of formal calls. Sylvester escorted her to the door. Why, he wondered, uneasily, did he feel he had come off a poor second?

A very different Lady Charlotte burst into the vicarage on her return, her bonnet awry and a bright spot of pink on each cheek. Geoff was still there, seated at the kitchen table with Marianna and Celeste, initiating Charlie into the mysteries of whist.

"He has called the Runners!" she cried. "What shall we do? They are coming for Charlie!"

"Me?" Charlie gasped. "The Bow Street Runners are after *me?"*

"And it was I who told him Charlie was here," Lady Charlotte wailed. "Inadvertently, that is my only excuse. I did not know what was at stake. Charlie, can you ever forgive me?"

Geoff had risen, scattering the cards from the table. "We must hide Charlie at once, or his life is not worth a ha'pence."

"He said it was to frighten him only," Charlotte went on. "But surely the Runners are—"

"—are humorless where highwaymen are concerned." Geoff's face set in grim lines. "If he sent for them this morning, they could be here before evening."

Charlie gazed into space as though in a trance. "The Bow Street Runners," he whispered. "After me. If only Jed could hear this, wherever he is."

"No doubt the flames crackle too loudly for his ears."

"They sold his ears," said Charlie absently. "I could not afford one. A man from our village tried, and he told me they went for a pretty penny. I doubt mine will ever be worth as much."

"They are worth more to you, idiot, right where they are." Geoff turned to Celeste. "Where can we stow the body of this vainglorious young cock? Where will he not be found in a thorough search?"

Marianna already had started. The settles by the hearth

were wood boxes, and she raised the seats. "These are almost empty now that summer comes, but they are the first place they will look."

Celeste opened the door beneath the stairs. "Here we have the broom closet." Geoff gave her a look. "No, no, I am grasp at the straw," she apologized. "Me, I cannot think yet, but soon I will."

"I should hope." Geoff spoke as one with experience. "Charlie would surely knock over buckets and mops, making a clatter that would alert the Runners at once. We must find a foolproof place."

"Charlie is not a fool!" Marianna exclaimed. "It is just that he is sometimes careless. What about the attic? He hid there once before when Lady—that is, when we wished him out of the way."

Lady Charlotte, so perturbed she missed the *faux pas,* caught up the idea. "There are trunks, are there not? One we could empty, and put him inside?"

"They will open everything," said Geoff.

Celeste tapped her chin with a slender finger tip. "Now I begin to think. There is nothing behind which he could take cover, but—ah, I have it! There is stored an old rug from the parlor. We must roll him up inside."

"You forget it is Charlie we hide," Geoff told her. "He would sneeze from the dust just as they came near."

Now Lady Charlotte grasped at straws. "A pity we cannot disguise him in some way."

Marianna shook her head. "We do not have a beard or an eye patch. Oh! Why do we not put him in Lady Charlotte's bed, under the mattress, and pile her quilt and pillows on top? They would not dare search her room."

"They will dare search anywhere, child." Geoff looked

out the window at the cemetery beyond. "We should find a place outside."

Marianna was seized by an inspiration. "Charlie, can you climb with your wounded leg? The apple tree by the back gate is so full of leaves, I am certain it would conceal you completely. I was always used to hide in a tree in our yard when I was wanted."

"Ah, yes," said Geoff. "I remember. You fell out once and sent your governess into a fit of the vapors. She thought you dead, until you sat up."

"I never fall out of trees," Charlie informed her loftily.

She flared at him. "You are not hampered by petticoats!"

"I like this idea," Charlie mused, ignoring her. "While I am up in the tree, I could eat the apples and throw the cores at the Runners."

They looked at him. He probably would be unable to resist such an opportunity. The apple tree went the way of the broom closet and the attic rug.

"The vicar!" exclaimed Lady Charlotte suddenly. "He must be told. Where is Mr. Brinkman?"

"He is in the church," said Celeste. "He gives comfort and solace to one of his parishioners who has come in great affliction. It is the poor natural from the Aultmere gardens. I found him this morning, weeping in one of the pews, in terror of a ghost that pursues him. He had been there all night, *le pauvre.*"

Lady Charlotte ranked Charlie above feeble-witted gardeners. "Mr. Brinkman must come at once."

There was no need. Having seen Tom-Tom off to the tavern to spend his silver in the light of day and his nights at home in his bed, the vicar came in through the passage between the vicarage and the vestry. His eyes were bright with curiosity.

"What's toward?" he asked. "I fear I have missed a momentous development."

They all proceeded to tell him at the same time, and he held up both hands for silence. "You, Sir Geoffrey, seem the sanest of the lot. Explain to me the cause for this hubbub."

Geoff did, in a few succinct sentences, and Mr. Brinkman pursed his lips. "Are they likely to search the church itself?"

"But no!" Celeste cried. "The church is a sanctuary! Charlie cannot be taken from there."

"By the same token," Geoff told her, "it is open to all, the Runners cannot be kept out, and if they once set eyes on Charlie, he is lost."

"But could we not better hide him there?" asked Lady Charlotte. "There is the choir loft—the vicar's anteroom—the bell housing in the steeple—"

"And if one playfully pulled the bell rope, anyone hidden up there might be deafened for days."

Charlie was becoming impatient. "Why do you not bury me in the cemetery and be done with it?"

Mr. Brinkman studied him over the top of his spectacles. "You are overly tall," he remarked thoughtfully. "Gentlemen of two centuries ago did not reach such great heights as the young men of today."

"What has that to do with anything?" Charlie sounded pleased nevertheless. "I know I am of a good size, and I have not yet filled out."

"That is an advantage." The vicar walked around him, considering. "I think we can manage."

"Manage what? What have you in mind?" demanded Marianna.

He blinked at her. "Why, the sarcophagi in the crypt, of course. It came to me when our young man suggested we bury him."

"The crypt? What crypt?" she asked. "Do you mean the Ault mausoleum?"

"No, no, my dear. Charlie could not walk so far. I refer to the crypt beneath the church. Four knights from the Crusade lie there. They came from this district, you know, and their families claimed the right. There were previous inhabitants, but no names were affixed to the stone sepulchers, no one claimed the skeletons, so the churchmen of the time had them removed to make room for the knights. The story is in one of the volumes of our Book of Recording."

Lady Charlotte had been looking out a window at the ancient building next door. "How old is your church?" she asked.

"Oh, this is not the original construction. I believe it is the third or fourth laid on the same foundation. Only the crypt below remains of the first, which was destroyed in the civil wars of the twelfth century. King Steven, you know, and his cousin, the Empress Maud. The faith was Catholic, at that time. It has since been rebuilt, devastated by fire, rebuilt again, and converted during the Reformation to Church of England by Henry VIII." He beamed with pride. "It is an honor to be vicar of so truly venerable and holy a site."

"Ah," said Celeste. *"Le bon Dieu* of a certainty dwells in its shelter, and our Charlie will be most safe."

"With a little help," amended Geoff.

Charlie seemed uneasy. "What about those skeletons that got thrown out? I'm not going down there with a bunch of angry ghosts."

"There have been no hauntings recorded, ever," the vicar assured him. "The remains were handled with all dignity and reverence. They now lie in a place of honor in the cemetery proper, marked by the old, Saxon-carved churchyard cross on the side nearest the lych gate. You need have no fears on their account."

Lady Charlotte had a fear. "I do not think a crypt, no matter its age, to be secure. It is open space, is it not, like a vault? If the church is searched, they will surely look down there. Charlie cannot hide behind a coffin."

Mr. Brinkman blinked at her. "I did not mean *behind* a coffin, my lady," he said in mild surprise. "I propose we place him *inside* one of the sarcophagi."

Charlie yelped, revolted. "With a skeleton? Oh, no you don't!"

"Let me explain, Mr. Charlie. The skeletons are not loose. They are nailed into wooden boxes sealed with lead from those days, for they were not embalmed. Now, the one I would recommend for you has an extra advantage. Sir Jonathan Weil expected his lady to join him, but she remarried after his death, and he was left with a large, double sarcophagus. I've often thought it was a shame to waste the space. There is room for you to lie beside his wooden coffin. Sir Jonathan won't mind after all this time, and may even enjoy the company."

"More than I will! Why must I hide at all? Those Runners could never catch me."

"Oh, could they not!" exclaimed Marianna. "An old

man hobbling with a cane could do the job! You can hardly walk, let alone run, since Ault shot you."

Lady Charlotte gasped. *"Ault* did this? He shot a lad for what he must have known was only a schoolboy prank? Indeed, it is high time and more that someone took the man in hand!"

"Actually," said Geoff, "it is just as well that Charlie is damaged. Only think of our trying to keep him still were he whole!"

This bit of flattery turned the trick. "Perhaps they have me at a disadvantage," Charlie admitted, magnanimous. "But had I both my legs in proper order, they'd not lay a hand on me."

"Quite," Geoff agreed. "But you've not, and they can! Let us inspect this crypt."

"We shall need a lantern." Mr. Brinkman wandered vaguely about the kitchen until Celeste produced one and handed it to him, with a tinderbox. "Thank you, my dear. Very dark down there."

They trooped through the short passage to the church; the vicar led them to a back corner and the stone steps leading down into the darkness of the crypt. "Go carefully," he advised. "The stairs are uneven and slippery."

They crept round two sharp turns before reaching the bottom, where they clustered behind the vicar. The light from his lantern shone on a small room with a low, arching ceiling, carved from the native bedrock and redolent with damp and must. The floor had been leveled by primitive means, and rough projections tripped their feet as they moved on in. Marianna and Charlotte caught at their skirts, holding them away from the black, slimy walls. There were only four stone sarcophagi, but they filled all the space. Not the glorious carved creations of the Ault mausoleum, these were simple boxes with flat lids bearing brass plates to identify their inhabitants. One, twice the size of the others, had a chunk broken from the corner of its lid as though it had been dropped on the rock floor at some time.

Mr. Brinkman exhibited it with triumph. Charlie would be able to breathe inside.

Geoff walked around it and nodded. "It should do nicely. Is that cover heavy? Can we move it?"

"We need not take it off." The vicar began to shove on one corner. "We have only to slide it a bit to one side, so Charlie can get in."

"Right," said Geoff, and went to his aid. It moved with surprising ease, grating on crumbled stone with an eerie screech that sent shivers up their spines.

Charlie hung back. "How'll I get back out?"

"Oh, Charlie, you cannot think we'd leave you in there." Marianna gave him a push. "Do get in, so that we may see if it fits."

He hesitated still, but Geoff gave him a boost. After ascertaining that Sir Jonathan was indeed well inside a wooden casket, Charlie lowered himself gingerly down. There was room enough, with only a slight bending of his knees. He climbed back out.

"You needn't think I'll take up any permanent residence in here. Only in dire need, and I must be let out at once."

The matter settled, they went back into the vicarage to remove every vestige of Charlie's presence. His borrowed clothing was mixed in with the vicar's, his pallet rolled and stored in the attic, and his bedding distributed among the other rooms. Celeste found the bag of Charlie's own garments and proceeded to build a hot fire in the hearth. He stared in horror as she ruthlessly tossed first his black mask and then his worn hat onto the blaze.

"That belonged to Jed!" he howled. "And that!"

"They go to join him," she said.

"Better his possessions than you," Marianna comforted. "Besides, you do not need them. You are no longer going on the High Toby."

"But—"

"Believe me," said Sir Geoffrey. "You have reached the height of your profession. A price on your head, Bow Street Runners on your trail, and a hempen rope waiting for your neck. It is time to retire and rest on your laurels."

This aspect apparently had not occurred to Charlie. He made no more objections and watched the flames shrivel Jed's mementos. Celeste decided it would take too long for the fire to consume the frieze coat, his bloodstained leg-wrappings and worn boots. She bundled them into a basket and carried them out to the garbage midden where, with Sir Geoffrey's help, she buried them. When she had done, not a trace of the original Charlie remained.

During all this commotion, Geoff was far too aware of Celeste, remembering the feel of her soft body in his arms, the warm response of her kiss—and the fact that he now was making excuses to be near her, to brush her arm or shoulder. She avoided looking at him, which was just as well, because when their eyes met, betraying color flushed her cheeks. He knew a sudden fear that Charlotte would see and demand they take Marianna and leave at once. So far, Charlotte had been interested only in Charlie's safety and regretting her part in his discovery. That, however, could not last. Not with the heat of the tension growing between himself and the lovely French girl. He'd best leave for a while.

"I am going back to Aultmere," he said, "to see what Sylvester is doing now. Perhaps I can learn when he expects the Runners."

He had not been gone ten minutes when the London Mail rattled by the vicarage and stopped at Bob Hawkins' tavern. Celeste, on watch at the window, saw two men get down. Obviously strangers to Ault-in-the-Vale, they wore the city garments of the lower middle class, tailed coats, knee breeches, and low-crowned, flat-brimmed black hats. They stood looking toward the vicarage for a few minutes, then walked into the tavern.

"If I mistake not," Celeste announced in a shaken voice, "our Runners are here."

Fourteen

Celeste knew a moment of sheer panic. Oh, where was M. Sir Geoffrey when they needed him? She knew perfectly well why he had gone—but why could he not have waited a few more minutes? They needed him *now!*

Lady Charlotte echoed her thought. "Why did Geoffrey leave us? We need him!"

"We do not, Lady Charlotte." Taking a deep breath, Celeste rallied her forces. "We three can manage. It takes only that we are calm. M. Brinkman can help us put Charlie into the sarcophagus."

"But he has gone for his nap."

"We shall wake him, and quickly." Grabbing the reluctant Charlie by the arm, Celeste dragged him into the study.

"Why are you so sure it's the Runners?" he demanded. "Have you ever seen one? I don't want to go in that weird place unless I have to!"

"You have to." Ruthlessly, she shook the vicar awake. "They come, M. Brinkman, we must hide Charlie!"

The old man awoke in an instant and sat up. "Is Sir Geoffrey here?"

"No, that he is not. It is only we who must manage."

He got to his feet, and counted on his fingers. "We are five to slide the lid, and four to push it back. Enough."

With the vicar leading, Celeste pulling Charlie, and Marianna pushing him from behind, they hurried through the passageway to the church. Lady Charlotte, with remarkable presence of mind, caught up the lantern and tinderbox and gathered up her skirts to run after them.

Half an hour later, when a peremptory knock sounded on the vicarage door, they were seated sedately about the table, each holding an odd number of playing cards in their hands. Simultaneously, the back door creaked, admitting Mrs. Mudd. Celeste muttered something in French. It was too late to warn the woman to silence. The vicar already had opened the door to their visitors.

The two men Celeste had seen dismounting from the London mail coach stood on the steps. Mr. Brinkman, at his most benign and gentle, eyed them over his wire-rimmed spectacles.

"Good afternoon, gentlemen," he said. "May I be of assistance?"

"Bow Street," the taller of the men informed him. He hesitated, taking in the stooped, elderly clergyman with his utterly innocent features and halo of soft white hair. "My apologies, sir. We have received notice of a wanted man in this area."

" 'Ave to search the premises," put in the short, chubby one. "Orders."

The vicar blinked. "Search here? For a wanted man?"

"Yus sir." The tall Runner shuffled his feet, looking uncomfortable. "We are after a wounded and dangerous highwayman, last reported in this vicinity."

Mr. Brinkman shook his head. The three women behind him held their breath. The vicar, who took his vows

THE DUKE'S DOUBLE 193

to the church as absolute law, always spoke the truth. "I know of no *dangerous* highwayman," he said.

"Tall man," said the Runner. " 'Ardly more than a youth. Straw-colored 'air, limping, possibly from a bullet wound. 'As 'e been 'ere?"

Someone in the room gave an audible gasp, but Mr. Brinkman rose to the challenge.

"Oh, yes," he replied, completely calm. "I had such a young man, but he is gone from the vicarage." Which was true. Charlie lay under the church next door.

The Runner consulted a notebook he took from his pocket. "Charlie Makepeace, 'is name is." He asked a direct question. "Where is this Makepeace now?"

Celeste and Marianna clung to each other in horror. Lady Charlotte collapsed on the settle by the hearth in dismay, her fingers at her lips. A man of the cloth could not lie.

But he could prevaricate, and rather well.

He treated the men to his blandest smile. "I fear I cannot say," he replied with perfect truth. He turned to Mrs. Mudd, who stood by the dry sink, her ears positively flapping. "These gentlemen are from London, Mrs. Mudd. Bow Street Runners, I believe they are called. They say they are after a thief who may be hiding somewhere about." He looked vaguely around the room. "I see no one here we do not know."

Mrs. Mudd, whose husband was well known as a poacher, had no love for the law. She waxed indignant. "You may be sure, sirs, I don't allow no rabble to come into a house of the church."

Four collective sighs of relief disturbed the air, a breeze that swayed the kitchen curtains.

The two men at the door stubbornly held their place. "We 'ave our orders," said the short one. " 'Ave to make a search." They pushed their way in and began poking about the cluttered community room.

Mrs. Mudd glared them down. "You won't find no dirt in 'ere, no way you looks. Nor no thieves either."

The door had remained open, and now it was filled by another arrival. "What's all this?" the newcomer demanded, coming in. The three ladies greeted him with cries of delight.

"Uncle Geoff!"

"Geoffrey, I am so glad to see you!"

"M. Sir Geoffrey, these men say we hide here a thief!"

"They are Bow Street Runners," Marianna summed up the situation. "The idiots think a highwayman is somewhere here, Uncle Geoff!"

"What utter rubbish," he said, acting Sir Geoffrey to his fingertips. With an air of insufferable hauteur, he raised his quizzing glass and looked the two men up and down, from their flat black hats to their solid boots and back. He dropped the glass and let it dangle from its ribbon. "But in no case, Marianna, do we call people idiots until they prove themselves so." He turned to the Runners. "You may be sure if any such person is in the vicarage, I would remove Lady Charlotte and my niece at once."

Both men seemed somewhat awestricken by his lordly manner, but the taller one pushed out a stubborn lower lip. His partner, made of less stern stuff, hastily doffed his hat and made a half-bow to Charlotte.

"We begs your pardon for intruding, me lady. Orders, you know. 'Ave to be carried out."

Charlotte acknowledged his existence with a queenly inclination of her head.

Geoff wandered about the room as though helping to search, peering under the table, opening the broom closet, and removing Charlotte, but politely, from the settle in order to tip up the seat and look inside. "If you have a highwayman, Mr. Brinkman, where the deuce is he?"

"The only thieves around here," the vicar said firmly, "are safely underground."

Geoff had succeeded in making the Runners look a bit silly, but they were still determined. One headed up the stairs to the attic, while the other poked about in the parlor and the study. Mrs. Mudd had put a kettle on the hearth, and Celeste brought out mugs and the teapot. The residents of the vicarage pretended to ignore the invaders and appear at their ease. All seemed to be going well until the tall one, who had remained downstairs, gave a shout to his partner. He had discovered the passage to the church.

"Where's this go, yer 'oner?"

"Oh, dearie me." The vicar fluttered his hands. "Do you think he might be hiding in our church? It is a sanctuary, you understand. If he is there, you cannot take him."

"Mebbe not, but 'e can't lie in there forever." He glanced away as the other Runner clattered down the stairs. "Come along, Eben, 'e may be in the church."

"Indeed?" Mr. Brinkman threw open the passage door. "We must look at once! I cannot have miscreants where they might frighten my elderly parishioners. Come, gentlemen, this passage leads directly into our new vestry, which adjoins the vicarage. So handy for me. Added during the incumbency of my predecessor."

The vicar's passage was narrow, and they had to proceed single file. Celeste and Sir Geoffrey brought up the rear.

"How came you here so quickly?" she whispered over her shoulder.

"I was at the tavern waiting for Jobbs to bring up my curricle, when the mail coach arrived. I went out the back to the stable to tell him to wait, and then walked over by way of the cemetery. I collect all has gone according to plan?"

They bumped into Lady Charlotte and Marianna, held up by the vicar and the Runners who had come to an abrupt stop at the entrance to the vestry. Mr. Brinkman, taking on the mien of a tour guide, was happily displaying the addition to his church.

"As you see," he declaimed, "we are a small but exquisite example of a village church, having only the nave, the chancel, this new vestry, and at the front, our square stone tower. It is low, but gains height from the timbered belfry added, I understand, in the fourteenth century."

"Aha," exclaimed the taller Runner. "A belfry!" He strode toward the small stone room that formed the base of the tower, next to the oaken church doors. "That's where we'll find our man."

He gave his short companion a push. "Get you up there, Eben."

"There is a ladder on the wall for access," the vicar offered helpfully. "Indeed, you must see our bell. We have only the one, but it is an excellent specimen. Medieval, you must know, long and narrow with a prayer inscribed about its circumference. Its name is Rudolph. I don't know the derivation."

He paused to admire the agility displayed by the stocky

Eben, who had started up the ladder. A long, heavy rope, with a loop at its base, hung down in the center of the little room from a circular hole in the roof above. It ended a few feet above the floor.

"This is the bell rope," Mr. Brinkman explained. "The stirrup loop at the bottom is for the ringer's foot. It takes strength and skill to ring a proper peal."

Sir Geoffrey had been standing back, admiring the vicar's performance, but at the sight of the little Runner scrambling up the ladder like a fat spider, Rake Cole took over.

"Shall I demonstrate?" he asked. He put one foot in the rope loop and gave a hop on the other, producing a mellow bong from above. Eben, who had disappeared through the hole at the top of the ladder, came tumbling back down and sat on the floor, clutching his ears.

"M. Sir Geoffrey," exclaimed Celeste. "You should not have done that!"

"I know," he said. "It was very bad of me, but I could not resist. I did not realize what it would do."

"Dear me," murmured the vicar. "I should have warned you, but you gave a very light pull. You really should hear our bell when Bob Hawkins tolls for events. He is our regular ringer, and I understand he can be heard for miles."

Sir Geoffrey kindly extended a hand to help the dazed Runner to his feet. "My deepest apologies, sir."

"Eh?" said the Runner.

Sir Geoffrey thumped him on the back and shouted in his ear. "It will go away in a few minutes. All will be well." He steered him after Mr. Brinkman, who was already herding the others down the nave toward the vestry.

Working his way up beside Celeste, Geoff gave her

waist a companionable squeeze under cover of the vicar's next speech.

"M. Sir Geoffrey," she hissed. "We do not play a game. This is of the most serious."

He tried to appear contrite, but the teasing warmth in his eyes quite spoiled the effect. She pulled away, her own eyes on Lady Charlotte, who presented an appearance of not having noticed. A deceptive appearance? Uneasy, Celeste moved farther, putting Marianna between them.

The taller Runner again consulted his notebook. "Says here, you 'ave a crypt below." He looked up at the sound of a collective catching of breath. "Aha," he said. "We'd best 'ave a look-see in that crypt."

"No!" cried Marianna. "Not down there!"

"So?" said the Runner. "And why not, missy?"

"You can go," Marianna told him, clinging to her uncle. "Not me. It is full of ghosts!"

"Now, now," the vicar chided. "You must not listen to the village tales. There is no such thing as an earth-bound spirit in my church. I do not allow it."

"Nothing but rats," Sir Geoffrey assured Marianna. "All damp, dark holes in the ground have rats, and naturally they make odd sounds when disturbed. Show the gentlemen your crypt, Mr. Brinkman."

"Certainly," said the vicar. He pushed the two Runners ahead of him to the very back corner of the chancel, where the rough stone steps led underground.

"Here we have a crypt," he announced, "well worth the seeing, for it is the last remaining piece of the original Saxon church that stood on this ground for several centuries." He took down a lantern from its hook and struck it alight. "Very dark down there," he explained, and led the

vay, waiting at the foot of the steps until they were all
huddled in the tiny pool of light around him.

"You see here four knights of the crusade," he told
he Runners, pride radiating from his beaming face in
he yellow glow. He passed the lantern in turn over the
arcophagi, and introduced each as though meeting
guests at a party. "Sir Germain Howe, Sir Adelbert Der-
vent, and Sir Edward Conan. And here is Sir Jonathan
Neil, whose wife fitted him with a double stone coffin
hat she might eventually lie beside him."

The wavering lantern light created an eerie atmosphere
n the ancient, dank crypt, and Eben already had begun to
peer over his shoulder into the black-shadowed corners.
As the vicar ceased to speak, a sudden sound broke the
ilence, rather like a stifled sneeze issuing from Sir
onathan's stone resting place. Marianna let out a despair-
ng wail and fled. Eben, his hearing miraculously restored,
scrambled after her, back up the rough stone steps, tripping
over his boots, with his compatriot at his heels.

"Rats," Sir Geoffrey shouted after them. "Only rats!"
But he was unheeded. The two wanted only to get back
up into the sunlight.

The Runners took their leave, apologizing profusely
for all the pother. "It was 'is Grace as set us on," the
aller man explained.

Sir Geoffrey nodded gravely. "Ah," he said, taking out
his snuffbox. He placed a pinch of his private sort on
his wrist and sniffed delicately. "Very nervous sort of
man. No doubt he has been listening to the servants'
gossip. Would you believe," he went on, "I hear his people are even saying they have seen a ghost at Aultmere."

This accomplished the complete rout of the Runners.

They headed for the tavern, the shorter man still shaking his head and pounding his ears. As the rest of them left the church, Geoff emptied the silver from his pocket into the alms box by the door.

"I do hope they enjoyed the tour of our church," said the pious clergyman as they entered the vicarage.

Marianna, overcome by giggles, gave a little skip. "No more so than we."

"M. Brinkman, you were *formidable!*" Celeste threw her arms about him and kissed his cheek.

"A Trojan," Geoff agreed, wringing the vicar's hand. "I have but one question. Why?"

Mr. Brinkman hesitated before he answered. "I feel we should not be too precipitate in this matter of Mr. Charlie and his—er—borrowing of the duke's signet ring. Surely, Ault is far too anxious to be rid of the boy. I have always believed the Makepeace family left in the night because Jed was caught poaching, but suppose instead—I cannot help wondering—could there be something in the odd rumors that floated about the village at the time of the little duke's unexpected death?"

Geoff frowned, his eyes intent. "What rumors were these, sir?"

Once more, the vicar hesitated, as though assembling the rights and wrongs of what he was about to say. "If all is innocence, I have no desire to blacken the character of one who is no longer of this world."

"Go on," said Marianna. "If it will help Charlie, blacken away. Do you mean his stepfather Jed?"

"No, no." Mr. Brinkman smiled, suddenly looking quite human. "His character is black enough. Though these rumors do involve him further."

Lady Charlotte moved to her favorite place, the settle by the hearth, and seated herself, her hands folded primly. "You may be sure, my dear vicar, nothing you say will leave this room."

Geoff didn't agree. "That we cannot promise until we have heard. Pray speak freely. I daresay it was common enough gossip in the village at the time."

"Yes, of course." Mr. Brinkman brightened. "It cannot be a secret. It was being rumored that the duchess, Sylvester's mother, you know, had connived at the little duke's death, with Jed Makepeace actually committing the foul deed! Naturally, I did my best to quench the rumor, but now I cannot help feeling there is something very peculiar about a recent affair at Aultmere. All is not right."

"Do you mean about the ring?"

"I do not think it is a matter of the ring," said the vicar. "Rather it is the person of Mr. Charlie. Sir Geoffrey, I knew the Makepeace family well. That boy is not the son of Jed Makepeace."

"He knows that. He said the man was his stepfather."

The vicar pursed his lips. "I believe he is of the family of Ault."

"Yes, I agree. Of that there is no doubt, but on which side of the blanket? And why is Sylvester so set on removing Charlie permanently—simply to retrieve his ring?"

"It is no longer his," declared Marianna.

The men looked at her, taken aback, having forgotten her listening ears.

"He gave that ring to me," Marianna continued. "And I gave it to Charlie. Sylvester cannot have it back."

Lady Charlotte spoke up from her seat by the hearth,

breaking up further discussion. "Are we not forgetting something? Poor Charles is still in the crypt."

Before returning to London, the Runners dutifully reported to the Duke of Ault.

"No sign of any 'ighwayman, your Grace. We searched that there vicarage from attic to cellar."

"He is there, I tell you!" Sylvester exclaimed. "He has been seen. You cannot have looked."

The taller Runner stuck to his guns. "We looked, your Grace, never leaving a stone unturned."

"What about the church, did you search in there?"

"Yus, your Grace. Very thorough we were."

"Even the belfry," put in Eben. "Nothing in't but that bloody bell."

The taller man kicked his shin. "Watch yer languidge," he muttered.

"Under the altar?" demanded Sylvester. "Do they have a confession box—no, I suppose they don't. But I've heard there's a crypt beneath the church. Did you go down there?"

Both men paled a trifle and shuddered. "That we did," said the tall one. "Nothing down there but a bunch o' skeletons in stone coffins."

"And ghosts," Eben added. This time he was not kicked.

"That there is no place for no 'uman beings," his companion went on. "But we went down there. We knows our duty," he added virtuously.

There was nothing more to be got from them. Utterly useless, the men Bow Street sent out. Probably kept their better Runners for more important affairs in London proper. Sylvester dismissed them to spend the night at the tavern and catch the morning coach back to town.

After they left, he retired to the library and paced the floor, deep in thought. He knew the Makepeace youth was still there. He could feel it in his bones. Somehow Sir Geoffrey and that Frenchwoman had hidden him somewhere. Those two were in a deadly plot against him, he was sure, but why had they become involved in his affairs? Did they want money? Blackmail or extortion? But of what could they charge him? As long as that coffin was never opened . . .

He went out on the terrace and pretended to admire his view, though it was not as soothing to his spirit as usual. Not that it mattered, for his thoughts were busy elsewhere. He didn't notice the general air of gloom that pervaded the landscape. Dark clouds had gathered above, threatening rain, but his every nerve was tuned to possible observers, for he intended to see for himself that the coffin still lay safely hidden, waiting for him to dump it down the well. Not an agreeable task, and he would have to do it tonight after all were abed. He shivered.

What if his mother's ghost had found it? What if the spirit of the little body inside clung to its remains? He gritted his teeth. One quick drag from the bushes, one hasty shove into the black depths of the well, and both wraiths could hover over the spot forever if they wished. The Duke of Ault would never go near that place again.

But he could casually walk by the spot now, just to reassure himself that the coffin was undiscovered. No one was about the place who'd notice his movements.

The domestics inside were involved in the preparation

of his evening meal—which Sir Geoffrey would attend. It seemed very important to Sylvester that Sir Geoffrey did not suspect he knew of his treachery. Above all, he himself must seem innocent of *anything*. He wandered—innocently, of course—toward the back and the kitchen gardens. He could see the spot where the abandoned well lay covered with planks, and the thick bushes behind. With difficulty, he kept from going over to push aside the shrubbery to assure himself that the coffin was still safely hidden. He couldn't go near it now. There were servants in the garden. Meanwhile, his awareness of its presence held him as though on a leash.

As he stood there dithering, the first drops of rain began to fall on his head. If he remained outside during a shower, his interest in the area would be noticed for certain. He ran for cover. His other problem intruded, weighing as heavily on his mind as the coffin, the pressing matter of Charlie Makepeace and whoever he might be. Sylvester knew he could never rest easy while that young man lived; he must be removed—and forever.

What could he do? What if that damned Sir Geoffrey and the Frenchwoman, who must know of his mother's sacred confession to her French priest, had put two and two together and decided he was not the real duke? One certainty overwhelmed him. He could not give up being the Duke of Ault. He'd be cast out, homeless, into the streets—if not haled into prison as a usurper.

But that was ridiculous. It had to be. He was becoming desperate and losing what wits he had. The immediate solution was to discredit his double—have him hung for a highwayman—and then, why, he was the heir in any case! Legally, he'd be what he was now. The sixth Duke of Ault.

He began to scheme, pacing the covered terrace as he had paced the library. If the man could be brought out into the open, if only he could be found in Town and caught in the act of thievery by the London Watch . . .

An idea came to him, so momentous it stopped him in his tracks. Young Makepeace—Sylvester refused to think of him by any other name—when Makepeace held up their coach, he wrested Marianna from himself and Sir Geoffrey; would he do it again if she were once more being forced into marriage?

He continued his pacing, this time with quick, decisive steps, as he worked out the delightful details of a complex, diabolical plan.

This one, he was certain, could not fail.

Fifteen

The light rain of the evening had become a downpour by the time Aultmere began to settle in for the night. Sylvester sat by his window in his night rail, for he couldn't have Prouty suspect his intention to go outside. All that was ruined now. He stared out at the storm. Rain pelted against the casement, strands of loose ivy scraped like clawing fingers across the glass, and no moonlight pierced the thick blackness of the cloud cover. How could he venture out into such a maelstrom?

A deep sigh escaped him. Would it never stop? Frustrated, he squinted his eyes, trying to perceive a lessening of the tempest. Here he had worked himself up to his hideous task, and all nature contrived to impede him. He'd have to wait for another night, and he wondered if he could stand the suspense. Almost, he considered bundling up and going anyway, but he'd be drenched to the skin and how could he ever hide a pile of rain-soaked garments from Prouty? The man had the curiosity of a cat.

One comforting thought, the heavy rain might have spoiled his foray for tonight, but at least no one else would be wandering about the grounds. And if that coffin was not waterproof, what did it matter? It was destined for a well. He retired to his bed and lay awake, going over and over the details of his marvelous plan.

That marvelous plan kept his quill busy the following morning, as he composed a number of missives. The day had dawned clear and calm after the night's near cloudburst. Sunshine sparkled on fresh-washed leaves, vivid green against the blue of the sky. Flowers opened their petals in a rainbow of colors, and bits of fleecy white cloud replaced the overcast of the day before. A perfect day. And perfect for his plan.

He finished his last letter, and read them over. The first, the one essential to the success of the others, was an invitation to the ladies at the vicarage—graciously including Marianna's French companion, Mlle. Moreau—to ride about the countryside in his open carriage to view the beauty of the land after the rain.

The second, to be held until a favorable reply came from the vicarage, was an anonymous note to Bow Street in London, beginning: "Owing to information received, I take leave to inform you—"

The third, even more vital, was addressed to Mr. Charles Makepeace, in care of the vicarage, to be delivered by hand. He had written and torn up half a dozen before achieving one he felt struck just the right note. He sealed it, and gave it to Prouty, along with a penny, to be carried by some unsuspecting child.

Sylvester's invitation, suggesting they all take advantage of the excellent day, was delivered by a footman in full Aultmere livery, arriving during nuncheon. Sir Geoffrey, who spent a great deal of his time at the vicarage,

was among those present. It was he who took the message. After a quick glance at the contents, he ordered the
footman to await an answer and shut the door, leaving
the man outside while he read the missive aloud.

"Now what is Sylvester up to?" he wondered. "I see
he only includes the ladies for this delightful excursion."

"I believe I should be offended," said Mr. Brinkman.
"I am the only resident not invited."

"How about me?" Charlie complained. "I would enjoy
a breath of fresh air. I grow quite tired of being cooped
up indoors. What say I borrow a mobcap and gown and
go along as Mrs. Mudd?" He ducked as Marianna threw
a cushion at him.

Geoff eyed him, frowning. "This has all the earmarks
of one of Sylvester's tricks. I have a feeling you'd best
keep under cover, if you are left here alone. It seems almost
as though he wishes to clear the decks for some scheme,
but then why does he not include you, Mr. Brinkman? I
can understand his not mentioning Charlie, who does not
exist, but he specifically writes only to the ladies. All of
them."

"Except Mrs. Mudd," put in Charlie. "Thereby spoiling my chances of going along." He threw the cushion
back at Marianna, who caught it easily.

The vicar seated himself on the settle opposite Lady
Charlotte, and steepled his fingertips. "This all may be
quite above board, Sir Geoffrey. We must not judge the
man too severely. I daresay he might feel I would put a
damper on his party. I have found that many people consider my vocation a barrier to innocent fun. I do not mind."

Celeste had been sitting quietly, her gaze—in spite of
herself—following Geoff's every move. She gave herself

a tiny shake and turned to Charlie. "But yes, M. Charlie. It is well M. Brinkman remains, for someone must be on guard for you at all times."

Charlie grinned at her. "Do not fear for me. I shall be on the alert for anything untoward."

Geoff still frowned. "See that you are, young man."

"But what can happen to me, when Ault will be occupied with the ladies?"

"Charlie, you do not think!" Marianna exclaimed. "What will you do if those Runners come back while we are all gone?"

"Why, the vicar will be here. He will secure me into that sarcophagus, and if one of them comes near, I shall sneeze again."

Marianna heaved the cushion at him in turn. "You give no thought to the safety of Lady Charlotte, Celeste, and myself."

He returned the missile. "What can happen when you are all together?"

"Enough of that." Lady Charlotte confiscated their cushion. "This is a serious matter. Geoffrey, I believe we should go. It is a chance to discover what those Runners told him, whether they have actually left for good, and what he plans next."

Geoff felt uneasy, but it was an opportunity not to be missed if Ault could be induced to confide in Lady Charlotte, as he had done before. He might consider Marianna to be unsuspecting. And Celeste? Under the watchful eye of Charlotte, he had been careful not to glance at Celeste, but he did so now and caught her looking at him. Her face flamed, and he remembered the man who had seen them at the edge of the field. Had that incident been reported to Sylvester? He knew well the servants' grape-vine, word could have reached the duke, but Sylvester knew of his reputation. Rake Cole would naturally take advantage of so pretty a housemaid—housekeeper. A weight lifted from his mind. He'd never expected to be thankful for his shady past. She would be safe from suspicion of anything but harboring a wounded man who had now left the vicinity, and being the innocent victim of one known to be a scoundrel.

Lady Charlotte interrupted his thoughts. "The man waits outside for our answer, Geoffrey. I shall send a note to the duke, accepting for us all."

He still was uneasy. A nagging sense of something wrong persisted, but surely it would be aimed at Charlie, not the ladies. It should be safe for them to go.

"You must stay here, Uncle Geoff," Marianna ordered, echoing his thought. "We will not leave unless both you and the vicar are here to guard Charlie. I cannot but feel that those Runners may come again, and Mr. Brinkman will need help with the heavy coffin cover."

He nodded. "For once, young lady, you may be right."

All being decided, Lady Charlotte penned her note.

In due course, Sylvester arrived in his open landau, dressed to the nines in full ducal regalia for the benefit of the villagers who might see him pass. The ladies, in fresh gowns and carrying parasols, took their seats; the carriage departed, and the vicarage settled down to peace and quiet.

Charlie, determined to learn enough Latin to eventually be able to read Ulysses for himself, took up his books in the study behind a closed door. The vicar, looking forward to a nap with his home in silence for a change, retired to his bedchamber. Geoff pulled Mr.

Brinkman's easy chair up to the hearth and put his gleaming Hessians up on one of the settles. Mrs. Mudd, who had a tin ear, began to sing her favorite hymns in a monotonous monotone as she prepared vegetables for a *pot-au-feu,* known to her as mutton soup. Lulled by the comfortable drone, Geoff first dozed, then joined the vicar in gentle slumber.

The sightseeing party had not been gone above an hour, when a village child appeared at the kitchen door with a note addressed to Charlie. Mrs. Mudd accepted it, unaware of any danger. She tiptoed past the sleeping Sir Geoffrey and carried it into the study at once.

"For me?" Charlie put his English translation of Ulysses aside. "Who would be writing to me? Unless"—he grinned—"unless Ault has thought better of not inviting me, and suggests I run behind his carriage and catch up."

His sally was wasted. Mrs. Mudd, her mind on a boiling mutton bone, had already left. He unfolded the paper, a note written in Sylvester's most feminine hand, had he only known.

"My dear Charles," he read. "You must come to my aid. I have been abducted by the Duke of Ault and am a captive in his house in London. Come to my rescue tonight at midnight, and break a window after the domestics are asleep. Yr. obt. servant, Marianna Cole."

Charlie let out a few remarks regarding Ault's ancestry, culled from Jed's vocabulary. Had his wits been about him and his brain not steeped in the heroic deeds of the ancient Greek, he might have read the message with more care and detected a few glaring discrepancies. As it was—

"The devil!" he exclaimed. "That abominable screw still means to force her into marriage!"

He crumpled the paper into a ball and flung it across the room, missing the hearth. Catching up his coat he, like Mrs. Mudd, tiptoed past Sir Geoffrey, who snored softly. Limping out the back door, he headed for Bob Hawkins' tavern and the stable where the piebald cob named Dauntless resided. As noble as any hero in mythology, he was off to perform a deed of glory.

Geoff, peacefully asleep by the hearth, did not hear the familiar creak of the door. Mrs. Mudd heard it, but it was none of her business where rackety young men chose to go.

The return of Sylvester's carriage and the entrance of three chattering ladies roused Geoff from his sleep. Marianna discovered Charlie's absence at once, and the ensuing bedlam brought the vicar down from his room and Mrs. Mudd from her stew.

" 'E slipped out," she announced, aggrieved. "So quiet 'e was, I never 'eard 'im, only the creak of the door. Off to Bob 'Awkins' tavern, 'e went. I seen 'im through the window."

"Why did you not stop him?" cried Celeste.

Mrs. Mudd waxed indignant. "Why should I? Iffen the lad wants 'is pint o' ale, why, let 'im, I says."

Marianna turned on Geoff, pounding on his chest with both fists. "Uncle Geoff, how could you sleep at your post?" she wailed. "It's all your fault!"

"I quite agree," he said, catching her hands. "But recriminations won't help. We have to find him before it is too late—if it isn't already."

Celeste, at this moment, saw the crumpled ball of paper on the floor and picked it up. She read it, and with a cry of dismay, handed it to Geoff.

Rake Cole's vocabulary came near to taking the shine from that of Jed Makepeace. Lady Charlotte clapped her hands over her ears, but Mrs. Mudd eyed him with something akin to admiration.

Marianna hopped up and down with impatience. "What does it say? Is it from Charlie?"

Geoff handed her the paper. "No, my dear, it seems to be from you."

Mrs. Mudd's earlier indignation was nothing to Marianna's. Wherever Sylvester was at the moment, his ears must have burned.

Geoff took back the wrinkled sheet before she shredded it, and perused it again. "No doubt Sylvester has also sent a message to those Runners, telling them he has learned a notorious cutthroat will be breaking into his London town house tonight. Midnight seems to be the witching hour. If Charlie is going to be lying in wait in Ault's shrubbery, I had best go there at once and apprehend him myself." He caught up his hat, preparing to leave.

Lady Charlotte, who had been contemplating the folded hands in her lap, raised an unhappy face. "Geoffrey, is there not some way to put an end to this Bow Street fixation of Sylvester's?"

"Perhaps," Celeste suggested diffidently, "it would be the thing for the duke himself to apologize to these poor Runners for playing his tricks."

Geoff grinned at her. "Indeed it would, but how do you think to convince Sylvester of that?"

"M. Charlie will do it. Why do we not take advantage of his resemblance to *M. le duc?*"

Geoff's eyes sharpened. "Go on."

She did so. "It may be we can also take advantage of his continuing to cry the wolf, and discredit him with officialdom for all time."

"How?"

But Marianna had caught on. "Yes, Uncle Geoff! The very thing! You must hurry to London and intercept Charlie. Then dress him in Sylvester's most dandified town coat and one of his silly beehive hats, and meet the Runners at his front door. Charlie can pretend to be the duke and dismiss Bow Street from the case. He can tell them it is all a plumper, and they were quite taken in. They will be so annoyed, they will pay no attention to his claims ever again!"

Geoff rubbed his chin. "It might work, if I can get to Charlie in time to make the change."

Celeste glanced at the mantel clock, which for once had continued to tick. "Midnight, the *billet* reads. That must be the hour the Runners are ordered to arrive. It is now nearly six by our timepiece."

Geoff, skeptical, took out his watch. It agreed. "I can be in London in two hours."

"Yes," said Marianna, "no doubt you can, but how do you suppose Charlie means to travel?"

"Can you ask? I'll check with Bob Hawkins' stable for that blasted multicolored excuse for a horse. We have four hours. Even that plow horse should make it there in time."

He set off at once to retrieve Jobbs and his curricle at the tavern, where he had parked them as usual. The piebald cob was missing from his stall, and he breathed a sigh of relief. From what he had seen of Dauntless in action—or what that slug considered action—he might even catch Charlie on the road.

Stealing Sylvester's best coat and favorite beehive hat proved more difficult than Geoff had expected, for Sylvester had worn them on the afternoon excursion. By the time the duke had been changed into garments more suitable for an evening at home, Geoff's nerves were raw. At last, Sylvester emerged and headed down to the library, where Wapshott was already setting out a tray of preprandial drinks. It was another fifteen minutes before Prouty came out, bearing a pair of inexpressibles with a smudge of dirt on one knee.

When Geoff finally sneaked out the drawing room French doors, with the coat and hat rolled into a ball—ready to be stuffed under his curricle seat—he had only two and a half hours to intercept Charlie. He set off for London, driving his pair *ventre á terre*.

Geoff saw the piebald cob first, tethered to a gas lamppost a few doors from Sylvester's town house. He drew his curricle up on the other side, just past the front entrance, and hitched his pair to a neighbor's kennel fence.

All seemed unexpectedly quiet. No lights shone in Ault's prestigious establishment. A section of wrought iron fence on each side of the steps enclosed a small area from the road. On the left was a bit of shrubbery and a tree, on the right, stairs led down to a basement entrance past a street-level window, through which a butler could observe anyone standing before the door. Leaving his curricle, Geoff moved to stand beneath the single tree.

"Hist," it remarked.

A startled gasp escaped him.

"Hist," the tree repeated. "Sir Geoffrey!"

"Charlie?"

The leaves above his head quivered. "Have you come to save Marianna, too?"

It *was* Charlie. Geoff drew a relieved breath. "Certainly not. I have come to save you."

Branches rattled, and Charlie's head appeared for an instant. "What the devil do you mean?"

"I mean you've walked—or ridden—into a trap. Marianna is safe at the vicarage. Ault has probably notified the Watch that his house is to be broken into, and I'll lay you odds the place will be surrounded before midnight. Come down from there."

"Are you telling me that note was not from Marianna?"

"She denies it, quite vehemently, and she is fearful for your safety."

"For me?" Smug satisfaction tinged the voice from the tree. "She is, is she?"

"Come down at once," Geoff ordered, losing his scant patience. "I'm getting a crick in my neck from conversing with you up there."

Branches rattled again, and a shower of dusty leaves fell on Geoff's face. First two legs, then the rest of Charlie appeared on a lower limb. He sat, swinging his feet. "Are we just to go home then? Nothing will happen?" He sounded vastly disappointed.

"No, there'll be excitement enough before we are through." Geoff brushed at the debris that had landed on his coat. "I have a scheme," he went on, ruthlessly claiming Celeste's idea as his own. Charlie, he felt, would accept it far better from him than from a female. He had observed that young man's opinion of Marianna's suggestions. "We are about to thwart Ault's conniving for tonight, and perhaps sour Bow Street on any more of his attempts to call them in."

Charlie's feet ceased swinging. "Really? Wonderful! What are we to do?"

"Come down, dammit. We haven't much time, and we have the devil of a lot to accomplish if this is to work."

Charlie promptly slid down the tree trunk, ripping the knee of a pair of the vicar's weekday breeches. "I hope it involves something to eat, I haven't had any dinner and I am starving."

"So am I, thanks to you."

"You are sure Marianna is safe?"

"Of course, I am sure. I left them all at the vicarage. Mrs. Mudd," Geoff added regretfully, "no doubt served one of her excellent ragouts. We'll get boiled mutton and cabbage when we get home, if we are lucky."

"I like mutton," said Charlie. "Why are you trying to take off my coat?"

"Because we are in the deuce of a hurry, and we are going to turn you into the Duke of Ault."

Charlie was agreeable, but still curious. Filling him in on the details of his impersonation, Geoff divested him of his—or rather, one of the vicar's—coats, as they walked back to the curricle. Charlie donned Sylvester's nipwaisted garment, but objected strenuously to the beehive hat.

"I'll look a confounded quiz!" he exclaimed.

"So you will," Geoff told him. "That's the idea. Now, let's see you walk like a Bond Street beau."

"A what?"

"Damnation, I didn't think of that. I daresay you have

no knowledge of London dandies. Walk—no, do not stride, take mincing steps—and do not swing your arms! Hold them so, with your hands high, as though showing off an array of jeweled rings."

Charlie dove into the pockets of the coat he had removed and drew out Ault's signet ring. "This is the only one I have."

"Good god, put that back! That's the one you are thought to have stolen! Now, try the walk again . . . oh, hell."

Geoff soon despaired of getting him to ape the duke's mannerisms or stance, nor could he imitate his conversational style. Even in Sylvester's fancy Town toggery, no one could ever suspect Charlie of being a dandy.

Geoff ran his hands through his hair, dislodging his own curly-brimmed beaver, and had to rescue it from the gutter. "I wish I'd reached here sooner so we'd have more time."

"I was late, too," Charlie comforted him. "Old Dauntless is not much for speed, and we got lost on the way; a kind farmer put me right. Then I didn't know London was so big. I had to ask my way to Ault's house several times."

"Thereby ensuring that you and Dauntless would be recognized by a large number of witnesses. I see," said Geoff, amazed at the calmness of his tone. He noticed that Charlie had put on the signet ring and was admiring the effect in the light from the gas street lamp. "I don't suppose," he suggested tentatively, "you would consider returning that bauble and perhaps saving us all a lot of trouble?"

"No," said Charlie.

"I might even be able to convince Sylvester to call off this vendetta."

"No," said Charlie. "This crest is the only connection I have to my key."

Geoff gave up. He could think of only one way they might have a chance of surviving the coming encounter and coming off victorious. Charlie could never manage a sober duke, but one deep in his cups would not require a haughty manner. He reached under the curricle seat and removed a flask of brandy.

"To keep us warm?" asked Charlie.

"To save your life," Geoff explained, and proceeded to pour a goodly amount down both their shirt fronts.

"You are wasting it!" Charlie howled. "And ruining one of the vicar's best shirts!"

"Perfume." Geoff looked at the shirt more closely. "It is one of mine," he said. "And we are not drinking, though we must seem to be drunk as wheelbarrows. We'll need clear heads, but we are going to pretend to be too jug-bitten to stand on our dignity. It will be the only way you'll pass muster. Can you act as though your back teeth are awash?"

"Oh, I can do that easily. Jed was a great boozer. I've seen him quite castaway many a time. Like this?" He let his face go slack, and staggered. With one hand he tried ineffectually to straighten the beehive hat, setting it artistically askew.

As he took a few wavering steps forward, two members of the London Watch moved into the pool of light from the gas lamp.

" 'Ere, now," said one. "What's all this?"

Geoff drew himself up and then staggered artistically against the wrought iron fencing surrounding the nearest kennel. "We are minding our own businesh—ness— which is more than I can shay for you."

"I know 'im," said one of the men. "That there is Rake Cole."

They both peered at Geoff with interest. "Izzat so?" asked the other. "And 'oo may be the young 'un?"

Charlie heard his cue. Putting on a haughty air, he stepped forward, nearly falling on his face. Geoff caught him about the waist and stood him on his feet. Charlie looked down at the shorter officer with a fatuous beam. "I am the Duke of Ault," he announced.

"Oh, yus?" said the first man. "And I am the Emperor of Araby. 'E wouldn't 'ave said 'e's the duke," he explained to his companion. " 'E'd just say 'e's Ault."

A grave error. Geoff had not reckoned with Charlie's ignorance of the mores of the nobility. He jumped in. "He'sh—he's not only the duke," he explained confidentially, "he's also corned, pickled, and salted."

"Three sheets to the wind is what he is," agreed the officer. He regarded Charlie, who had draped himself over the fence. "Can you prove you be Ault?"

Tempting fate, Charlie held out his hand, displaying the signet ring on his finger. Geoff choked, but apparently Sylvester had neglected to include his stolen ring in his report of an expected housebreaking.

The second officer had been sniffing the air about them. "That's good brandy, that is. Costs a pretty price. 'Aven't been at no Blue Ruin."

The quality of the liquor Geoff had poured on their shirts seemed to go far to substantiate Charlie's claim to be Ault, but the men were not finished.

"We 'as a report 'ere of 'ouse-breakers. Got to check on every suspicious character."

Charlie drew himself upright and put on an imitation

of Sir Geoffrey at his most supercilious. He did it rather
well, and Geoff glanced at him with grudging appreciation, but surely he himself had never appeared so odi-
ously stiff rumped!

"Show them your card case," he suggested. "In your
pocket. That will prove who you are."

Charlie slapped his sides, produced a snuffbox, a handkerchief, a comb, and finally a flat silver case.

"That's it," Geoff told him.

Charlie fumbled at it, not finding the catch. Geoff took
it from him, extracted one of Ault's cards, and handed it
over. The men studied it.

"Ah," said one. "That's all right then."

"This housebreaking tale is all a take-in, a hum,"
Geoff explained. "Some of his friends cutting a lark,
making a pigeon of him."

"Curst rum touches I've got for friends," complained
Charlie. "Mighty queer cronies I have, setting me up to
be lagged by the pigs for milling my own ken."

If the officers thought Charlie's vocabulary odd for a
duke, they accepted it in one accompanied by the notorious
Rake Cole. The man who recognized Geoff nodded sagely.
"I knows the likes. Bunch of peep o' day boys running a
hoax. Up to every havey-cavey rig and row in Town."

"I'll serve 'em trick and tie for this," Charlie muttered
darkly. "Make no doubt of it."

"Give us your key, your Grace," one of them proposed
in an indulgent tone. He held out a hand in a friendly
fashion. "Best we get you inside."

Charlie began slapping his pockets again. Geoff knew
a moment of terror. Would he produce the vault key? It
would be just like Charlie to make a mish-mash of the

affair at the last minute. But that key must have been left in the coat now under the curricle seat. Charlie cast him an agonized look.

"What?" Geoff exclaimed. "Did they steal your key as well?"

"Damn them!" Charlie wailed. "Shtole my key so I'd be jugged for breaking into my own house for sure!"

"Come on," Geoff shoved him toward the curricle and boosted him up into the seat. "You can sleep at my digs. Get your key back tomorrow." He unhitched his reins from the fence and climbed up after him. "Good night, gentlemen. Pray acsh—accept our apologies for your trouble." The curricle weaved down the street at an erratic walk, leaving the Watchmen on the road.

"You did me proud!" Geoff exclaimed as soon as they were out of earshot. "Charlie, my boy, you were born to be an actor!"

"Rather go on the boards than be a duke, if they're all like Ault. He has nice coats, though." He had been looking behind them. "They've gone, turn around. We have to go back."

"For God's sake why?"

"Dauntless. We've left him tied back there."

"Someone will find him. He'll make a dustman very happy."

But Charlie, who was honest in his own way, refused to leave the piebald cob in London. "I only borrowed Dauntless, I have to return him."

"You mean we have to lead that clownish brute? He can't move above a walk," Geoff complained. "By God, I ought to make you ride him back! It will be after dawn before we reach Ault-in-the-Vale."

"Good," said Charlie. "Then I can sneak him back into his stall while Bob Hawkins sleeps. I neglected to tell anyone I was borrowing Dauntless," he added apologetically. "Hadn't the ready for his hire."

There was no help for it. To say Charlie could be stubborn was an understatement. They waited around a corner until they were sure the officers were gone, and then went back. After waking up Dauntless, who had gone to sleep leaning against the lamppost, they hitched him behind the curricle and began the long walk back to Ault-in-the-Vale.

Charlie promptly went to sleep, and Geoff's thoughts drifted to Celeste. To her quick mind, and to the success of her scheme to confound Sylvester. A woman in a million. His thoughts wandered on their own . . . to mischievous brown eyes . . . a soft, yielding body in his arms . . . the feel of her pressed against him and the heady taste of her lips. . . . Never had he met a woman with her combination of adventurous spirit and sensuous appeal, one who was such a delightful companion and fitted so perfectly in his embrace. His heart quickened at the thought of seeing her again, seeing that dimple deepen in her cheek when she tried not to smile. So lovely . . . and so warm . . . he lived over that night in the vault and kissed her again by the side gate to Ault-mere. He enlarged on that memory, played it over and over—and came to a conclusion that left him shaken.

Sixteen

After a sleepless night, Sylvester was on tenterhooks. Had the affair in London gone well? Had that blasted highwayman—he could no longer call him Makepeace, his conscience would not permit it—had he taken the bait? Was he even now in the "stone jug," as the Newgate gaol was known?

Through his window he watched the rising sun turn the sky to pink and gold—and heard footsteps tread firmly past his door. Now, when it was too late, Sir Geoffrey had come home. All night, Sylvester had lain awake waiting for the sound of those boots in his hall. He hadn't dared sneak out and rid himself of that damnable coffin, until he was sure Sir Geoffrey was in bed and not roaming about the woods with that Frenchwoman. Another night wasted, and he'd have to lie awake again this night, hoping for his chance to dump that casket down the well before some idiot—like Sir Geoffrey—stumbled upon it. The confounded thing haunted him; it had become an obsession hanging over his head, a millstone set to drop about his neck and destroy him.

His fingers plucked at his coverlet. He shoved it away and turned over, seeking a dry spot on a pillow damp with nervous perspiration. It would be hours before he could pay a casual visit to the vicarage to see what he could learn there. Turning over again, he tried to sleep.

Prouty—rung for at the unheard-of hour of eight in the morning—came in full of conversation as usual.

"Awake bright and early, I see, your Grace," he began. "Unlike one as I could mention. Our guest 'as left a note on 'is door, your Grace, asking 'e not be disturbed."

"Indeed," said Sylvester. "Where is my tea?"

"Coming right up, your Grace. Sleeping in, 'e is," Prouty went on, his H's fleeing in the face of his news. "And not to be wondered at. I 'ear from the stable hands as 'ow—" he caught himself "—as *how* it was full dawn before his curricle came in. They said he was carrying a bundle, your Grace. I wonder what it could be."

A wild vision of a bag of dried bones floated before Sylvester's eyes, blinding him for a moment. "How—how big a bundle?"

"More like a folded up coat, your Grace. And 'e—he—was carrying an extra hat."

Relief shook through Sylvester. Not a bag of bones. Then he suffered a violent reaction. Only the skull would be needed, and it was a very small skull! A coat might hide it. He had to check that coffin, and at once.

"Never mind my tea," he ordered the startled Prouty. "Lay out my clothes, and be quick, I—I feel like a morning walk," he added, ignoring the expression on his man's face. "Fresh air."

He forced himself to betray no need for haste, allowing Prouty to array him in garments suitable for a morning visit to the vicarage. "Have my carriage waiting at eleven," he commanded. "I shall leave directly after breakfast." He shrugged into the coat Prouty held. "A short walk first, and then I shall be ready."

Prouty was eyeing him queerly, making him uncomfortably conscious of the fact that he never walked. His sudden passion for the outdoors must be arousing curiosity in his staff. If only that coffin was undisturbed, after tonight he'd never have to venture out again.

Half an hour later, he approached the shrubbery where the coffin lay. It had taken a while to get there, for he started out first in the opposite direction, and didn't double back until he was out of sight in the woods. He crept up on the spot, afraid of what he might find. But the place seemed undisturbed, the coffin so well screened he almost couldn't find it himself, and its lid still nailed securely down. Even so, he spent some time and a good deal of energy shoving it even deeper under the bushes, and piling on fallen branches and leaves to further conceal it. Satisfied at last that it was safe, he dusted off his hands and clothes. Tonight, no matter what, it was going into that well.

At the proper hour for a morning call, he presented himself at the vicarage where Marianna and Lady Charlotte welcomed him with every sign of pleasure. The Frenchwoman had just made a pot of hot chocolate for the vicar, who came in from the passage to the church as Sylvester entered. Cordially, Mr. Brinkman invited him to join them, and the French girl fetched another cup.

The vicar droned on happily about church matters that could not interest Sylvester less, and the ladies listened politely. Left on his own as he sipped his chocolate, Sylvester noted with some satisfaction that Mlle. Moreau's eyes were drooping, as though from a sleepless night, confirming his belief that she and Sir Geoffrey had been together.

In his vault, he thought with a touch of irritation, or perhaps canoodling in the moonlight by his mere. Why could they not stay off his property and let him get on with his coffin-dumping?

On the drive the day before, he had been occupied with impressing Lady Charlotte and Marianna, and had not paid much attention to the Frenchwoman. He studied her now with a new interest. Indeed, she had all the qualifications to attract a man of Rake Cole's inclination. She was, of course, not at all the type to intrigue a man of his aesthetic sensibilities. Lady Charlotte, however, was utterly wasted on a man of Cole's vulgar tastes. However had he managed to be the uncle of as lovely a damsel as Marianna? Looking at that maiden, who was munching a biscuit with demurely downcast eyes, he knew a twinge of unease. She appeared so very innocent. Why did she always give him the feeling that she was up to something? If she weren't exactly the nonpareil to set all London into the throes of envy, he might have wished he had not been in such a hurry to declare himself.

But a nonpareil she was, and wealthy at that. Her dowry would make a pleasant addition to his coffers. He reminded himself that charming Miss Marianna was not the purpose of this morning's visit. At the first break in the vicar's monologue, he set down his cup and came right to the point.

"I understand," he said, "a wounded highwayman was sheltered here." He could have sworn someone in the room caught her breath, but Mr. Brinkman, who he was sure could be no expert in the art of dissimulation, beamed at him placidly.

"Yes, indeed," he affirmed. "He has gone to London." There was no reason to add that he had returned.

Marianna spoke up cheerfully. "He left behind a note." Equally true.

Lady Charlotte added her bit. "I daresay the young man may have become homesick."

"More chocolate?" the Frenchwoman asked, raising the pot.

It was all so calm; they were so tranquil, they could have had no news from London. And if the highwayman had not come back, he must be safely in the hands of Bow Street. He was gone. Sylvester's knees went weak with relief. As soon as he felt able to stand, he took his leave, reassured. There was nothing left but to destroy the last bit of evidence. After tonight, he would be the Duke of Ault forever.

Lady Charlotte, standing at the vicarage door, watched Sylvester's carriage jounce away up the rutted street. When the duke had arrived that morning, they had been able to greet him calmly because Celeste had seen the coach enter the village and Charlie had been hustled into the crypt.

Charlotte was the victim of perplexity, an unusual occurrence for her. She didn't know all of Charlie's story, only that he carried out the holdup as a lark, egged on by the incorrigible Marianna. Sylvester seemed to be getting rather childish. She felt someone should take him in hand and cure him of such dangerous pranks. She had been shocked to the core when the scheme to trap Charlie in

London was revealed to her. No wonder Geoffrey was so determined to protect the boy. It showed a benevolent side to the character of Rake Cole that she had never suspected.

She had grave doubts as to her future happiness when she agreed to accept his offer of marriage, but as an impoverished maiden lady of no particular charm and beauty, she had seen no other choice. Her father never had a feather to fly with, nothing with which to support her, and when he died, she would be both destitute and homeless, for the estate was heavily mortgaged. Marriage, even to a dissolute rake, was preferable.

She had come to like Geoffrey, now that she knew him, but she had not failed to see the looks that passed between him and Celeste Moreau. Such dawning love was not for her. Indeed, she believed such a vulgar emotion as passion to be quite beneath her. However, it was high time she gave serious consideration to her own situation.

Still standing at the door, watching the receding dust cloud from the carriage, she decided on a drastic course of action.

Geoff awoke at noon from a nightmare that left him sunk in a black depression. It took him a minute to realize he was no longer dreaming. The nightmare was real.

The revelation that had come to him on the long drive home the night before had plunged him to the depths of despair. He had found the one woman on earth who could make him forsake all others—except for the one to whom he was irrevocably bound. He was betrothed to Lady Charlotte.

By honor, he could not cry off and leave her to be a

subject of pity and derision for every gossip-monger in her world. Even such a rake as he—as he *had* been—respected the basic code of an English gentleman. He had given his pledge freely, presumably after due consideration and being in his right mind. He was in the suds, trapped by his own early ambition. To regain consequence in the *ton,* he had opted to offer for a pillar of society. Well, he had her, and now he was in the devil of a hobble. At fiddlestick's end, he cudgeled his brain but saw no way out. Desperately enamored of one lady, he would be buckled for life to another.

The reek of French brandy gradually attracted his attention to a rolled-up bundle on the floor beside his bed. Last night that bundle had posed a problem. How was he to return Sylvester's coat and hat to his room? And what would his man think when he saw them? Faced with his new and overwhelming personal problem, he found he didn't give a damn.

He also discovered that forming a violent, lasting passion didn't prevent the pangs of hunger. He dressed and headed for the breakfast parlor. Pausing on his way, he opened Sylvester's chamber door and heaved his bee-hive hat and brandy-soaked coat inside.

It was Prouty, not Sylvester, who found them, and noted the alcoholic odor. Only the other morning, he had come upon some of the duke's best garments in filthy condition, all dirt and twigs, and yesterday his coat had been damp with rain. These rumors he heard about Sir Geoffrey and the Frenchwoman—could it really be Ault they had seen? Not likely, the duke had never been in the petticoat line, but something was going on. He might be able to use this to put a stop to the nasty remarks he'd heard regarding his master's virility. Scooping up the evidence, he carried it off to be cleaned, and incidentally to drop a hint in the proper ear. Wapshott? Or Cook? Perhaps both.

It became a very long day for Celeste. Sir Geoffrey did not come to the vicarage. Being female, she knew why.

In the brief few minutes when he delivered Charlie the night before, he had glanced at her only once. It was enough. The look in his eyes had set her very being ablaze, and for a short moment her spirit had sung to the skies—until she remembered Lady Charlotte.

She fully understood Sir Geoffrey and the hopelessness of their situation. Because she loved him, too. She admitted it at last. And he would not jilt Lady Charlotte, for her baronet was no longer wicked. How could she have been so silly as to believe in those stupid novels? Hot tears stung behind her eyelids, and her hands trembled as she checked the bandage on Charlie's leg to make sure he had come to no harm.

Charlie was full of his adventure, which he told and retold to Marianna and Lady Charlotte.

"What do you suppose he will do next?" Marianna asked, clasping her hands in excitement. "Oh, Charlie, do you think Sylvester will try to murder you?"

Charlie had not thought of that, and he paused to consider it. "I'd like to see him try," he decided at last. "I shall ask Sir Geoffrey to get me a bullet for Jed's gun."

Lady Charlotte stepped in to put a stop to such foolishness. "Do not be nonsensical, the pair of you. Shooting, indeed! I daresay Sir Geoffrey would have a few words to say about that, and you will get no bullet."

"But, Lady Charlotte!" cried Marianna. "He mus have some protection should Sylvester come after him.'

"Ridiculous. The Duke of Ault is a respectable mem ber of the nobility. He is not about to murder anyone."

Marianna frowned. "Perhaps he will not go so far, bu he is bound to catch Charlie eventually. He wants him away from Ault-in-the-Vale, and I am sure it is becaus the vault key is the clue to some tremendous mystery We must go back there and investigate."

Celeste tied a final knot on the bandage. "No. Si Geoffrey has forbidden Charlie to go anywhere near th castle. And the wound here is already inflamed." Sh looked at them, all seriousness. "I believe this duke i dangerous. He hides something and is afraid. Even th cornered rat will fight to the death, and look what ha happened to M. Charlie already."

"Nothing," said Charlie. "Am I not here?"

Celeste patted his bandaged leg. "We have here som evidence of what has happened. You will not venture ou of this vicarage. Either of you."

The young people grumbled and complained, but Lad Charlotte coaxed them into a game of spillikins, whic soon bordered on the bloodthirsty and occupied them fo the rest of the day.

Celeste, had she not been so absorbed in her own tu multuous thoughts, should have realized they submitte to her orders rather suddenly, and were unnaturally com plaisant. Hindsight, she thought later, is utterly useless

The long day passed somehow for Celeste, and at las they all retired to their rooms. Something woke her shortl after she had drifted off to sleep. The full moon, perhaps shining bright in her window. She slid quietly out of be

and crossed to pull the curtains, but she hesitated. It was
so lovely in the silent cemetery outside. Her thoughts,
never far from the subject that most interested her, turned
to that other moonlit night, when she and Sir Geoffrey
walked through the field to the Ault mausoleum. Sir Geoffrey occupied entirely too many of her thoughts of late.
He belonged to another woman, she told herself, fiercely.
You are an *imbecile, sotte, fou!* It did not help a bit.

She had begun by thoroughly disliking Lady Charlotte.
Now, that had changed, but the woman was humorless,
wrong for a man of Sir Geoffrey's nature. Only misery
lay ahead for him—and for herself. Somewhere that night
other lovers lay in each other's arms. She wished them
well, but . . . staring down at the moonlit churchyard,
she blinked back tears. And stared again. Was that movement in the shadows of the yews?

It was. Two figures slipped out into the graveyard and
hurried toward the lane. One wore a hooded cape, and
the other moved with a decidedly uneven gait. Turning
quickly, she looked at Marianna's bed on the other side
of the room. It was empty.

Those idiotic youngsters were heading for the vault.
She should have known they gave in too easily! Snatching up her dressing gown, she pulled on her half-boots
and ran to catch them, with her hair in curl papers and
nightgown flapping about her ankles. By the time she
reached the lane, they were already over the field and
entering the side gate to Aultmere.

"Le bon Dieu," she prayed as she ran, "do not let M.
Charlie be seen!"

When she reached the vault, she found no sign of the
exasperating children. They must have seen her pursuing

them and were hiding somewhere, for the ornamental iron doors remained locked. They had not gone in. That meant they were outside, in the woods, perhaps watching her. She waited, holding her breath and listening. From the depths of the grove, nearer to the castle, she heard stealthy sounds. As quietly as she could, she made her way toward the noises and caught a glimpse of movement, a pale garment, far ahead.

"Ah, you are there," she murmured. "Now have I discovered you!"

She began to run, pushing her way heedlessly through the undergrowth—and fell over something in the dark. It seemed to be a box, buried beneath a pile of leaves and dead branches. What was it? And what was it doing out here? She rubbed the shins she had banged on the box, and then felt along it, trying to identify the shape. Smooth, finished wood, about four feet in length and two feet high, with ornately carved metal handles on each long side—for carrying?—as in a funeral parade? She ran her hands over it again with a growing sense of horror. It must be—it could only be—a child's casket.

The millstone of the coffin in the woods, hanging about Sylvester's neck, bode fair to keep him sleepless until he could drop the blasted thing down the old abandoned well. Tonight, at last, he was sure Sir Geoffrey slept peacefully in his bedchamber, a fact that roused his envy as well as promising him a clear field.

He slipped out, a bit nervous in the brilliance of the moon, but all seemed quiet. Carefully skirting the edges of the kitchen garden, he went straight to the well, for he must first remove the rotting planks that covered it. He had been unable to do that by daylight, for some one of his domestics seemed always to be picking vegetables or pulling weeds. No matter, he could see well enough by the moonlight, and no one would see him. Nevertheless, he slid the boards away as quietly as he could. Now there was only to find the coffin, drag it over, and push it in. After the brightness of the moon, he had some difficulty finding his way to its hiding place in the black shadows under the trees. Then, just as he came up to the casket, a pale, female figure rose from the ground beside it.

Good god, it was his mother's ghost! She had come for him because he had desecrated the dead! He shrieked like a banshee and bolted, shaking so in every limb, he could scarcely keep his feet. He had barely broken out of the trees when a hollow, despairing wail echoed through the night behind him. He stumbled, nearly falling flat, and began to cry. She was coming after him!

Celeste had just risen from her discovery of the casket when an apparition came toward her through the trees. It threw up its arms with an unearthly cry. Already unnerved by the coffin, she fled, crashing through the shrubbery.

A moment later, the ground beneath her feet vanished, and she plunged, down and down, into inky blackness and ice cold water.

Seventeen

Sir Geoffrey was not in his bed, peacefully asleep. He had been lying awake, agonizing over his love for Celeste, when stealthy footfalls passing his door interrupted his orgy of self-pity. Ault on the prowl? What could that cozening rascal be up to in the wee hours of the night?

Throwing on his dressing gown, Geoff silently crept out into the portrait-hung corridor. He was just in time to see Sylvester tiptoeing toward the main stairs, fully clothed, prepared to go outside. Geoff nipped back into his room and shoved his bare feet into his boots. No time for further dressing, he'd have to spy as he was.

By the time he reached the great hall, Sylvester was already slipping out through the drawing room French doors. Geoff went after him, waiting a cautionary few minutes for him to get well ahead. A mistake. Sylvester had already vanished. Had he gone around the terrace to the back? Or was he in the shrubbery, making his way toward the vault? Ever since they had identified Charlie's key, Geoff had been sure that vault was somehow connected with Sylvester's determination to rid the countryside of one Charles Makepeace. But why would Ault go there in the middle of the night? Or to the kitchen area at the back of the castle, for that matter. Which way should he himself go?

A minute was wasted in indecision—until the quiet night was shattered by an eldritch shriek, followed by a hollow, despairing wail which seemingly came from the bowels of the earth. Something crashed in the shrubbery at the kitchen end of the grove, and Sylvester burst into view, galloping as though the hounds of hell were at his heels. Geoff started toward him, but Sylvester passed him by as if he were invisible. Crossing the terrace in jack-rabbit leaps, he dove through the French doors and slammed them behind him, throwing the latches, incidentally locking Geoff out in his night rail.

What had so frightened Sylvester? What else but Celeste playing ghost in the vault, after he had ordered them all to stay home! Grimly, Geoff retied the sash of his dressing gown. The mournful howl rose again, echoing the despair of an animal trapped in the deepest of caves. The distress sounded too real, and there was no reason for it to continue now that Sylvester had fled.

But the eerie wails went on. Sudden urgency prickled up Geoff's spine, and he took off at a run for the vault. Had that damned idiot locked Celeste inside? Had he hurt her?

He had not. Celeste wasn't at the vault, but Charlie and Marianna were, clinging to each other in the shelter of the portico. Geoff seized Charlie by the shoulders and shook him.

"Where is Celeste? What has happened here?"

"N—n—nothing," Charlie managed. "No one is here but us."

"She was here," Marianna cried. "We saw her and hid

because she was chasing us, only all at once she ran away. Uncle Geoff, do something! Is that her calling for help?"

The desperate sounds came from some distance away, and Geoff detected a feminine tone. Now was not the time to lambaste the erring youngsters. There were a number of things he meant to take up with those two—but later. At the moment, his heart pounded in terror for his Celeste. He released Charlie. "Come on." He ran toward the hollow cries, leaving them to follow as they could.

When he reached the edge of the grove, he stared out over the kitchen gardens. Nothing moved in the weird shadows thrown by the brilliant moon. No sign of Celeste, and the cries had silenced. His heart sank. Where could she be? Was she lying unconscious somewhere out of sight?

"Celeste!" he yelled, and jumped back, startled, as an answering wail came from the ground at his very feet. He looked down at a black hole. One more step, and he would have been in it. He knelt and peered down into impenetrable darkness. "Celeste?"

"A moi! Sauvez moi!" The cries formed words and changed to hysterical sobs.

Marianna came panting up, Charlie limping behind her. "You've found her! Is she dead?"

"Don't be such a goose," said Charlie. "She's still yelling."

"A light," Geoff cried. "We need a light. Celeste, my love, we are here. We'll get you out. Are you hurt?"

His only reply was a torrent of French and more sobs.

"She sounds all right." Digging in his pockets, Charlie

removed two candle stubs and a tinderbox. "Here, but candles won't get her out of there."

Geoff already had one alight, and he held it as far down the hole as he could reach. Celeste's pale face, blotched with weeping, looked back up at him from about six feet below. She stood in some four feet of stagnant water, up to her armpits in the slimy, abandoned well, shaking with terror and nearly out of her mind with horror.

"Charlie," Geoff commanded, "hold that candle so she has a light. I'm going for a rope or something."

He finally located a long ladder in the garden shed and came back, dragging it behind him. Celeste still wept hysterically. Charlie had dropped the candle stub into the well beside her, but Marianna had lighted another so they could see. Geoff let the ladder down. It was too short by several feet, but between them they managed to get Celeste calm enough to climb to a point where Geoff and Charlie could reach down and seize her upstretched arms to haul her out. All the way up, she babbled in French of a shrieking *fantôme* who had melted the ground from beneath her feet.

When at last they had her on the surface, Geoff lost no time in gathering her soaking wet form into his arms and kissing her again and again, all the while murmuring ragged words of love: a form of therapy that proved effective.

Marianna squealed with delight, but Charlie lost his patience.

"Make her speak English," he demanded. "How'd she get into this devil of a hobble?"

Celeste turned her face away, albeit reluctantly, so she

could speak. "Sir Geoffrey, if you will but stop, I have much to tell you."

She began with seeing Charlie and Marianna start off, and chasing them when they hid from her in the woods.

"Of that," Geoff interrupted, glaring at the guilty pair, "we shall speak in the near future. Go on, my love."

There he went again. The term of endearment made her lose track for a moment before she could continue. "I was running, pursuing one I thought to be Charlie, and I fell over something in the bushes. *Un cercueil,* a coffin. For a child."

"A coffin!" exclaimed Geoff. "What is a coffin doing out in the woods?" He stopped, arrested. "I would very much like to see what is inside the sarcophagus of the little fifth duke in the vault. We may have here the solution to the mystery of Charlie's key. Where is this small coffin? Can you take me to it?"

Celeste shook her head. "I do not know where. I chased strange sounds and a movement of a figure. I had just found the coffin when—when—" she shuddered and Geoff hugged her tighter, "when an apparition, *un fantôme,* appeared before me. It threw up its arms at me with a great cry, and I fled in terror! It opened the ground before me, and I fell in. I thought to be swallowed to the bowels of the earth."

Geoff found it necessary to comfort her some more. "That was no more a ghost than you were playing yourself," he explained after several minutes. "It was Sylvester. I met him running back, and from the looks of him, you probably frightened ten years off his life."

"But the ground, he opened it up!"

He kissed her again. It seemed a good idea, so he

repeated the gesture. "Only an old abandoned well, I believe, though I fail to understand why it has been allowed to remain uncovered."

Charlie had discovered the rotting planks. "Here is the cover. I'll lay a monkey Sylvester pulled it off."

Marianna, as usual, was ahead of him. "To hide that little coffin!" She danced beside him, excited. "Come on, Charlie, we must find it. Which way did you come, Celeste?"

"I do not know." She looked about. "But not from the gardens there. I was under the trees."

"We'll find it." Marianna grabbed Charlie's arm. "Do come on!"

"Sir Geoffrey, do not let them go!" Celeste protested.

Too late, they had vanished into the shadows of the grove. Geoff stripped off his dressing gown, which was by now nearly as wet as her nightclothes. Unconscious of the fact that he wore only a nightshirt and his boots, he wrapped it around Celeste.

"Here, my girl, you are shivering from the cold."

"But, Sir Geoffrey, those children are out there—they will become lost."

"In this tiny woods? I say it serves them right for starting this escapade. I am taking you home."

"But—"

He enfolded her in his arms again, closing her worried eyes with kisses, kissing the tip of her nose, her cheeks, and finding her lips once more. After a long time, quite pleasantly spent, he realized he, too, was very damp, and a cold breeze blew up the tails of his nightshirt. He ignored it and gave her one last crushing embrace, nuzzling his nose into the soaked curl papers above her ear. "I've

fallen rather deeply in love with you," he remarked conversationally. "I did not realize how deeply until I saw you in that well. I cannot lose you now, and you may succumb to an inflammation of the lungs, if I do not get you dry."

She pulled away. "Sir Geoffrey, you must not say such things to me. You forget! You are betrothed to the Lady Charlotte."

He *had* forgotten for a few mad moments, but he remembered now, and felt the world crash about him. How could he have been so stupid?

"And you cannot take me home like this. You must go inside and dress."

Sunk in his own black well of hopelessness, he looked down at his damp, clinging nightshirt, and remembered something else. "I cannot. I am locked out." He shrugged. What did it matter? Nothing mattered anymore. "I shall borrow back some garments from Charlie," he said.

Both in the depths of misery, they began the walk in silence through the trees, then past the vault and over the field. Celeste mourned for what might have been; Geoff writhed in mental agony, alternately furious with himself for declaring his love to Celeste, and dismayed as he contemplated his future with the wrong woman. He had no hope that Lady Charlotte would give up her one chance to marry.

At the vicarage, he relieved his feelings and his temper by administering a blistering set-down to Charlie and Marianna, who had given up coffin-hunting in the dark and followed them home.

The two miscreants listened with becoming gravity for several minutes, until Marianna spoiled it by breaking

out in uncontrollable giggles and pointing to his costume. In a fury, he left them and stamped inside to raid the vicar's wardrobe for some of his own garments.

Hearing the commotion, Lady Charlotte, muffled from toes to chin in a flannel robe, was coming down the stairs. "What's toward?" she demanded. "What is going on?"

At the halfway point, she met Geoff coming up in his wet nightshirt. She took a firm grip on the banister rail and did not faint. "My dear Geoffrey!" She turned her eyes away and struggled to maintain a calm and detached attitude. "Explain yourself!"

With the mood he was in, Geoff took pleasure in pouring out the entire story to both her and Mr. Brinkman, who had also come out and stood at the head of the stairs. Charlie and Marianna interjected remarks and ended it by saying their search for the coffin was in vain.

"Oh, that," said the vicar. "I know about that."

The entire assembly stared at him, and he blinked, mildly surprised. "The young man who was ordered to move it from the vault came to me in some distress to ask for my advice. He is not—ah—intelligent, but deeply religious, and though he had been commanded to tell no one, he felt that could not include a representative of God. He feared it smacked of the desecration of a tomb, and it was not right to attempt to lead the poor ghost lady astray."

"Why did you not tell us?" exclaimed Marianna. "We could have looked for it then."

"I did not care to betray his confidence, but I must admit, I am most heartily relieved that Miss Celeste's finding it has taken the matter out of my hands."

"And put it into ours!" Marianna grabbed Charlie's arm. "Come with us, Mr. Brinkman. We shall find it at once."

It was not easy to rise above being garbed only in boots and a nightshirt, but Geoff managed. "No one," he thundered, "is setting a foot out of here again this night. And I am remaining to ensure you all stay inside."

In the morning, Charlie was limping badly after his night-long activity. While Celeste renewed his bandages, Lady Charlotte asked to see the letter that had come with his key.

"A waste of time," Marianna said, retrieving what was left of it from the mantel clock. "Celeste's uncle gives us no clues."

Lady Charlotte, always literal-minded, mused over the letter. "He writes here that he has kept his promise, and that she has taken her secret with her to the grave." She glanced up, puzzled. "Why have you not thought of looking in the duchess's coffin?"

After a blank moment, Marianna cried, "Stupid! How could we all have been so hen-witted?"

Wasting no more time, they all paraded to the vault, which Charlie unlocked, using his own key. He and Geoff slid the lid aside on the duchess's sarcophagus. There, on top of her coffin, was a folded sheet of paper. Fr. Francis Moreau had placed his confession inside her stone sarcophagus, thus letting her carry her secret with her in death, as he had promised. He must then have arranged to have the key with the Ault crest conveyed to

Charlie Makepeace, in hopes its use would be figured out without his having to further break his vow.

Celeste read her uncle's words aloud, translating them into English. " 'In this year of our Lord, 1799, there came a plague into our village of Ault-in-the-Vale. The young duke became ill, and his nurse fled in fear. A woman from the village, already exposed by her own child, was called to nurse the duke, who recovered. The village woman's child died, and to her everlasting shame, the Duchess of Ault succumbed to temptation, taking advantage of what she believed to be a heaven-sent opportunity. She paid the woman to switch the children. A doctor, called in from the next town, declared the woman's son dead of the plague, and that boy was interred as the duke. Well-recompensed, the woman and her husband, one Jed Makepeace, a discharged poacher, left town taking the noble child with them. The duchess's son, Sylvester, thus became the sixth duke by means of this cruel trick. I am here breaking the sacred vow of the sanctity of confession, but in a cause I cannot ignore. I go now to the monastery, where I shall spend the rest of my days seeking God's forgiveness.' "

Celeste looked up, her eyes wide with wonder. *"Mon Dieu!* Can this mean that M. Charlie—"

"Indeed, it does!" Marianna squealed with delight. "I was right all along! Charlie is the Duke of Ault!"

Stunned, the others stared at Charlie. That young man, a picture of disbelief, shook his head.

"A Banbury tale. That is all a concoction of rubbish! I am not Sylvester, and I don't want to be."

Celeste handed the page to Geoff. "That is what it says, you see it here. My uncle has violated the vows of his church by revealing a confession. He would not have done so unless it was to reveal the truth. I see now why he retired to France to pray night and day for forgiveness. But he rights here a great wrong. Surely, *le bon Dieu* will understand."

Lady Charlotte stared at Charlie, bewildered. "Does this mean that Sylvester is not the Duke of Ault? That Charles—CHARLES—!"

Charlie backed away, a cornered animal, his eyes shifting from one staring face to another. "No!" he said.

Geoff caught him by the shoulders. "Charlie, think back. What can you remember?"

"Nothing."

"Come now." He gave him a shake. "You know the Makepeaces were not your parents."

"No, I don't. That is, I always called her Nana, and she said Jed was my stepfather. I wasn't very old when Nana died and Parson took me in. He taught me to read and write and speak proper, so's I wouldn't grow up like Jed. But I *liked* Jed!" he burst out. "He brought me things. Clothes and sometimes money. He left me his pistol and his mask."

Geoff let him go. "We need more proof than this. I think we must learn what body lies in that coffin."

"It will not be me," said Charlie. "I don't want to be a duke!"

"You may not have a choice." Geoff paced the length of the vault and back, stopping beside the sarcophagus of the fifth duke. "Help me move this lid a trifle."

Mr. Brinkman stepped forward at once. They had to shift the heavy stone cover only a few inches to see that it was empty.

"The coffin in the woods!" Marianna exclaimed. "Oh, do but think, Celeste, where did you find it?"

"I do not know. I ran from here—but I made many turns—"

Geoff shook his head. "We must face Sylvester first with this confession, and bring him with us to the opening of that casket."

He folded the sheet of paper, put it in his pocket, and they slid the cover back over the duchess's sarcophagus. While Sir Geoffrey decided how to best go about establishing Charlie's claim, they walked back to the vicarage.

Charlie had been unwontedly silent and suddenly spoke up, sounding worried. "If the duke is not Ault anymore, what will he do? I would not wish him homeless, he is not bred for it, and he could not make it on the High Toby, he has not the proper attitude."

"Be at ease." Geoff cuffed him lightly on the shoulder. "I suggest you grant him a competency."

Charlie, still dubious, hung back until a thought occurred to him. "Will I have much blunt to sport, if I agree to be a duke?"

Geoff smiled. "Quite a bit, I believe."

"In that case," said Charlie, "I'll do it, for then I shall be able to give Bob Hawkins his three pounds to buy Dauntless."

Lady Charlotte had been watching Geoffrey and Marianna's pretty French companion closely, noting how Celeste shrank into the background when he was present and how he avoided looking at her. The time had come to draw the curtain on this melodrama, before those two made a Cheltenham tragedy of it. She requested a private interview with Geoffrey in the vicar's parlor. He looked at her unhappily, certain she wished to set a definite date for their wedding.

"Geoffrey," she began as soon as the door was closed, "sit here beside me on the sofa." She patted the place.

"Yes, Charlotte."

"I have been observing you carefully these past days, Geoffrey, and I have come to feel you have a regrettable tendency to perpetrate larks and pranks. This penchant for treasure hunting and interfering with the lives of others should not concern one of proper breeding. I fear it shows a frivolous side of you that is not at all what I want in a husband. I am very sorry, Geoffrey, but I do not believe we should suit."

His mouth dropped open. "Charlotte—are you—can you be crying off?"

"It is most inconvenient, of course," she went on. "I will have to place an announcement in the London Gazette at once that the arranged marriage will not take place. I shall look about me for another more suitable *parti*. It will not be easy to replace you. Do not look so amazed, Geoffrey. I am more than seven, I cut my wisdoms long ago," she explained with paralyzing candor, "and I could not fail to see that you will be better suited with another, not too far from here."

Geoff grinned. "Thank you, Charlotte. I wish you the very best of luck in finding another to take my place."

She also smiled, a closed satisfied smile. "As a matter of fact, I have been giving the problem much attention of late, and I believe I shall marry Ault."

He gave her an anxious glance. "But you know he may no longer be the duke."

"No matter." She shook her head. "The mere presence or absence of a title does not alter his breeding or his manners—or his appearance." For a moment she looked a trifle dissatisfied. "I must deplore his tendency to dandyism, but no doubt a wife can direct his thoughts into a more serious vein, and I must marry someone. As for a title, I believe my consequence is great enough to sustain the position of both of us in the *ton*. I am certain we shall suit, for I find he thinks as he ought on all important subjects. He but needs the management of a respectable female."

Geoff knew a pang of sympathy. Poor Sylvester, he hadn't a chance! Another worry stopped him. "But when Sylvester loses Aultmere, as he will, how do you go on?"

She rose, signifying an end to their conference. "You need not feel concern, my dear Geoffrey. As you know, I stand to inherit a very tidy estate from my father, if the mortgages are paid off, and Ault—Sylvester—has told me he has a rather substantial fortune from his mother." She reached up to touch his face. "Farewell, my betrothed." She kissed him, the first caress they had exchanged. "Hello, my dear friend."

It was decided that only Lady Charlotte and an effervescent Sir Geoffrey, as responsible adults, should take their discovery to Aultmere.

When faced with the priest's written confession, confirming the catastrophe he dreaded, Sylvester broke down and collapsed in a chair.

"It is the end," he sobbed. "I shall shoot myself."

"No, no, do not do so," Geoff chided him cheerfully, clapping him on the back. "It would be a terrible waste, and we plan a far better use for you."

Lady Charlotte shook her head at Geoff, with a warning frown that failed to depress his good humor. She took Sylvester's hand and patted it. "You have only to lead us to the poor little boy's coffin, that all may be settled, and then you must come with me to Langham for a long visit in the country."

"But I shall be in prison," he wailed. "I cannot bear it! There will be nothing but bread and water and rats . . ." his voice trailed away amid hiccoughs and gulps.

"Nonsense," said Geoff, bracingly. "I am sure they no longer feed prisoners on rats. But you may perish such unpleasant thoughts, for I am sure Charlie holds no hard feelings."

"Indeed, he does not," Lady Charlotte assured him with further pats. "You will be safe at Langham. You must leave Aultmere to the ghost of your mother. She will not follow us."

He blinked up at her, a dawning hope in his streaming eyes, and he clutched at her hand.

Geoff had no patience with maudlin scenes, and he spoke briskly. "Your mother was to blame, not you. It is she who is irrevocably bound to Aultmere. I think, under the circumstances," his sparkling glance traveled to Lady Charlotte, "if you agree not to contest Charlie's claim and promise not to molest him in the future, it would be best to avoid scandal and not press charges. Brace up, man. Use your handkerchief, and let us get this over with."

* * *

The entire company from the vicarage followed Sylvester out to the coffin in the woods. Top o' the trees Corinthians do not skip along, but there was a jubilant bounce to Sir Geoffrey's stride. Celeste eyed him with suspicion, for there was a puzzling lilt to his voice and an irrepressibly rakish glint in his eyes, holding a promise that set her heart on a faster beat. What had he in mind?

She noted an uncommon bonhomie between Sir Geoffrey and Lady Charlotte. Obviously the two had come to terms. Why then did Sir Geoffrey look at *her* so? Surely, he would not—could not!—intend to offer her *carte blanche* after he was wed. But he was a baronet, a wicked baronet . . .

When they reached the little coffin, Sylvester would not stay to see it opened. The prospect of seeing that yellowed skull again sent him into a convulsion of shudders. Lady Charlotte led him back toward the castle, announcing she would send Wapshott for tea.

Thus it was Geoff who tossed aside the dead branches and brushed the leaves from the ornate casket. He pried up the lid and confirmed the presence of the child skeleton with dark hair. All the dukes of Ault had been fair.

"Then it is not me in there," Charlie exclaimed, relieved.

"No," agreed Geoff. "But according to the nameplate, the coffin belongs to you."

"I don't want it! I'm not ready!"

"It is too small for you, anyway," Marianna told him. "You will have to get a larger size."

Geoff grinned. "You will indeed. I suggest you leave this with the little one who already inhabits it, but we must remove the brass nameplate and replace it with his true name."

"What's that?"

"Why, I expect it will say Charles Makepeace."

Charlie shuddered. "No!"

"But yes, M. Charlie," Celeste soothed. "I will ask M. Brinkman to have the child buried where he belongs, in our village churchyard, and you shall have a new name."

Charlie looked at her, all at once a lost little boy. "But—who am I?"

"Let us see." Geoff leaned over and read the name on the coffin aloud: "Henry Edward Gareth Alston, Fifth Duke of Ault, Marquis de Verel, Baron Champleigh."

"Good god!" said Charlie, wrinkling his nose in distaste. "I prefer Charlie."

"So do I." Marianna made it a firm statement, and Charlie glanced at her sideways, a mischievous gleam in his eyes.

"Can I count on that?"

Her cheeks flamed, but she retained her composure. "Oh, yes. You see, I am already betrothed to the Duke of Ault, the announcement has gone out—and I much prefer *you* as my duke."

It was Charlie's turn to blush violently, and Geoff came to his rescue. "We will see how you feel about that in a year's time. You are both too young to marry."

"But you are not!" Marianna told him, with a speaking glance towards Celeste.

"Silence, chatterbox!" Geoff turned to Charlie. "Allow me to congratulate your Grace."

Charlie gaped at him, reality beginning to sink in. "Grace! But I don't know how to be a duke!"

"Uncle Geoffrey will teach you, and so will I." Marianna clapped her hands in glee. "And I shall show Celeste how to be a baroness, for I know all about it."

Stunned, Celeste stared, first at her, then at Sir Geoffrey. "What can she mean?"

Frowning ferociously at Marianna, Geoff folded his arms across his chest. "I had rather planned on asking her myself."

"But, Uncle Geoff, you are so slow!"

"Charlie," he commanded, "take that baggage away— and see her back to the vicarage. Come here, Celeste, for this we must be alone." He waited until the youngsters were out of sight. "Now that we are free of the brats—"

"But Lady Charlotte!" she gasped, coming up for air.

"Charlotte is going to wed Ault—I mean Sylvester, poor chap—so I find myself short one fiancée. It is my dearest hope that you will take on the job. My love, will you have me?"

It was hard to protest when her very being bubbled like French champagne, but she felt obligated to make a token effort. "But me, I am a commoner, I am not of your world—think of the advancement of your family!"

"I'd rather not." He pulled her closer and tipped up her chin with one finger. "As a matter of fact, I have thought of no one but you this past week or more. When I thought I might lose you—oh, my love, never have I seen anything more beautiful than your face when we pulled you alive from that well."

"Mon cher Sir Geoffrey, if you can think me beautiful

soaking wet in slime and with my hair in curl papers, you are out of your mind!"

"And I intend to stay that way." His arms tightened about her. "Actually, my love, I have never been more sane." He buried his face in her hair, nibbling at her ear. "For the first time in my life, I know exactly what I want. I will never let you go, and we shall live happily ever after."

This so exactly agreed with her own plans that Celeste snuggled against his chest with a tiny gurgle of sheer happiness. The women who wrote those marble-backed novels were fools! Dukes! Only a wicked baronet would do for her. She turned up her face, and for several long minutes, time stood still. . . .

ZEBRA'S REGENCY ROMANCES
DAZZLE AND DELIGHT

A BEGUILING INTRIGUE (4441, $3.99)
by Olivia Sumner

Pretty as a picture Justine Riggs cared nothing for propriety. She dressed as a boy, sat on her horse like a jockey, and pondered the stars like a scientist. But when she tried to best the handsome Quenton Fletcher, Marquess of Devon, by proving that she was the better equestrian, he would try to prove Justine's antics were pure folly. The game he had in mind was seduction — never imagining that he might lose his heart in the process!

AN INCONVENIENT ENGAGEMENT (4442, $3.99)
by Joy Reed

Rebecca Wentworth was furious when she saw her betrothed waltzing with another. So she decides to make him jealous by flirting with the handsomest man at the ball, John Collinwood, Earl of Stanford. The "wicked" nobleman knew exactly what the enticing miss was up to — and he was only too happy to play along. But as Rebecca gazed into his magnificent eyes, her errant fiancé was soon utterly forgotten!

SCANDAL'S LADY (4472, $3.99)
by Mary Kingsley

Cassandra was shocked to learn that the new Earl of Lynton was her childhood friend, Nicholas St. John. After years at sea and mixed feelings Nicholas had come home to take the family title. And although Cassandra knew her place as a governess, she could not help the thrill that went through her each time he was near. Nicholas was pleased to find that his old friend Cassandra was his new next door neighbor, but after being near her, he wondered if mere friendship would be enough . . .

HIS LORDSHIP'S REWARD (4473, $3.99)
by Carola Dunn

As the daughter of a seasoned soldier, Fanny Ingram was accustomed to the vagaries of military life and cared not a whit about matters of rank and social standing. So she certainly never foresaw her *tendre* for handsome Viscount Roworth of Kent with whom she was forced to share lodgings, while he carried out his clandestine activities on behalf of the British Army. And though good sense told Roworth to keep his distance, he couldn't stop from taking Fanny in his arms for a kiss that made all hearts equal!

Available wherever paperbacks are sold, or order direct from the Publisher. Send cover price plus 50¢ per copy for mailing and handling to Penguin USA, P.O. Box 999, c/o Dept. 17109, Bergenfield, NJ 07621. Residents of New York and Tennessee must include sales tax. DO NOT SEND CASH.